Eternal Search for Hope

(A Collection of Short Stories)

Rama Gupta

STERLING

STERLING PUBLISHERS (P) LTD.
Regd. Office: A1/256 Safdarjung Enclave, New Delhi-110029.
Cin: U22110DL1964PTC211907
Phone: +91 82877 98380/ +91 120-6251823
e-mail: mail@sterlingpublishers.in
www.sterlingpublishers.in

Eternal Search for Hope: A Collection of Short Stories

ISBN 978 93 93853 19 6

Printed in India

Printed and Published by Sterling Publishers Pvt. Ltd.,
Plot No. 13, Ecotech-III, Greater Noida - 201306,
Uttar Pradesh, India

Foreword

To write the foreword of Prof Gupta's book is a matter of pleasure and delight for me. Having interacted with her and Colonel Gupta on occasion, I have found them to be a balanced and creative couple. Colonel Gupta loves clicking pictures and Prof Gupta clearly loves the art of writing.

Her stories are insightful and deeply touching at the same time. She writes with style yet is compassionate in her thought process. She brings out the traits of the characters of her stories capably and starkly. I particularly like the story titled "Confessions of a Mother" in which she has somehow managed to draw the reader into the mind of a mother who is torn by the shock of what she and her daughter have had to face for years. Her anxiety, her love and her angst are enmeshed in her description of the highs and lows of being a mother who worries and worries, but comes out triumphant in the end. Her daughter too displays resolve and grit to a magnificent extent and she emerges a victor against the turbulent forces of life.

Another noteworthy story is titled "Progress of Love" and this tale brings to the fore the inevitable roller coaster ride that each love story must go through. We have all at some point undergone similar uncertainties and tribulations but love triumphs more often than not, and that is what Prof Gupta's story portrays so delicately.

All in all, Prof Gupta is a writer who carries a bundle of compassion and understanding for the intricate fabric of human existence. She writes with a rare sense of care, emotional intelligence and depth of perception.

Indeed a book to savour and cherish, but only another milestone in the literary journey of Prof Gupta.

Vivek Atray
ex IAS

Motivational Speaker and Author of
"It's Still a Wonderful Life"

This book is dedicated to
Daisaku Ikeda
President of Soka Gakkai International

Contents

1

A Devoted Son

Shreya was beautiful with fine dark hair and big black eyes, good features. She had a pleasant frankness and an air of candour that was very taking. She was easy to talk to and was brilliant enough to understand what other people were talking about. She was quick to take a joke and she was not shy. She had a happy placidity that suggested a good temper. She was in the first year studying with Aditya in Chicago Booth Business school in Chicago.

Aditya found himself under her spell — a spell cast first by her beauty, then by the constellation of personal qualities from which her life radiated. The rapture filled his heart when for the first time he walked up to her at a party and asked for her telephone number and she shared it coyly.

Sometimes it so happens that the instant you desire a woman you believe you cannot live without her for the rest of your life, though later on her possession might always follow by disgust but not in the case of Aditya.

He was aware early in life that to spend your entire existence you need not a raw physical appetite which is quickly sated but a rapport of souls, moods and temperament, so in yielding to seduction you have to determine whether it is a physical thing, an intoxication of senses, or a profound spiritual attraction.

Aditya felt Shreya was, in fact, a godsend to him as she combined all the traits, and, of course, he would get on capitally with her till they were both old people. Frequent visits followed over the next two years as their apartments were three miles apart and they saw each other quite often discussing the universe with a bottle of wine and talking deep about time and eternity, things of this world, books and all possible and impossible matters.

Eventually after graduating from business school, he married her in early twenties, thinking she was going to be a real treasure. And that was precisely what Shreya turned out. From that time onwards he and his wife lived in almost perfect felicity in Chicago where Aditya got a job in McKinsey and Shreya in American Bank.

Yes, theirs was a perfect marriage. They were the most devoted couple anyone had ever known. When a man marries, his wife sooner or later estranges him from his old friends, and in-laws but Shreya on the contrary increased his intimacy with them. By making him more tolerant she made him a more agreeable companion.

They had classmates, colleagues, lots of friends to enjoy their weekends with. Aditya would arrange a list of songs on his phone – Beatles, Abida Parveen – and get ready chilled beer bottles. Aditya liked red wine and made sure he had a few bottles for the parties at home which were most frequent on Friday night, that along with snacks from the supermarket, created a feeling of nostalgia as if it were a scene from one of the old films.

They chaffed one another a great deal and laughed a lot; every now and then their eyes met more significantly and they seemed to exchange a little private message in parties. She knew exactly what tone to use with persons with whom she conversed in the party, she was always polite as she was quick, silent and watchful.

Occasionally they would drive across the city to explore New York city and its pleasures. They made a lark of their life. No one has known a more devoted couple. They had never had much money as they were settling down the house filling it with objects of comforts and they never seemed to want any. Their life was a picnic that never came to an end. They had a tiny car which whenever Aditya had a holiday, they took it across the city.

Once someone asked them if they ever quarrelled. "No," she said, "we never seem to have anything to quarrel about. Adi has the temper of an angel." They were sweet together and were very happy in one another's company and were never apart if they could help it. They say complete happiness is very rare in this world but these two people seemed to enjoy it. Aditya was always full of spirits and extremely amusing and Shreya was peaceful and easy. They lead their lives as each one wished without interference from the other; in this way the seasons shifted and the months passed.

Then after two years Aditya was transferred to Australia and along with Shreya moved to Sydney. They initially stayed in Hotel Weston for few days then hired a big apartment. Shreya also got a job in Macquarie University and after four years was also blessed with a daughter Kuhu. Aditya lived joyously and pictured how exquisite, poetic, and even holy, life might be.

Goodness knows why, one still regrets something, one still longs for something. In short, a man is never satisfied with what he has. One autumn evening Aditya alone sauntered along the beach where the moon was pouring its light into the shimmering water. He began to think he would grow dull and old, die in the end, as the average man usually does die, in a decrepit, soured old age, making everyone about him miserable and depressed.

He was also faced with the eternal challenge of knowing what we want. After a long while he understood that he yearned to do something for his parents and this dream he had nourished since childhood. The very thought thrilled inside him desires and mysterious strivings which immersed his mind, dipped him in happiness.

Aditya was devoted to his parents. He had something of excitement at the idea of taking part in the opening up of a new life for his parents. It is rather splendid, isn't it? He said to himself. Their life seemed very humdrum and commonplace and of course, it was lonely. The companionship of son and daughter-in-law and bubbly Kuhu would be worth having for his parents.

There was nothing that pleased him more than the prospect of serving his parents in India. He was too anxious to help them in their old age and wanted to be in the thick of their difficulties. For others also he was a sincere friend in adversity. He was considerate and of a generous disposition. He looked upon it as his duty to see to the welfare of his colleagues. It was a satisfaction to him that Shreya could be trusted to share his passion of helping others.

He was always ready to oblige a friend and after this job he was now sufficiently well off to be able to indulge himself in the pleasure of helping others. You could find him somewhere confidante or counsellor in a conflicted relationship of his friends. He had turned unhappy marriages into happy ones; he had given health to the sick in spirit; he had saved friends from suicide.

He was a friendly man, affable to his juniors, considerate with his colleagues and popular with the neighbours. He was an excellent father, kindly but strict. Now he wanted to serve his parents; he had that humane faculty that enabled him to do things for which others could offer no explanation.

One Sunday night in November, a restlessly excited Aditya communicated to Shreya with a coy pinch of the eyes that he had something to tell her: "I have decided to quit the job in Australia; I am needed in India I want to go to India; my whole ambition is to serve my parents in old age. I have money, I have rank, I can claim that no honour, no personal advantage, no thought of self would induce me to swerve by a hair's breadth from my duty. Now service is my aim and it is within my reach. I must go there because I want to so intensely. I want to seize this opportunity. My mother has lost her father; during this visit to India, I had seen her agony I want to be with my grandmother and my parents. Besides, I love living there because that is where my roots are, those profound and delicate roots that attach a man to the soil where his forebears are born and died, that attach him to what people think and what they eat, to both customs and food, to local phrases to the smells of the earth and of the very air. I am very fond of my native land it seems to me so beautiful and so snug. I love the fresh greenery, the still, sunny mornings and chiming of the temple bells that peal through the beautiful morning, reaching me with their sweet and distant metallic booming, their brass chanting carried to me by the breeze, now stronger, now weaker. I know the weighty positions have weighty responsibilities. I am aware of those responsibilities and would strive to fulfil them with all my strength, no matter the cost I am prepared to do so."

He told Shreya he was sorry but they had to build a life in India and added intensely that he was his parents' only son. By now Shreya knew he was too hard working, too ambitious, and it must be added too devoted to be tempted by any pleasures that might interfere with decision/calling. He radiated unshakable determination. Without such commitment one cannot achieve great things.

Women are always sensitive to the beauty of the self-sacrifice of others. When he shared his decision with her Shreya did not say anything; no inevitable scene erupted as he had apprehended (he was continually watching out her for any expression), no expected reproaches, no tactless recriminations, no tears. She was not irritated with him who expected her to listen to his arguments or wished to hear the reason for his decision. It hinted at a subtle intimacy that asks no question but takes liberties with its love.

He could imagine a life in which Shreya encouraged him to be a better devoted son. He could imagine accomplishing quite a lot with her at his side. There was a silence between them, a promise of things to come.

Shreya voluntarily assumed the responsibilities of a willing and loving daughter-in-law. To accomplish that she left her job of a professor in Macquarie University, her home she had settled with such efforts, sold the heavy furniture and electronic appliances. It was the second time she was doing it; firstly when they moved from Chicago to Sydney because he liked a peaceful and relaxed job in Australia, the land of open spaces.

Women are easily attached it was rather difficult for Shreya to give up a secure and settled life but what made it possible was her love (the great love of her life) for him whom she thought the best husband in the world, tall and handsome, for her love marriage she was prepared to do anything. She understood it was not easier for him either to leave a high paid prestige job of senior manager in McKinsey. There were a lot of people who resented him having achieved the position at such an age when even the cleverest of men were content with the situation of relative obscurity. He had many good qualities he had courage, insight, determination. He had so much self-assurance, so quick and a decided mind that he was never at a loss to do the right thing at the right time. He booked the container in the ship and his luggage was to reach after a fortnight and they left by Quanta's flight to Bangalore.

In Bangalore his friend Amit from Bishop Cotton School Shimla had already selected a flat within the convenient walking distance from his office of Inmobi, and Aditya and Shreya liked it at first sight because this beautiful apartment overlooked a swimming pool and lot of palm trees.

Poplars covered with dew, filled the air with fragrance; it had a sitting room which he lined with books and a sofa, a dining room into which his Chippendale furniture just fitted, a big sized bedroom for himself for which he bought teak wood furniture from the local dealer, beyond his kitchen was a maid's room and he applied at a registry office for a housemaid. He got a maid of irreproachable character, sober, honest, reliable and of pleasing exterior. He offered her good wages, reasonable liberty and ample holidays.

Now it is a funny thing about life, if you refuse to accept anything but the best you very often get it; if you utterly decline to make do with what you can get, then somehow or other you are very likely to get what you want. After settling down in the new house and a new job in Bangalore his life seemed perfect, he called his parents and his grandmother to live with him. Now his life at home brimmed with uncontainable gusto for life he had just begun – a life he would purposefully pursue.

The anticipation of their smiles, the taste of Lipton Yellow Level whipped with fresh cream became the high point of Aditya's day, a gracious morning ceremony with his parents and after he was back from his office in the evening and in the breakfast, he devoured two eggs omelette studded with onion and green chillies and Shreya sipped tea before going to office. They dined together at night. On weekends he took them around the city looking at the sights of the town, its gardens, museums, zoo, theatres. His friends liked his parents, they were affectionate and easy to talk, called them for picnics and dinners.

Aditya would spend most weeknights out either eating with friends or taking them out for dinner in different eating joints in the city because his father was fond of good food and enjoyed a great deal on weekends. His mother was a religious lady who loved visiting temples so he made it a point to take them on Sunday morning to the neighbourhood temple in rickshaw because the streets were very narrow and traffic was heavy that side.

He would talk to the rickshaw puller and listen to his blaring Hindi songs and was happy to give him a generous tip. Not that it was a kindly thing for him to have done, it was a very agreeable sensation to give anyone so much real pleasure. His benevolence warmed him and for a moment he felt a great love in his heart for the whole human race.

He told his mother, "This is what he likes about India. The rickshaw puller is happy with his life and makes others also happy with his conversation. When I see small children playing in the mud and hear their shouts of joys it lifts my mood, I also want to be happy like them, this is my India."

"Such a depth of tenderness, such a boundless sympathy with all forms of beings, such a generous love renders my son singular in the whole world," told his mother at the dinner table that night.

When Aditya took long holidays, he took along his parents, they stayed at good hotels and visited churches, he hired the rental to show them Mysore palace at night fully illuminated with lights and sound that was picturesque with its palace gardens and forts, and Tipu Sultan's palaces, galleries, museums, temples on the hill top. Sometimes they went for picnics in gardens. Whenever he got the good opportunity to show them the movie that he had heard talked about he would take them to the cinema hall in spite of their continual no. And there it diverted them vastly to hear peal upon peal of joyous laughter.

There was a feeling of gaiety in the air and the people who poured past them, one way and another, seemed filled with a pleasant elation. He was a little amused at what he was doing and pleased too; it was nice to be able to make someone happy with so little trouble to himself. Rather than seeking happiness in some kind of heaven apart from this world, he tried to establish indestructible happiness right where he was, within the reality of his daily lives.

He told his parents that they must rest now, that they must not worry, they must sleep and rest their old bones. Tranquillity all around pushed their anxieties away and his words fell on their tired ears like the light rain of spring upon the freshly turned earth. He would go to his grandmother and could allay certain pains by the touch of his cool, firm hands; by stroking her weary forehead, he could soothe her perturbations, resolve the conflict that distracted her and banish her phobia and could induce sleep in her who was suffering from sleeplessness.

There was a fragrance of spring and a fragrance of happiness-everything seemed to say: "Here is a man who loves, labours and has attained at last the happiness possible on earth."

He was so certain of himself that he infected some of his friends with his own devotion, high spirits, his vitality, his confidence in the future, and his disinterestedness There was no reason in the world why he shouldn't be a happy man and if there had been in him a trace of self-complacency he might have claimed that he deserved to be.

Good parents make good children he said gaily when his parents appreciated him that he was the child who had returned to them he was the balm of their old age. His mother watched Aditya and Shreya; her heart swelled with pride and peace.

She marvelled at Shreya's ease, her interest in his land, his parents. In the dining room she spoke appreciatively of Shreya: "Shreya is a very sensible lady who manages the house uncommonly well. She does the groceries, makes sure the gas and electricity bills are paid on time and does our laundry twice a week and teaches Kuhu regularly as she herself has been a scholarship girl and later gone to the best university in USA. She is even tempered, a good hostess and good daughter-in-law, happily doing all chores for us; we like her."

"True," said Aditya about Shreya, "She's perfection. I should be lost without her. I do not know if she likes my shifting to this place but she has never complained. I've often wondered why it is that she never says no to my decisions. She has every quality in the world she is an excellent mother, kindly but strict. She does not bother how she looks; she wears no makeup but when she dolls herself up for a party, she looks quite attractive. She has been a nice woman, good wife to me and is at ease with her in-laws as she is with her parents."

Her mother-in-law also helped her in her household chores. In the kitchen she would say at times, "I will cook one of Aditya's favourite dishes: butter chicken, *sarson ka sag* with corn roti, mutton kababs off the spit, vegetable *biryani,* Kabuli chickpeas with a heap of chopped coriander, green chillies and ginger tonight," and made Aditya's favourite drink of lemonade with soda and his father took seat at the head of the dark teak table and his mother regaled them with his childhood stories.

Aditya beamed tightly, "My mother has a delightful knack for stories. Kuhu, listen what Dadi is telling when I was child like you." While all the family members shared their meals at night, his mother would say to Shreya, "Eat, you must eat. No wonder you're so svelte. You do not eat. What would you like to eat? I've cooked your favourite biryani tonight."

Shreya had never missed her breakfast with her, a ritual dear to her mother-in-law. Whenever she was free from routine of household she would sit by their bedside, talk to them and arrange nutritious snacks for them. Aditya knew she did it with devotion and her actions were buoyed up by her old and fixed notion of respecting the elders.

Aditya's eyes would light up with laughter when he was happy. There were no issues as happens in *sas bahu* relationship in India. There had been no scenes, she had no quarrels with her in-laws. She had enthusiastically adopted the manners and customs of her in laws' family with elegance. She seemed to take it for granted that she would serve her in-laws faithfully.

Aditya noted it with approval that his wife was carrying it off in just the right way. No wonder then her vivacity and determination had given her the position she held now. Shreya, one night sitting in the bed, acknowledged, "I have never seen a more united household. They were merry, industrious and kindly. It had a completeness that gave it a beauty as definite as that of symphony by Beethoven or a picture by Titian. They were happy and they deserved their happiness; she liked his mother who was of seventy, tall, upright, and dignified with grey hair and though her face was much wrinkled, her eyes were bright."

His stay in Bangalore was a period of ecstatic happiness. The world, the dull, humdrum world of everyday, blazed with glory. The music/songs both devotional, ghazals and rock flowed from his house. There was a great deal of talking, laughing and sharing.

Things had been proceeding happily for nearly six years, but now things didn't pan out according to schedule. Eventually it was a shock to Aditya to discover that his daughter Kuhu had developed asthma. As he heard the doctor say that the pollution and damp weather of Bangalore was damaging her health, suddenly sullenness darked his face like a thunder-cloud.

She was the only child and he adored her with a fiery passion that demanded an immediate care of her in the world. He could not sleep that night and lay thinking what he should do now. Her health deteriorated over a short span and doctors put her on inhaler even when Aditya consulted every renowned doctor in time. They went from pillar to post in search of unconventional cures; they tried homeopathy, ayurvedic but nothing helped her. Immediately he took her to Delhi and showed her in the premier institute of AIIMS. He was equally disappointed there as well when doctors recommended Kuhu to be immediately shifted from this climate. He searched Google and discovered Bangalore climate is injurious to children of such tender age in this acute condition, and asthma was the common problem here. Aditya felt aversion to this Bangalore weather, the filthy damp air.

In the months following, every doctor suggested change of place now. Until now he had imagined his life in Bangalore to be so picture perfect yes it was so till Kuhu developed this disease and life became so insufferable.

Is it not strange that a simple malaise, a minor disturbance in the so imperfect and so delicate functioning of our human machine, can turn the most joyful of men into a melancholic? Aditya was faced with the dilemma – he could either leave the job and his parents or let Kuhu suffer.

He started thinking if he was forced to leave Bangalore and his lucrative job, where could he go? He consulted his company for the options: he could go back either to America or to Australia but they were far off places and leaving parents behind was inconceivable. Shreya was anxious to show him sympathy but was afraid of saying the wrong things. She did not seem to extract confidences from him. She did not know how to give him a lead to share his innermost thoughts and frustration.

Then one evening after he came back from office, Shreya sat with a cup of tea with him and he, (ruminating of his past, his hopes) suddenly said in a sullen tone, "Shreya I have lost everything that made life meaningful and lovely to me. You already know that to have this opportunity to be with the parents meant the world to me. Losing this chance of serving my parents, I feel the future dissolving in a moment like salt in a weakened broth. What I held important, what I counted significant has gone before I knew. I was riding the bus of joy and hopes, journeying through life with plans I woke up with sorrow as the deepest thing."

Suddenly the enormity of what had fallen upon him hit Shreya she said, "It is okay to feel miserable," but he responded very irritably, "It may be okay to fall in other people's estimation but I never want to fall in my own. I think of the startling direction in which our life has slid. Shreya, I have made myself the laughingstock of the whole world. Isn't it true that everything around us, everything we see, everything we brush past without knowing it, everything we touch without feeling it, everything we encounter exerts rapid, surprising and inexplicable effects on us, on our organs and through them on our ideas and even on our hearts? You may say it doesn't seem much good to make a lot of fuss about a thing that is beyond my control but it impacts all aspects of your life."

Shreya understood that Aditya suffered from a typical Indian guilt of a devoted son who unlike the mythological figure of Shravan Kumar failed to serve his parents in old age. It was this idealized time spent with them he missed and the real joys of intimacy, fun of family jokes, the exchanging of vulnerabilities, helping him become a better version of himself while holding them and comforting them; presently he felt a zero in life, wretched for having to desert them.

He told Shreya, "With all the work I have; I must be in control of all my faculties. I need rest; sleep brings me none. I no sooner fall asleep than my dreams begin: they are grinning at me, mocking me, despising me. Sometimes I had a notion of the people looked at me in rather a funny sort of way, I have the impression that colleagues are talking about me and they titter after I pass. It's a monstrous persecution. I have no strength left, no courage, no self-dominion, no power even to stir my will. I can no longer will; someone controls all my actions, all my movements, all my thoughts. I am nothing on the inside, nothing, but an enslaved spectator terrified of all things I do.

Leaving Sydney to look after my parents was the real joy I knew it then, know it all too well now but leaving them is the real blunder I am incapable of making. Nothing has prepared me for this. Everything was surrounded by a halo of romance I had expected something wholly beautiful and less complicated but now this inevitable disillusionment I have reached here after so long a journey from Sydney and now so many charming associations are attached to this place, I did not know that I had formed in my mind. Every exact picture of what I expected is causing me not only great shock but also giving me a tremendous feeling of guilt. We are meaning-making creatures and I am facing the terrifying prospect of its meaninglessness."

He spoke without life and one had the feeling that for the sake of the family he forced himself to speak, his thoughts were elsewhere. Shreya's thoughts were in turmoil, she was aghast. There is nothing more awe-inspiring than when a man reveals to you the nakedness of his soul. There was something in his expressions that she did not understand. There are hundreds of youths who enter upon the calling of youth with extravagant high hopes but come to terms with the vagaries of destiny and find somewhere in life a niche where they can escape. His shattered hopes, dreams had broken his spirit, his disappointments shattered him and his lost illusion ground him to dust. What a lamentable object he looked!

She thought: Women are different they will talk to one another without embarrassment of the most intimate matters. It is always difficult for a man; he neither wanted Shreya's glance nor sought it. She asked herself if nothing could be done. She was afraid she had lost him. In her desperation she went to her father-in-law and shared Aditya's predicament. But the good thing about being parents is that even in their gloomiest moments they could transform their mood at a moment's notice. His father knew that self-sacrifice appealed so keenly to Aditya's imagination that the inability to exercise it gave him a sense of disillusion.

His father said coolly, Aditya, "I understand your condition. It is true when we are unable to live our expectations there is protracted mourning for it or an endless tantrum; it is natural. There is nothing wrong with the expectations but you have inextricably tied them up with the self-image and self-worth and the result is there is a pressure inside your head all the time leading to anxiety. Besides, your life bears witness to the challenges of a devoted son; in India the need to be a devoted son is drummed into us from childhood. I remember you grew up hearing your Nani's stories of *Ramayana* where Shravan Kumar carried his parents for pilgrimage and she affectionately calling, 'You are my Shravan Kumar and your mom saying 'you are the balm of my old age.' To top it all you have grown up watching us serving our old parents. Do you remember when I had brought you sketchbooks to draw in, you sketched an old man and boy holding his hand; you had written papa at the bottom of the old man and Aditya under the boy?"

"Yes, Papa I had saved those drawings and had showed Kuhu also," Aditya wanted to say but kept quiet. His father continued, "Imbibing of Hindu norms and culture were of utmost importance to you from the beginning; you were brought up in a traditional way. You need not think that your pain and your heartbreak are unprecedented in the world. In every life, there comes a time when we are razed to the bone of our resilience by losses beyond our control, as you have read in classical writers like Dostoevsky and Dickens and I have seen in real life.

Of course, chance plays such dice with the universe. No one knows the meaning of why anything comes to be or does not. We are aware of your sacrifices Aditya. You abandoned a stellar career in Sydney after your mother lost her father. You changed your life around, moved to India to be with us. You are most kind, upright and humorous. Do not crank now within carrying these unknown reserves of guilt and fear. You are the privileged few who won the lottery of serving their parents even for a short time against all odds, how dare you whine at your inevitable return to the state from which the vast majority have never stirred?

Your physical presence is not the only way to measure your devotion. We know you are our devoted son but we also understand your compulsions. We are with you whatever decision you take. Can we ever be happy if you are making yourself miserable? Our real prize is to see you grow and evolve into a better person with a smile on your face at the end of the day. The only thing is that you have to open your heart to the possibilities of whatever may emerge." What train of thought his father's remarks had suggested in Aditya no one knows but he began to speak.

Aditya spoke in a low voice, without any expression, "After coming to India it is I who said to you that I would be looking after you now. Since I am here, I will go with you everywhere like a shadow. Now they tell me to leave this place. Papa, it is hard to get over the expectation of yourself. Who can comprehend my abominable anguish?"

His father was startled by the expression in those sombre eyes of his, an expression of intolerable anguish, that betrayed a tragic depth of emotion of which he had never thought him capable.

His father calmly said, "Yes, I understand your anguish. We were also reliving the joys of parenting – a much gentler model than our own. We value your unspoken but obvious plans for us to live happily our setting years with you in Bangalore. We are also upset. One of the many inconveniences of real life is that there is no human being on earth capable of ever knowing with certitude what the future is. Therefore, all of us have to move on whatever may happen. Although to move on or to let go sounds simple yet is rather one of life's most difficult tasks and requires a triumphant feat of maturity. The difficulty lies in our attachments, insecurity, fear or simply the desire to control everything ourselves. Do not think papa is preaching but I want to share this secret that it has taken a long time for us even to achieve this maturity. It has grown through so many obstacles conquered, so many serious illnesses cured, so many griefs appeased, so many despairs overcome. It has grown through so many desires, so many hopes, so many lapses, so much love. Not only you but we (me and your mother, grandmother) have to accept the situation and stop contemplating these existential immensities. Actually, we should learn from the migratory birds in the blue sky when to fly to the sun. No one tells them the seasons. Your whole future is in front of you and you must decide for yourself; all I can tell you is that there is no future for Kuhu in India. Big cities in India are full of pollution and small towns have no job for you. And life is something that you can lead but once; mistakes are often irreparable. Go now and begin a new life in Singapore and move on through this impasse. I know your unwillingness to walk away from us is rooted in your belief that you won't be able to help us from afar. Singapore is two hours away by flight, and my boy difficult situations demand different responses and difficult decisions. In fact, the rightest choice can present itself shrouded in uncertainty and doubt at the outset, its rightlessness only crystallizes in the clarity of hindsight.

Do not underestimate your innate ability to deal with setbacks. We, human beings, are more resilient than we often believe. In fact, invariably, it is in such situations that we learn and grow most. Do you remember the film *Shawshank Redemption* we saw together sometime back last year during the Christmas holidays? I may remind you:

In the film, Redding, called by jail inmates as Red, towards the end of the film reads a letter which he found buried under the rock where Andy, his jail mate had written long time back; "Hope is a good thing, may be the best of things and no good thing ever dies." Andy goes to Zihuatenego (in Mexico which is warm and has no memory) and he was hopeful, he and Red would finally meet and they did.

Your Nani is ninety-eight, and you cannot count on many more years of her life. It is for her that we are here. We will come to you in Singapore and live in a foreign country with you forever. Being away from us also allows you to love us and if need be, come to help us. You only told us how your friends in Singapore helped their parents in COVID times with doctor's advice and even managed to deliver the medicine and other kits and pathological services at home. You need to understand that chances of helping us would come in unexpected shapes for you too."

His father was the only person in his life whose strength and sunniness had always warmed his heart. There was in his bearing assurance and dignity. Aditya watched him, he understood how he had swayed men's minds and touched their hearts. It seemed to Aditya a tremendous moment when he captured the optimism of his father in his hurtful voice and with an effort, he pulled himself together. He forced a smile to his shaking lips and hoped this time, he would not disappoint.

2

A Mango Tree

Riten Mandal was a man in his forties with a head full of thick black hair. He was not tall but had well-built shoulders and a broad chest. He was one of the fortunate ones who by nature was overcharged with breezy spirits and vigorous health; cares and troubles would slide off leaving no impression on him.

From his father he had inherited light-heartedness and boundless gaiety that made him very popular amongst his neighbourhood for his good humorous nature. He had a younger brother Amitav, twenty-two years old. He was very joyful, smart and playful as a child. He had not completed his schooling and dropped out in elementary school. He had migrated to Bangalore as a skilled carpenter whereas he worked as a farmer on the piece of land he had inherited from his father in a village named Gaighata of North Twenty-Four Parganas in West Bengal. Gaighata is 60km from Kolkata.

The village of Gaighata is made of few pucca houses and old huts of soil. The lanes are deep in mud during wet weather. There are no factories, no railway and no library; only a small temple which folks have constructed with mud and a primary school that is half an hour walk from his house. It is a remote region far removed from the busy world and the interests that animate it. It is full of green trees of mango, jackfruit, wood apple, Krishnachura, mahogany, and an almost two-hundred-year-old banyan tree.

The Mandals lived in this village. They were the oldest residents in Gaighata. Neither they nor their forerunners for two generations had known any other place. The land didn't yield much but Riten worked the fields himself and with his own family. He had been farming for a long time; he ploughed, sowed and reaped. He was never bored doing it and never frowned with disgust and was easily reconciled with this life of toil. He thought that they had all that was necessary for life.

He had a lovely, young, intelligent, fascinating and beautiful wife Meeta in whose eyes he – her husband, was everything a man ought to be, in spirit and body beautiful. They got married when she was sixteen years old. Everybody felt her to be someone close, familiar, and cordial as if they had met her before.

They had two very dear children, Ashutosh nine years old, and Basu six. They had not been happy in the beginning but were a happy family now. Presently they had no problems, nor were they expecting any. They were well satisfied with their lot.

One night Riten told Meeta, "Recently I have constructed one pucca room with a kitchen, now I am planning to construct a pucca house this summer when Amitav would come home. He can help with woodwork and the rest I would manage with my savings and the money Amitav was sending every month."

Meeta was very pleased to hear this and said, "One pucca room we have already made for him now; I would also show him the girl I have selected to be his bride." Riten said, "Amma had taught us work is worship. Amitav and I have been worshipping at the altar of hard work believing that hard work brings more money, more happiness and a better life. Isn't it true, Meeta?" He fell asleep dreaming of the pucca house and good times ahead.

They were in no way prepared for this terrible thing. The ordeal started at 12:30 pm on Wednesday when Riten's neighbour Ganesh Ghosh got a phone call: "Tie your water tank with rope and fill it with water."

It didn't come as surprise for Ganesh Ghosh as he was tracking the updates of cyclone Amphan for the last three days. The wind picked up at 2:30 pm when they began to hear a hissing sound. The beast was on the prowl and the sound went up steadily.

Doors and windows started creaking. A fearful uproar arose both inside and outside. Every living thing in the neighbourhood of Gaighata began to rush, stomp up and down the rooms. The names of Satan and God and angels were overheard. There was an eerie feeling that windows panes would come out and this stormy wind would get you.

This was happening in strong pucca houses and destruction in Riten's mud house was much beyond comprehension. His mud house was washed away; he was rendered homeless with the house destroyed, roots blown away, crops submerged under waist-high water and livelihood snatched away.

It was a terrifying experience; hundreds of dwellings fell instantly to the ground. There was not a building that was left with four walls intact. The proper roofs of buildings were hurtling around like projectiles and electric poles uprooted by the cyclone fury were acting as speed breakers. Nature's fury was unleashed full-blown as the severe cyclonic storm Amphan battered Bengal with a wind speed of up to 165 kmph. It could not have come at the worst time with the country already battling the Covid 19 pandemic.

They had endured the trauma for more than four hours and patience was starting to run out. Hope was giving way to fear, and a deep sense of helplessness was gripping each one at home. Finally, around 10:15 pm the wind started to subside. "The cyclone has passed us but Amphan had exposed yet again our helplessness against nature's fury," said Riten.

The next morning Riten sat in the yard of his Gaighata home which had collapsed like a pack of cards under a large mango tree that had uprooted. He seemed lost in his thoughts comparing the devastation wrecked by Cyclone Aila to Cyclone Amphan that had pounded Bengal on Wednesday evening.

"It was in May eleven years ago when Aila hit, and we were robbed of a roof over our heads overnight. We struggled for months before we could get back on our feet. I don't know if we can survive the damage this time as we have nothing left," said Mandal. He was devastated by the destruction but still grateful that his Ashu, Basu and Amitav were not among the four members from North Parganas who were dead. The four had died after the corrugated sheet roof collapsed on them when a tree fell on it. He remembered how his mother had died when she ran out but could not run. They tried to save her but in vain. Her lifeless body was found under the debris the next day.

How their village had gone underwater and they along with thousands of people were shifted to relief camps. As the day progressed Riten and the people of Gaighata realized that the 30 km stretch of Jessore road from Duttapukur to Gaighata was the worst hit. The cyclone had wreaked havoc in the area, large trees had uprooted, smaller one flung away and homes reduced to rubble. He learnt later that according to the estimates of the district administration at least 80,000 people had turned homeless.

The following day Riten along with his sons and wife jostled outside a relief camp for two loaves of bread and a tarpaulin sheet to spend the night at a cyclone shelter. It was near impossible to maintain social distancing in cyclone centres. Evacuation would have adverse consequences; it was almost impossible to carry out large scale evacuations while observing social distancing. It was a humanitarian disaster of epic proportions.

Riten returned to his village. "Meeta we have to start from scratch. There is no trace of any help. We cannot reach any relative. Even your parents, cannot help us as they are suffering the most in Sunderbans. Their villages have been inundated; their dwellings swept away. Arable land was swamped with saltwater and won't be cultivable for years. Freshwater ponds are also flooded with seawater.

Many fishermen had lost their boats and nets. Bridges were blown away; wharves were carried off by the surging waters. Godowns and stores were all gutted with water and even houses. Rivers overran farmlands throughout the Sunderbans damaging acres and acres of standing crops. O Meeta! Such a misfortune! What am I to do? My sons are hungry." Riten was grieving with all his heart that he was a father who could not feed his children.

Where's his brother any way he thought. Then he said to himself, "Do not get excited. You told him to take his time to come home when the trains start. Don't get nervous now."

But he was nervous, it made him angry at himself. Riten was engrossed in thinking, "What should I do now my crops are washed, what should I give my children to eat?" Riten looked pale, his inflamed eyes darted in all directions, he took long strides, he was obviously waiting for someone.

He was looking up the street for someone who had not arrived. Yes, his brother Amitav, a migrant labourer was returning home exhausted and hungry after a fortnight of trudging the roads and rounds of relief camps. On returning to his village, Amitav stood still, his bag fell as if on its own volition, silence fell, and they stood looking at each other.

This catastrophe was incomprehensible to him. He didn't understand how much had come to an end. Granting that he was young he could not help being shocked by something so massive. A scene of such devastation transfixed him, and he began slowly scratching the back of his head, as if trying to solve the problem where he was, all the while sighing and looking around apprehensively.

All the devastation, the ruined homes, debris all seemed to look at him reproachfully. He was quiet, diffident and shy; besides which at this time he was looking paler than usual.

Apart from shame, bewilderment and surprise he felt empty and disillusioned as if someone had taken a pair of scissors and cut out of him all dreams of future happiness.

"What is the matter with you?" Riten asked. "Are you sick? You do not look yourself," glancing at his white face and faintly trembling lips. After the first shock, he did not let anybody see a thing. "0h nothing. Here I am. I am sorry that I took so long to reach you. Bangalore is too far away and then after such a long wait I got the train."

"I hope you are fine," said Riten. After hesitating for a moment then with the gesture of despair he replied, "I was happy to be reunited with my family. After an arduous journey of 15 days by foot, truck and bus I managed to reach home. When I reached home I thought my sufferings were over; I was hopeful that everything would be fine but I was wrong the worse was waiting to happen," said Amitav.

His hopes and happiness disappeared suddenly as he looked carefully at the ruined house and along the street. "I must have known just like everyone else. It was just I had no idea. My territory had altered and cyclone has gone through it and skimmed off all meaning except loss and ruin. Our home has been destroyed by Amphan. The lock down took away my job and this cyclone took away everything we were left with. I don't know what we would do next."

On seeing his younger brother so distraught, Riten said to himself, "He looks dispirited. Last summer when he came home he was looking younger and very confident. He was full of eagerness and talked together for hours a great deal in the quiet domestic surroundings. Now we are silent, each thinking his thoughts. I never mentioned my fears to him, he never mentioned his to me. Each of us thought it would break the other's hearts. Look what this catastrophe has done to him!"

Riten looked at Amitav full of forlorn feelings and suddenly blurted out. "I have never seen such a fierce storm in my life," pointing at the twisted electric pole lying on the road. "Look at that. It seems like a toy flung into the air and trampled on. When the thatched roof of our kitchen was blown away, we ran out to take shelter in a pucca room. In the morning we found a heap of debris that was once our own home.

We took years to build it but it was wiped out in a matter of a few minutes. In our village, a house is rare to come by that has not been damaged. Electric poles were uprooted and overhead wires snapped; our paddy fields are flattened, embankments breached, water sources are contaminated."

Suddenly the sight of the naked stumps where once there had been a mango tree broke Amitav's heart. He stood staring at the mango tree in disbelief. He paced the length of the ruined mango tree several times as if he had not noticed his brother, then he stood in front of the mango tree, stared intently at it for some time and began fumbling about in the broken branches as if he was searching for something precious that was now lost. There came a moment in his life when everything seemed to have something to say to him, all in a flash, all in a rush and he could not concentrate.

He said to himself, "For others, the loss of a mango tree may seem trivial but for us, it was a family tree. It carried our special childhood memories that anchored us. Our grandfather had planted it in the memory of his mother."

Amitav's heart was beating in big thumps, like howls happening in his chest. He burst into tears and went straight to hug the broken tree whose branches were strewn on the ground, few green mangoes rolling in the mud like spilled marbles.

Riten looked at him with surprise and said, "Look at him! What has happened to him? Has he gone quite out of his mind? He is a very quiet person by nature."

Meeta said, "Let him mourn this tree, this is the only way he can wrap his head around so much loss, so much heartbreak. What do you expect of him when his heart is so troubled I heard his sighs? The mango tree seemed to him not a plant outside his house but presences rooted in the ground. He had scratched his names on its trunk like freezing moments in an album. As a little boy, he didn't venture too close when his father through the summer afternoon sat with old men on the wooden bench placed under this benevolent mango tree, talking as old people talk of the past. He kept discreetly in the background as his father had delicately hinted that children were to be seen but not heard. He had wept when he lost his mother and shared his grief when his father passed away. As generations pass, trees reassure by carrying on. Now he is feeling rootless."

"True." said Riten, "It was a place to gather, for the road barber to set up his shop, the street dog to nap, shade for the domestic help and the rickshaw puller. We had taken them for granted just like loved ones."

Riten went to Amitav and folded him in his arms and they both wept. While sobbing Amitav said, "Do you remember how I grew climbing those branches? Amma used to tell us stories of the ghosts that dwell in these branches and ghosts with feet that turned inward. When I used to pick the raw mangoes with slingshot she got very irritated.

Baba used to say, "Don't fell trees they also have life." They also groan when hurt. All through the storm, the tree must have groaned, its branches flailing against the whipping wind. It was a treat to walk under the shady trees after school and then rest in the afternoon under the mango tree. It was home to crows, sparrows, orioles and tailorbirds too. When the mangoes fell due to storms, mama would have mangoes charred over the fire and turned the pulp into tangy *aam pora* and sometimes made spicy pickles."

Suddenly their eyes met, their spiritual fortitude deserted them both. Riten took him in his arms and pressed his face against his chest, tears flowed from his eyes and he kissed his forehead, his shoulders, his hands wet with tears. With a burning pain in his heart, he realized how deceptive, how petty, how unnecessary it was to conceal their feelings at this crucial time.

Riten had the courage to love more, to give more, in the face of even the most heart-breaking devastation. Perhaps the deepest measure of our character, of our very humanity, is how much we go on giving when what we most value is taken from us. People who lead a solitary existence always have some things in their hearts they are eager to talk about.

Amitav also told Riten that throughout his journey he heard passengers saying Kolkata woke up to the macabre sight of 11 bodies floating down inundated streets. Hundreds of houses were destroyed and embankments were breached at many places leaving scores of villages swimming in misery.

Many of the casualties during the cyclone's nine-hour march through seven south Bengal districts on Wednesday were either caused by electrocution or houses collapsing. The trees that took years, even decades to grow toppled over in just one night's fury. An almost 200-year-old banyan tree that had survived Aila, Phani and Bulbul had its canopy ripped apart by Amphan.

Mamta Bannerjee (CM, West Bengal) said all she was seeing around was destruction and misery. It was not easy to gauge the scale of destruction as roads were either blocked or blown away. Thousands of villages were beyond the reach of rescue personnel and government officials.

When evening set in Riten became so mournful with sad thoughts that his searching eyes were fixed on Amitav. He didn't understand what was passing in his soul. There were miseries he could bear, those connected with migrants' life in Covid-19. And others' miseries connected with Amphan that he could not.

"Bhai it is worse than Covid-19," said Amitav. While Covid-19 has infected 1,20,000 people in India in three months, Amphan in three hours destroyed a few million livelihoods and uprooted as many families. With Covid you could still save yourselves with proper behavioural hygiene, social distancing and early detection but against Amphan you could be sitting ducks waiting to be pounced and tormented."

Riten said, "We know the roads have gone underwater, trees are blocking the roads, the relief workers cannot reach our affected area to repair damaged embankments and houses and restore water supply, communications and power.

Amphan has come at a time when the resources of the state are already at breaking point, battling diseases, fortifying health systems and providing relief to the poor amid an economic standstill. The CM said that the disaster could not have come at the worst time for Bengal. "We also have to deal with the pandemic, migrant labourers' problems and the rising cost of quarantining people." True they are battling Covid, enforcing lock down and social distancing but it seemed as if the state had receded all together from Amphan. A litany of woes can be heard from almost everywhere."

Different circumstances are likely to produce different reactions.

"But the question is can we reclaim the life that was and can we continue to stay afloat amidst this gloom?" Amitav asked. "I came to this village when the act of taking responsibility is most difficult, and the impulse toward evasion and escapism most intense. Nevertheless, I must devote my adult life to sharing in its responsibilities, its atonements, it's healing. I am young; I am of this village, and a carpenter. Whether or not I am a victim of this hostile fate I cannot avoid responsibility for what has happened, is happening. What am I waiting for? Oh God, what am I waiting for? I am responsible for it, must fulfil my obligation to it, I must contribute to its restoration. And I am not alone I have my family."

It was a moment of reflective repose before he devoted himself to action. This was the most logical thing, by the undiluted logic that most people had relinquished.

"As there are no mobile connections, no power, no drinking water, everyday basic needs are to be restored first and as soon as possible. Let us start by clearing trees and electric poles first," he said.

Riten, Amitav, Meeta, Ashu, Basu all joined hands! Amitav was a diligent carpenter; he worked day and night to restore some normalcy to their life.

Seeing them working Ganesh his neighbour, his family and their neighbour's families also got down to work. In a village or small town, some men are always around to help others in need and you know them by their faces. Abhijit and Ganesh and friends of his were like this.

Nobody said, "Look here, come around to work;" all went without asking. Other villagers started making all efforts to push aside broken branches of tree trunks from their homes. Riten said to them, "But let me tell you things happen all the time. The only thing to do is to get along and to remember you are not the only one and you are not alone. There is no denying the fact that what we had always taken for granted is now under threat. Our foundations of normal life have been shaken. It is normal to mourn loss but we cannot remain transfixed there. We have to adapt to it, make some necessary changes and adjustments, and move on."

"We human beings have the gift of biological and psychological plasticity, the ability to adjust to the changing environment. Once we face it with courage and mindfulness, the worst would get over and new possibilities would sprout up. In the present circumstances, we cannot simply sit back and wish that reality changes. We don't want the divine to perform miracles and take away all our difficulties. We need to deal with the after-effects of Amphan ourselves. You know telecommunication systems are down in several areas, electricity is cut off, we are left without electricity and clean drinking water. We the people have to deal with fallen overhead wires and threats of electrocution; trees precariously fell on or in front of our homes and crashed electric poles. And for many of us, there was nobody to reach. The state machinery is failing, as also no help is at home. It is not Bengal's misery, it is India's misery, it cannot be left to state or NDR, and it needs your coordination and people's participation at every level to start the revival."

It was then that people themselves started to cross their hurdles and come forward. They gathered together, all the peasants, all the men, women, children from the village and the work of rehabilitation started at a tremendous pace. Now people did not look at these trees as obstacles to normalcy, impediments to the restoration of electricity.

The villagers got busy chopping trees into chunks of wood; their mango tree was also hacked to pieces. Amidst the wreckage of the tree they found half a dozen more mangoes that had eluded the mango scavengers. Women made mango rice with mango chutney. Women would get them some tea and meagre lunch and elderly people cooked food. As they had no bed to sleep, they slept on the broken sledges in the barn or ruined dwellings wherever chance took them.

All joined hands with them in ways that reminded of the days of Swadeshi movement and the nationalist struggle — Bengal's era of Tagore, Chittaranjan Das or Subhas Bose when self-help was a motto, when all countrymen were called upon to stand shoulder to shoulder in the face of adversity.

Riten recalled his grandmother's words, "In Bengal Famine of 1943, I would cook rice and broth and your grandfather with his friends would go to feed the poor starving on the streets."

His father would have joined hands to clear the streets if he were alive. Riten felt sad when he saw elderly people cooking meals and feeding civic bodyworkers working through the day in their neighbourhood. They motivated the people around with Mahabharata stories.

Ganesh related a story of Pandavas, the rightful heirs of the kingdom but their uncle gave them Khandavprastha — the infertile, rocky and arid part of the kingdom but with the motivation of Krishna and consequently with the fearless and optimistic attitude they developed that barren piece of land into Indraprastha – the most elegant city of the world.

They too could change the face of this village. Nature in itself is neutral, neither good nor bad. It is we who create value. It is for us to determine the good life, not for Nature – not even for Nature personified as God," he said smilingly.

Watching them struggling Ganesh seemed very happy as if they were his children taking unsupported steps or a first lone wobble on a bicycle. They also fed animals. Where there was no sarkari help available the villagers themselves started to rebuild inundated embankments to save themselves from floods. They held the hands of their neighbours and used their own resources to get respite to people.

Just like in the past when they would give selflessly to the cause of freedom and the nationalist struggle. A spirit of compassion and understanding showed itself that is very rare in modern times where needs are easily met and deprivation is alien. So when confronted by the very same deprivation, in the face of calamity that was unprecedented, they suddenly became more affected by the sufferings of others and more so of those who were of lesser means than them and therefore less able to combat or endure the ravages and misery.

The cyclone was a great leveller. All joined hands against this calamity. There were many frayed nerves, but people quietly acknowledged the enormity of the crisis, squared their shoulders and got going without waiting anymore. It happened without anyone saying or asking. Only because people knew that they had to take their own lives into their hands. The days of their sorrow were to end in time. They felt it and they knew it in truth. So they endured, they struggled and were patient.

Amitav was surprised above all by the self-assurance and confidence of the people, by their apparent happiness and apparent adjustment to the world around them. When all aspects of reality were disagreeable, irrational or repugnant, they refused to see themselves as islanded in the river of time. They seemed to carry a history of troubles borne, lesson learnt. They had air too of gallant accommodation towards whatever choices had gone wrong or chances had not panned out.

There was some sense of triumph about them which was not hard to understand. Luckily or unluckily there is nothing in our lives that does not end sooner or later said Riten to himself. Soon the signs of the fury of nature would be completely wiped out. The mango sapling, they had planted would bloom into a big tree and Amitav would marry in a few months and his children would play with him under this tree.

It seemed to Riten then, and it still does, that Gaighata is a village that wants to realize its ideals, has no wish to exchange them for others, and is confident of surviving, no matter how dark the future may appear.

"I do not know whether this attitude is justified by reason and reality; I simply want to point out that it exists, I found it in the actions, the words and even the faces of almost everyone I met. You can also see it written; you've got to be as clear-headed about human beings as possible because we are still each other's only hope. Anyone who has looked hope in the face will never forget it. He will search for it everywhere he goes, among all kinds of men."

The feelings of pain and helplessness were not there; there was reckless determination to go on.

3

A Visit to Family

One Sunday morning Priya was looking at the blue hills, listening to the leaves rustling so lonely in the trees. She started thinking of her home in Bahrain. It is the place where her father, thirty-four-year-old Vivek, had gone from India with his wife Savita, his elder daughter Preity, his younger daughter Priya and his son, Saurabh. There he sent them to public schools and Preity became a doctor and she, Priya was sent to IIT Delhi while Saurabh was still in school.

After almost two years in IIT Delhi Priya met Ajay a fellow IITian and slid into infatuation and slowly developed deep feelings for him but the fellow was not sincere. After a few months, she was jilted and Ajay left her. This scene was replaying in her mind: how she had become distraught and spent nights on the floor mattress crying and, in the morning, would go to the theatre, wait for the teacher to teach sitting in the last row. She didn't write down any notes or care to hear anything the professor was saying. She didn't participate; she would not take her bitter stare off Ajay.

He sat in the first row untroubled and her reticence, seemed a blessing to him. Nevertheless, she was still so stuck on seeing him. Feeling desolate and depressed, she followed him through streets, hostel, classrooms, college canteen. She was convinced that he would turn around and recognize her love but nothing like that happened.

When these memories were crowding her mind, she was surprised to see Amit coming to her hostel by himself. She was anxious not to turn into a sorry spectacle in front of Amit whom she had met while graduating from IIT Delhi with a degree in electronics. Now he was working in McKinsey; her cousin had introduced her to Amit. They had met quite often and he was moved by her pleasing smile, her earnest enquires about his health, friends, family, his interests, work and her painfully careful details about his life.

Amit was honest, open minded and kind to people, soft spoken, well dressed and was always ready to offer his large shoulders to cry on. Not in the beginning perhaps but at least as things went on, she confided in Amit about her breakup with Ajay.

He said, "Of course, that selfish brute has deceived you, destroying your self-respect and self-confidence. Your heart is broken". "Who cares?" she said. He said reassuringly, "I do. Tears wouldn't help you. You are an intelligent girl. You have to get over these things on your own. I can only say it is silly to expect from a flirt acts of kindness and sacrifice. He kept on assuring her that break ups are common in the contemporary world and asking her to take it easy. I think it is still better he had left you. Anything worse could happen."

Many a time Amit lifted her pride, catered to her fragility by offering affection that he really felt. Eventually, she began to think about herself when the sense of injustice wore down. After a few months it became clear to her that she had stopped loving her boyfriend. She never thought about him every day and night as she used to do.

"After today I might believe Amit and I to be friends but now I am not too sure," she said to herself. Ever since he met Priya, Amit had liked her. She was a tall, broad-shouldered girl and her hair were dark black and she wore them down to her shoulders. Whenever Amit met somebody from his old life as he sometimes went to IIT and was asked how he liked Priya, he would say, "I cannot tell you how much I like her. It makes me happy to think that I do have a true friend in the world that is her."

Of course, they became good friends and she graduated from IIT with a degree in Biotechnology. He wanted to propose to Priya and marry her with a feeling of buoyant expectation. He wanted to tell his parents about her but before he could do so, she had already moved to Germany for doing her PhD in genetics in Heidelberg.

In her imagination Priya had gone to Heidelberg with a lot of expectation that her apartment would be bright, open and comfortable but it was a dark narrow room, built of raspberry-coloured bricks, with shelves of books, dark, unpretentious tiled floor with a low window and an oak door. There was no dining room, no fireplace and only a small balcony outside. She couldn't afford a luxurious apartment nor did she want to share an apartment with other fellow students. Besides she was an immigrant who was unable to speak German and unable to communicate even in the supermarket. This made her a very sensitive and lonely student.

The situation in the university was also not encouraging. Her professor was slightly older, grimmer, with a stern face and short-sighted eyes. It took an unusually rare pupil to come through with anything like a creditable performance. Priya worked hard in the laboratory and library and after a few months went to show her assignment. The professor screamed at her work and called it useless, an hopeless attempt and asked her to redo it without any suggestions or guidance. She felt not only the embarrassment but also so discouraged that the thought of giving up the research occurred to her frequently.

After a few days she learnt that other research students were also complaining about the fuss over their thesis. Later on, she discovered that her professor continued to publish papers, serve on committees and made progress in his career. But he had no intention of helping Priya to finish her PhD in time. After persevering hard for months, she again went with her complete manuscript that he did not read completely, before he remarked "Too trash to inflict on other people," and threw it away.

She furtively slipped beneath her shawl the manuscript she had patiently scribbled with so much difficulty. In tears she crept out of the office humbly. She was reminded of Ashu who had committed suicide because of the rude behaviour of his professor and the many dishonest things that had been done to him. The many irresponsible persons or research scholars who plagiarised from others' thesis and published their research work under their name and some she could never have thought upon or planned to do.

At such times she missed her parents but she had no money to visit them frequently; she lacked the moral courage to ask for more. Travel costs money and frequent visits cause interruption in studies too. At such times if you are deprived of seeing people you care about; you do feel sad. She was also sad, sullen and spiritless.

When she was feeling lonesome and friendless in Heidelberg, Amit visited her. He lived with her in Heidelberg for a fortnight and was tender and reassuring to her. He did not go for any guilty intimacies, none of the pleasures as he had not considered these escapades with anyone for whom he had some respect or any fondness. Anyway, they would talk late, fall asleep very tired about two in the morning and had sound sleep, woke up quite refreshed and fine. "There is no need to keep your sorrows to yourself, you could pour them into my heart which is quite open and ready," he said to her and she did it. He dissipated her self-doubts so that she could concentrate on her thesis with a quiet mind.

As long as Priya was in Germany they were constantly in touch through phone, e-mails and letters. Talking to Amit on phone brought pleasure to Priya who admitted to herself, "If I received his email it sent a thrill of pleasure through and through me. Amit is the person I love and honour most in the entire world. Look how strongly he influences me! Now I am focused on my thesis; I can persevere to fulfil my goal."

After coming back from Germany, he talked to his parents about Priya, and when they insisted on seeing her, Priya visited them with her parents in Delhi during the Easter break and eventually they were engaged. The diamonds in her engagement ring glittered on her fingers. The wedding was arranged for the month of September that was to be celebrated in the old Indian way. They were perfectly happy.

She said to herself, "By this time I would have finished my PhD and then I would go to my parents to Bahrain to rest and recuperate." Now in Germany she continued to perform or work for her goal even if she failed many a time in her attempts and was tired of trying. She did not give up when the going got tough and kept on moving forward to succeed. Perseverance always pays. She succeeded in completing her PhD and went to her parents in Bahrain.

Within two months of her stay with her parents, strict regimen of dieting and strenuous workouts she lost weight and looked quite young, slender and graceful creature. But now for some unknown reason, she had begun to experience fear and anxiety as if something uncertain awaited her. "Perhaps every fiancée feels the same way before their wedding. Who knows? Or is it the influence of Preity's abusive marriage. But anyway, why can't I get Preity out of my head? Why?" she asked herself. Her mother addressed her concerns and helped her to overcome her anxiety that she told her that every girl experiences before marriage.

After their wedding in India, Amit with Priya moved to Chicago where he got a new job. One day while moving out the gate of Millennium Apartments in down town, Amit met his old friend Abhisek from DPS Delhi with his wife Lakshmi. Priya liked Lakshmi They became friends, they had dinner in each other's house and listened to their husbands' talk about their school days -- the jokes, the fights, the conspiracies and disasters, the bullies and the victims, the terrifying or pitiable school fellows, the teachers, treats and the humiliation.

When they had talked enough about school, they talked about movies, politics and public personalities. And the places they had travelled to or wanted to travel to. Priya and Lakshmi also joined them. Amit strongly believed that women were every bit as intelligent as men. Priya and Lakshmi talked in each other's kitchen over coffee. They had lunch in cafes in downtown. Priya revealed how Amit wrote letters to his mother in India every week; he worshipped her as she had sacrificed a lot for sending him to Chicago business school. They spoke about their lives, childhood problems and husbands. Priya told how her sister Preity was in an abusive relationship.

First few months of marriage were fun and laughter. For that time life was perfect, there was nothing to mar it. Amit would say, "Let us go for a joy ride, let us go to the lake front we will sit on the logs". This was what they did. Priya would return home, strengthened and a lightened woman, woman in love and favoured by the universe. She told her acquaintances, "The most remarkable, the most important and necessary thing in the world is marriage and that only in marriage could one find true pleasure and evolve together and become humane. We have a good life, thank God. May God grant everyone the life like Amit's and mine."

Vulnerabilities increased as time went on and things progressed. They wanted to spend their money on travelling, no children. Life was beautiful and filled with joys. After all that nice time she must have been disappointed when Amit's parents came from Delhi to visit them in Chicago.

So, it always happened with these practical people. In spite of their calculations, their survival instincts, they might not get what they expected. Trouble began perhaps as soon as her mother-in-law entered the kitchen, corrected her, looked after the cooking part and could see a sense of drama in her ways and manner of dressing. Priya spoke disapprovingly about it to Amit and always went with some good explanation. With tears in her eyes, she would embrace him and beg him not to be angry. At first, he also felt sorry for her. "Aren't you my sweetie?" He said with complete sincerity, smoothing her hair. And they both would be happy.

Priya never had that much tidiness about the house as her in-laws wanted. After his mother talked to him about this, Amit pointed out to Priya and she said, "I don't want my living room to look like theirs -- clean, pale beige. Priya went around doing all the usual daily routine. At night they would come late after parties and she would get up late in the afternoon and did not care about her-in-laws' breakfast and other needs. So much so that at times Amit himself felt troubled and slightly humiliated that Priya had not let him know that there was no *atta* at home for his parents to eat chapattis. For if there was one thing, he feared was of neglecting his parents.

Priya wanted to eat out more often, which did not mean she liked eating in restaurants; it was that she grudged having to cook meals for her in-laws. And how Amit loathed to see his mother doing kitchen work as he knew she had servants in Delhi to do this. Here his mother preferred to do the work herself because it made life much more peaceful. Already there's had been a love marriage, much to her *sass's* chagrin, now emboldened by the free western atmosphere in USA, they had started holding hands which led to open display of kisses in public places that irritated her in-laws. Had they not married they would not have stopped there. Priya didn't regret what was said nor felt any shame. Amit didn't expressly say something challenging but his eyes became cloudy calm and sombre.

A divergence of opinion became evident between Amit and Priya. Some girlfriends sensed that there was some unhappiness in their marriage. Boys thought it was the *saas-bahu* thing. But the fact was that she had lived in foreign cities too long to have forgotten about filial duties for the only son in Indian context. Many times, Amit reminded her, "My parents are my saviour I am bound to serve them day and night. It is through them I got the best education in prestigious institutions in and outside India. I love my parents, I really do. They are nice and kind people. It is due to their blessings that I have got a job in Bank of America in Chicago after graduating from Chicago business school."

Nevertheless, she would tell him at length the complaints her in-laws made and the insults she had to put up with every day. "They treat me unkindly and you must forgive me to say but I am not happy about this. They talk so loudly and continuously throughout the day; you have apparently got accustomed to them since your childhood but I need some peace in my house." "It is all the same old boring stuff. Invent something newer," he said and got up. She said, "If you knew what's happening to me. I implore you to listen to me." Priya recalled how till recently he had considered her extraordinary and had proudly listened to her words but now he was indifferent. Now she would sit in the house waiting for his call or doing things to keep her busy. Her house had certainly not shown the benefits of her attention. She would stay up late watching the television and munching potato chips arguing. She would go to bed at her regular time thinking what a conceit on his part. Too stiff, too professional. He stayed near the phone, working on the computer but did not pick up her phone. It kept on ringing persistently. In those moods she left messages on the phone: Why are you dealing out these punishments? Why are you ruining our life for your parents?"

"I work, I do my best, I worry and I lose sleep thinking how to make things better. See what happens! You don't seem to see my viewpoint. Do you think what I want? Do you think you understand me? You behave this way, because, for some extra ordinary reason, you love to humiliate me in front of my parents," said Amit. "You are being cruel! You are being cruel," said Priya pulling at his hands. He pushed her away and went out. She couldn't understand that things had so stunningly turned around. Late that night she thought how happy they used to be. Now she would see tears running down before she knew she was weeping. This was because of some shadow she had glimpsed in him or some off-handedness or an oblique warning he had given her. She woke every morning hungry for the sight of him; she worshipped the back of his neck, the shape of his head and the frown of his eyebrow, his long feet, his gurgling laughter, his loud and confident voice and his smell and the sound of his car on the pebbled driveway. Now, there was no morning kiss, or a wave of bye-bye, or turning of the head towards her. He pretended that Priya wasn't there; he walked briskly and never even looked at her.

She thought to herself: It's like an earthquake or a volcano. The people can take a fit like the earth can take it if it was a periodical fit like married people have. In her case there was no breakthrough or reconciliation but now they were having serious argument saying the cruellest things to each other that they could imagine. "You are always telling what a raw deal you are getting or what some unkind thing someone said to you and your horrendously boring self-centred conversations," screamed Amit.

"I have thrown myself in painful and hopeless entanglement because there is rejection of the ordinary, decent contracts of life on your part. Even before marriage I have made you realise that even in marriage, I put my parents and my filial duties above everything else. You are insensitive to my concerns for my parents. You are very selfish. It is better we part our ways decently," he said with sincerity, effort and relief. By God, his words went through her like knife, she felt too shocked to say anything.

No doubt, Amit wanted to make everything right with his parents, perhaps he wanted to make sure that he became someone his parents would be proud of. He was committed to his ideals -- a devoted son. Unfortunately, high ideals come with a price.

Anyway, he left Chicago for Australia for doing a project of one month. His mother also accompanied him as she had not visited Australia before and his father had already gone to Delhi to sort out some court cases. When he went away, he paid no attention to Priya, not a hint of goodbye. His going away was like overturning the only pillar that hitherto had prevented everything collapsing for Priya into a boundless chaos, into a fearful nothingness, so Priya kept persistently ringing him up, he refused to talk to her. She was still thinking that there might come a time when their relationship could be mended. That night she did not go to sleep, as she was feeling uneasy. In the morning she received a message on her WhatsApp. She had received messages from Amit before but now for some reason she felt numb. With trembling hands, she opened the message and read. "Enough is enough. You are free to go to your parents." No one can imagine how sad and distraught life could appear to a woman who had been told to leave the house. The end of this shameful sort had not occurred to her as being among the possibilities of marriage, it took the romance out of it and dreams of happiness and glory turned into repulsive nightmares.

She realized clearly that her life had been turned around, that here she was lonely, alien and not needed. The old habit of reading, receiving and making phone calls and contended chat was gone, forgotten. She sat at home worrying and silent. There was no sound not the whisper of the leaf, this stillness, lifelessness and dullness of the house oppressed her spirit. Sodden with homesickness and emptiness of life, she lay awake and miserable waiting through the still eternities for the clock strikes.

She wept, "Amit, how could you go and leave your Priya? How am I to live without you, wretched and unhappy as I am?" She kept talking to herself, "Why didn't I understand how much has come to an end? She was alone but she could not leave Amit. Unhappy wives couldn't just go back home to their parents, expecting sympathy. Moreover, her elder sister Preity had already come back to her parents. How could they endure this agony again? I cannot even consider that I might see them in that situation. The only thing that held me back was the fear of what Amit's desertion would do to my parents' reputation. Word would spread through the community of Indian expats. Soon a distant country filled with aunts, uncles, cousins will know. Her parents would die of disgrace. Shame, for Indians, is worse than death. They could no longer endure it. Her mother and father would fall apart. She could hear her mother howl, "You let the whole family be humiliated like this." She saw her mother staring at her in horror, wondering how their daughter might be so arrogant as to ruin the marriage and come to them. My parents could not endure Preity's husband's beating, the wounds that made her bleed, the words that cut her open. Of course, that was a thing of shame, but at least, justified her returning to her family but I do not have that excuse. My parents know for certain there was one good thing in my marriage: my husband loves me and my mother had repeated it so many times. She is right even I remember what Amit had said, "I met you. You were everything I'd imagined -- Smart. Beautiful. Funny. I was proud. I loved you from the moment I laid my eyes on you. He said he had never met a prettier girl and he wished he could spend all his life with me. He had never thought about anything but me. Hadn't I experienced both love and duty, delight and exasperation, since he entered my life." She recalled how companionably they had managed their married life, the times they had laughed together, moments when their bond had felt true, strong and those nights of love. "He had been a part of my life for so long. To quash those memories would have been like pretending that my past life did not exist. If I had not met him and come to Germany I might still be wallowing in self-pity. Without his encouragement, who knows if I could have completed my PhD in time. I might never have reached USA and enjoyed all these luxuries of life and exceptionally enjoyable married life. I had lived for years now in America -- a place of my liking. The thought of countless good things passing out of her life occurred to her, she became desperate. She heard her mother saying, "I am repeating this to you: before you make any decision, can you evaluate yourself? You are not a very attractive woman. You are a foreigner in this country. You are hardly twenty-five and you are unemployed. So, don't be silly, stop daydreaming about another prince charming, that is not going to happen for you. Be realistic and wise." "Yes, I don't deserve his loyalty, just as I hadn't deserved the comfort, he had tried to give me. I thought I was successful but success was ephemeral and fluid as I found it hard way. It came, it went. It changed me from outside but not from inside. Inside I was the same girl who dreamed of a destiny greater than I was allowed. Do I really need this marriage or my ego to prove I had talent, intelligence?

What a mess I'd made of my life, his life. If I had not been so selfish this would not have happened. I have failed such a loving husband; I have ruined my husband I have done what I cannot undo. In fact, I did become troublesome.

Had I not behaved unfairly; I would not have suffered so much. I would not have been so powerless against an entire family. I didn't make a true change, long necessary for the voyage for the house of marriage. It was not too much to be expected of me. I couldn't accept readily and devoutly the role of the dutiful daughter-in-law that had been explained or agreed upon before the marriage. This was the only thing he had asked of me and he was ready to devote his life. I was stubborn, tried to be carefree and show an independent spirit; it was all my entire fault. I will never forgive myself." She could not come to reckoning with the loss, the grief, the awe, the gratitude, love, sorrow and regret. She kept feeling desolate and depressed for days and days together. The expedition to the university, science centre, exhibition and museums, treats in cooled restaurants of the malls didn't make up for the absence of husband or reconcile her to the tapestry of the home he had provided. She ate and drank as if against her will. She lost weight and looked lost.

Even now I have no ground for divorce. We have everything in common and there exists no issue of incompatibility. Amit has good looks, he works for Bank of America now and earns enough, he's good in crisis, good at survival and would give her a fancy lifestyle. Was he different now? No, it is me who had changed. I don't fit in with any of them. I don't wear the right clothes. I do not cook the right food and I am different now and they know it. Why am I trying to destroy the fortress I had pictured? Why do I want to ruin my life for lack of adjustment to a new sense of duty towards his parents? Why did I think I was not accountable to the hopes and expectations of his parents? Was he asking too much? Are his demands unnatural or too exacting? Of course not, then something is terribly wrong with me. Do I lack sense of adjustment or am I ignoring my duties to my in-laws? Since the time of marriage even I was aware I married into a traditional family where it is expected from *bahu* to care for the needs of in-laws. Moreover, my husband had made it clear to me before marriage how strongly he feels about his filial duties that was the only thing he had asked of this marriage. Can't I grant his solitary wish? Of course, I was brought up to obey my parents, my husband, not to defy, question or contradict. But the books have filled me with too many silly notions that I could make my decision and have an independent life. I need to learn to accept what I couldn't change. I do not know what would happen to me if I don't change.

And then the strangest thing happened, some thought directly got inserted into her limbic system. She was clinging to what she had just thought, the thing her brain had somehow comprehended. She understood for the first time that Amit was also exactly asking for his parents' happiness as she was herself thinking of her parents. What an irony! You expect from the person the same thing you had denied him without any compunction. You feel the pain of another person when you are also suffering. Now I have destroyed everything I have worked so hard to achieve. The only other choice available to me before I could reconsider anything else is to ask for forgiveness or I would come out worse -- a petty, vindictive and ungrateful person. And guilt is a hard burden to carry. Sitting here, waiting and knowing he will not forgive. I can see the future and how I have to live with this burden." For she knew finally that she wanted him and this was stronger than anything else -- that without him there would be no meaning in her life at all.

During Amit's stay in Westin hotel in Sydney with his mother, he didn't tell anyone about the change that has occurred in their relationship and tried to conceal it from his mother too but didn't succeed. One evening when the moon rays were flooding his waterfront facing room he confided in his mother. His mother listened to him gravely, silently. Sometimes tears came to her eyes. She understood he was caught between filial duties and his commitment to his wife. Despair was permanently engraved on his face and he aroused a deep and genuine feeling of remorse in her. She had always loved him and could not live otherwise. She could not see her son unhappy on their account. Her anger against Priya suddenly vanished and she now began to feel a little sorry and ashamed of herself for having put her son in such a difficult position. She suddenly seized his hand in the middle of conversation and said, "Do not worry, my son I would do something. Calm yourself, it will pass. It happens; you've probably had a falling out with Priya, lover's trials end in smiles. Do not have any issues with Priya on account of your responsibilities to us, save your married life and I want you to be happy." For a moment he looked at his mother in amazement, finally he understood and was happy as a child. "It takes courage to make such a resolve. He knew his mother is a woman who has integrity to keep her promise whatsoever may happen. Being a teacher, she had opened minds and world of possibilities for so many," he thought. His mother had again given him the gift of life that created a silent and eternal bond between them. However gloomy a day he was having, however sunken his young heart, his mother's conversation had always transported him to a buoyant world of sunlit possibilities. In that happy mood they flew back to Chicago by the Qantas flight the next Saturday.

And next morning as Priya saw Amit walking into the driveway she ran to him. Just for a moment both stood silent; then Priya said apologetically, "I am really sorry, truly sorry. I know you don't believe me. How can I say it so that you will? Please don't send me back to my parents' house. I won't do it again. I won't I promise. You and my in-laws, are more of a family to me than my parents." She said pleadingly while her body was shaking because, the whole of her life, all that she would become, depended upon it. Priya slipped from sensible remonstrance, earnest confessions into true and fearful regret. She talked to him of abandoning old bad habits, old deceptions, self- deceptions, mistaken notions about life and herself.

The more fixed Priya was in her resolve, the more grimly satisfied Amit was in his heart. Meanwhile his mother came to Priya, affectionately put her arms around her and wiped her tears. "You are not going anywhere. After marriage, you are my daughter, my responsibility," and embraced her. Time after time she looked at her mother-in-law who had interceded for her. She felt more guilty and ashamed, humiliation spread as easily as oil on wax.

Oh, she was offering her something more: forgiveness, understanding, respect. Priya was surprised and confused, but her mother-in-law's genuine outpouring of concern really touched her. In that instant she finally breathed a sigh of relief. At once she felt something she had never felt before -- the beginning of small hope and thought for the first time that things were going to be ok from here on.

4

Brown Bond of Love

Few are those whose contribution to humanity -- may be love, music, harmony in family or some other enchantment -- fills the heart with uncontainable gratitude for their existence. Tara Bua, my aunt -- my father's sister was such a person, a sweet blessing of a relation. My father would bear a witness to this blessing. It was such uncommon love she poured from the soul utterly besotted with his world.

Tara bua was a tall, graceful elderly lady with dark eyebrows on her long face. Her attractive and majestic smile was simply delightful and she was always happy to meet her brother.

With the news of Tara bua's coming home it seemed some sort of family celebration was going on in the house and we, the children, felt a pleasant flutter of excitement. I remember vividly when the morning mail was handed in and I glanced at her handwriting that sent a thrill of pleasure through me. It was Tara bua's; the sight of her handwriting reminded me that I was eagerly waiting to see her again.

I opened the letter. Good! Just as I had expected, she was coming. I said to myself I am happy and content now. She would bring gifts for everyone but her habit of paying compassionate attention to her brother's needs was remarkable. She from experience and familiarity, knew how cold Pratik felt during winter despite his living for many years in Delhi. Despite his showing the wardrobes and cupboards where he piled up heavy garments and shoes for all seasons and purposes, she knitted him a brown pure wool sweater with cables which he used on special occasions. He liked wearing that sweater and was comfortable in it. He liked to think about her whenever he wore it.

Tara bua, you may not call beautiful but she was attractive. There was something poetic in her that coloured her acts, her movements and everything about her. She was such a cheerful, hearty soul that it was no trouble for her to laugh than it is for the bird to sing. There was something so candid in her expressions, so courageous and independent in her bearing that made mere beauty just dull. When you are in Egypt you worship Goddess Isis and when in Anatolia you kill a lamb for Cybele. When you are in Tara bua's company you cannot help but adore her. There was a sensation of well-being when you were with her as though you could relax and be natural and need not pretend to be anything you were not.

It was impossible to think of her as envious of others. She seemed to have such a generosity of soul. You could confide about the most intimate things with her. She was always so nice to me and easy to get on that I never hesitated to ask her favours. Sometimes she would plead Pratik papa to give some pocket money to me. She was so simple, natural and helpful. She was the person I loved and honoured most in all the world. She had been my boyhood's idol, maturity which is fatal to so many enchantments, also I had not been able to dislodge her from that pedestal. She was so serene and cordial; she owned her beautiful serenity to a deep effort of the disciplined will of her own.

Those days were so grand and enjoyable, one could not think one could enjoy oneself so much. In the evenings one could play cards or turn on the gramophones. Her cooking was good too. It was a change from what we generally got. I could not help envying Tara bua and Pratik papa their life. With her coming it was so jolly and peaceful. They could talk whatever they wanted.

With Tara bua in the house Pratik was quite different from what he was when she went away. He was very pleasant and cordial. But Tara and Pratik were left a good deal to themselves and now they liked their society better than of others. They had a nice place; there was nothing grand in it but it was easy, homelike and comfortable. It was a very happy house then and we enjoyed almost all pleasures of modest home and hearth. These visits brought them closer together; they had plenty to talk about. They were more devoted to one another than I had ever seen any other brother and sister be.

The most interesting and intimate conversation happened over food. They opened up to sharing, nurturing and growing. They found joy in incredible ways. When they were occupied in separate affairs, they were pleased to feel that they were near to one another. They were wonderfully delighted. They told the truest, tenderest funniest things about themselves. They recounted the shared history, laughed at the memorable set pieces they had not laughed at when they happened, the tales of courtship, love, of fortitude, absurdities and many disasters and in the middle of it they recalled another story of driving home, scolding or event as it drifted in their wandering mind.

Pratik at times listened in silence and did not ask any questions pausing to allow a forgotten detail to add and surprising her with something she had forgotten to remember. The stories were changing with every new recollections and they were rearranging new additions. They shared many intellectual interests that made their life full and varied too. (At times I got the impression that

I was edged out of their conversation, as though I were a child who was expected to sit still and not interrupt the elders when they talked; I had also the notion that often my presence was unwelcome to them; they were more at ease when I was not there.)

At times Tara bua would recall Pratik's childhood, "You were such a quiet boy and played alone most of the time. You were fearful of dark and would ask me to come with you to the washroom at night and kept on holding my hand as you were afraid of allowing me to move out of sight. In your heart you guarded a sort of privacy of soul that no living being was allowed to know except at times I alone could pierce into your heart. You know, how sometimes you see clearly into the people's thoughts that you are more certain of them than if they have spoken them."

"Yes," said Pratik, "You would walk with me and play with me every game I asked for but if your attention strayed even for a moment how I used to rage and wail, clinging to you." At that Tara smilingly said, "At that time I would wish that someone else was there in the house, not to commiserate but cherish you with me, after all, you were such a sweet wonder of the world."

Pratik confided, "I was amazingly intimate with you. You know, you might be with a person you have known so well all your life that you never thought of putting on frills with him or her. It was so good having you around, who treated me so kindly, who made sure there was nobody to bully me or take advantage of me. That was the time we shared every confidence. We were together every day. You would take me swimming, and afterwards we would sit beneath the mango tree and watch people go about their business. You knew their history and would tell it to me. I asked you how you understood the world so clearly. You told me it was a matter of keeping still and showing no emotions, leaving room for others to reveal themselves. You were always serene, smiling and your kindly self."

They recalled their story in bits and pieces. I had to piece together what they said at one time and another and put them in words of my own. Pratik was an adorable brother who loved Tara bua and sought her counsel on trifles and hid behind her when he was scolded for his mischief. She remembered what he said and how he looked at her and saw pleasure in his eyes. He could listen to her appreciatively when she told him stories that he had not heard before and felt his fears and sorrows passing away and giving place to a comforting contentment.

At times Pratik would remind her that they always walked home after school, all the time talking that made her laugh and flatter her outrageously. There was so much he wanted to do, so much he wanted to experience like walking, biking, camping, racing, car exhibition, art festival but he dared not ask his father. Maybe he had not enough daring, perhaps, he was afraid of getting into trouble. His father would create a scene, he thought.

Those days he wanted his father's face to be open or readable, concerned or content or resolute as the situation demanded; not this inward gaze that made him afraid. Pratik wanted to talk to him, play with him, laugh with and not to fear him as much. There was so much he wanted to do and so much to experience. Of course, he followed him like a dog, content to suffer wrong and abuse if he might only be with him but he rather gave him such a reproachful look, you know what contempt was in that gesture and expression. At other times he would jeer at me, leer at me, sneer at me. He was nagging, badgering, fault-finding day in and day out, all forever and ever about little insignificant things or other and then he would fall silent. There was no sense in that and no reason in it. He did not do it with the honest intent to improve him; he did it simply because it was his business.

One evening even Tara told Pratik, "Yes, you wanted him to talk to you, to listen to you but instead of chuckles and kisses, he gave you directions and you did not understand that but was hurt by the withdrawals and instructions and thought it as a kind of rejection and he was very firm stiff and stern with you. Nobody of this age really is unafraid with so much happening to you." Her eyes filled with tears as she said this; it was frightfully unfair of him. Pratik was hurt by his father's withdrawal and he found even his silences daunting and those silences in turn made him afraid of him, his father never understood him. Pratik became withdrawn and that feeling of rejection had been with him most of his life, even when he had slowly begun to understand its several causes.

When father came home everything changed, too painful to live as an ordinary boy. Sometimes the anger would come over Pratik but the words curdled in his mouth. He bore his father's rage day after day and suffered while he turned his eyes away. He concealed the rage that lay under the surface waiting to break forth or the rough injustice of everyone else who mocked and despised him. It was impossible to forget anything, the most difficult was to forget his father. Tara noticed Pratik was upset and she assured him, "You are particularly of a sensitive nature; forget it I am there for you."

At such moments Tara would make efforts to remind Pratik that when he grew older, he made up his own stories, led his heroes on adventures or bested them with clever stratagem. Perhaps a child who had his sister only for the company could be so imaginative Tara wondered. Anyway, his face was rapt as he conjured up those visions. His gaze grew serious, his limbs tall and strong. He had the habit of tapping his fingers on the table as he liked best the stories of courage and virtue rewarded. His world was an easy place of right action divided from the wrong, of mistake and consequences, of monsters defeated.

It was no world Tara knew but she would live in it as long as he would let her. She would laugh and say you have more tales in you than she had. He sought all Tara could remember of his father, his lineage, his childhood occupations and his honours. The stories were vivid in her as they were when at first she told him but she found herself hesitant as her father's face with all the harshness shone before her. The few times she would leave the story as it was, he would frown at her. "You did not tell it correctly," Tara said, "There were moments of tension and many things we disapproved of in him. That made you retreat into silent spaces where you could not be reached."

In all her visits Pratik kept recalling and telling Tara how he watched his father like a dog, hoping for a morsel of understanding but the man of rage was his father. He told Tara you know my past was not some game, some adventure tale, it was a wrack that the storm left rotten on the shore. Of course, there was a kind of warmth in his mother's voice, an unforced kindness and a studied mildness that was intended to reassure and reconcile and that conveyed something affectionate and sympathetic and that was a relief in those dreadful surroundings. "Mother indulged your whims and let you watch TV. She also pampered you and we listened to music."

Now they smiled at the irritations and laughed about the worst moments and began to think with some satisfaction what they had done. Whenever they talked about their father I somehow got the impression that he was a man who wrecked his own happiness and was a terror to others connected with him. He was never used to having them around so much, yelling and tugging and bickering in the sweet way of children. He was busy at work, tired when at home. No one got to know much when he was in a good mood; that's when he was relaxed and comfortable; he was hard and frightening and a tireless man who always gave orders.

Pratik was always frightened and intimidated by his knowledge and power. It made him unsure and afraid and made him lose self-confidence. They were almost under a kind of scrutiny and they invariably failed to impress him however hard they might try. Notwithstanding that frustration of growing up in a small house with his indifferent parents became less urgent when he was with his sister. No one can imagine what living in that fear really felt like. He could not make himself say 'home' when he meant this house. I have heard Tara bua saying to Pratik, "I realize how sad it was to live with those things on your own. Don't distress yourself anymore about it."

Of course, he didn't worry about anything when she would tell him hilarious stories of adventure. He would shift to another topic. He would show delight remembering the times when Tara was preparing to cook the meal, he used to help her in peeling the vegetables and laying the table and cleaning it after the meals. Tara taught him to find dignity in doing honest work. In spite of all the things that were happening and that made everyone of his age unhappy. Tara was determined that he became clever, that he had something to look forward to something to do with his life after coming such a long way and having put up with so much. She could find the easy words of assurance that the moment required. She motivated him, "If you work hard you can make your way even if life has given you an unkind start."

Pratik was silent and hardworking about everything he did. It was grit – the perseverance and passion to achieve long-term goals – that made the difference.

Tara continued telling him, "But when you grew older and became a teenager you wanted the things to be done your way which was not his, that left father quite irritated. After a while you didn't bother to tell him about them either. Have you forgotten how irritated father was by our constant chatter, he could neither participate in our hilarities nor could tolerate us. Now I remember enthusiastically how college life suited you honourably; you became bold and independent and with a sharp wit that made you daunting and popular at the same time. You turned out naturally gifted at the small-town college scheming and intrigue and fine tuned into gossip and rumour.

One day I asked you where you went but you were preoccupied always running somewhere breathlessly, coming home flushed.

"Then suddenly one evening you were in a good mood and came beaming in my room but did not know how to tell me. After hesitating for a while you confided that you were besotted with Preity -- a girl with dark blue eyes and how incredibly sweet she was and how you felt about her when all the time you were aching for her." Tara understood that his face was full of bold hopes. His youth had swelled in him ripening. Dark curls hung over his face and his voice had deepened and he was sighing as he had fallen in love. Tara thought she had kept the face of the world veiled from him. Now it was too late to change it, now the bird had already flown. She saw the strength rising in his shoulders.

Let him go she told herself, "He is happy, he is growing, what harm can find him there." But the endurance had been her virtue and she kept on. She looked at him. Yes, it was ecstasy he wanted to lose himself in, pleasure so complete that it overwhelmed his whole mind and his whole body. Tara knew he entertained secret ambitions and desires. Sometimes he replayed happy moments and indulged fantasies of future achievements, his success and fame.

After a long while he said, "There is a chance of happiness that I shouldn't be stupid and lazy enough to miss this time." He wondered if it could be true and he would have stories to tell about these moments of his life. Tara listened silently when he went into those details, it was the first time he was to choose what he wanted to do with his life. He understood about the family, its responsibility, its affection and its silent pride. He had never felt like that before. He wanted to forget the humiliation and injustice of all these years like a scar that fades. He did not want to remain unhappy with the silent burden he was carrying around and bring newness and joy back in his life so he felt it important to share his feelings with Tara.

Even when I grew up Tara bua was regular in her visits to us and mostly I would find them sitting at the end of the long table drinking tea my mother brought from the kitchen. That was the thing about growing old together, you made space and learned to be comfortable with each other. I could see the drawn muscles relax, and the anxiety go out of the face, and rest and peace steal over the features like the merciful moonlight over the desolate landscape. And Pratik talked about his distinguished past, guided Tara all over the houses, showed her his valuable collections of paintings, antiques and rare curios brought from abroad, read out hand-written letters from important people and his children and display paintings and drawings of his children. Tara and Pratik were together laughing at each other while one of them became solemn about life's tragedies They wanted to keep things light to themselves. It gave them a mature sense of proportion that they refused to see their pain as exceptional.

Life passed easily till Pratik turned sixty-five, and he had a mild stroke. Tara listened to him compassionately and offered the sympathy that was probably the best she could offer and that was what he needed at that time and that was enough. She said who did not know a friend, sister, husband or neighbour who was not struggling with lingering illness and waiting for recovery. They listened to each other and the stories of the friends that made the tragedies tolerable blaming the doctors, fate or the unfortunates themselves for the miseries they described.

Tara did all the checks the doctor required her to do and fed him the medicine he prescribed. At times Pratik became abrupt and difficult, sobbing with pain and pushing her away. The older he became, the more childlike his wishes were at times. The longer he lived, the nearer his childhood drew to him.

The weariness descended on him inexplicably now at the end of the day and more so in recent times more than before, that made him wish he could sit down and do nothing until the weariness had passed away. He tried to work out the cause of fatigue and make sense of it. He thought, perhaps, ageing or wear and tear were irreplaceable worn-out parts. Tara would always say, things take the time they take. Don't worry. All's going to be well. She had a good sense of humour and a way of easing those around her. She was patient and understanding and knew she was a kind of friend he could open his heart to and spoke openly releasing a torrent of gloom and agony crushing him. She was also worried that we the children should not see him until he was calmed.

He became easily irritable with his own feebleness and spoke ill-tempered words to his wife Preity. Sometimes he could not bear it when she came in the room, chattering to him and fussing around. Sometimes he could not bear her not being there. Even in that state, when he spoke to mother, his voice was harsh and his words were cruel. I hated him and most of all I hated that he spoke to mother like that. He knew the unhappiness he had caused ma.

Notwithstanding that I sat beside him and did not want to think about these dark silences and those growling words. I wanted to think of father, to be strong enough to fight his assailant and to think of him as a laughing story teller who got lost in telling those tales.

During his illness every petty defect of the world enraged him, all the waste, the stupidity and slowness of men, and all the irritants of nature too ripped him apart. Now he was like this year after year, raging, beating, shouting at mother, turning our house to hell.

It even hurt Tara when he spoke roughly to his wife which was not his way, but she said to Preity she had to get used to it. He was so weak, so confused, so angry and so quickly reduced to tears and sobbing for no reason. Anyway, he was not well and shared the feeling she always had that things never turned out as badly as you expected them.

Pratik always resisted going to hospital and I would become irritated. I told Tara bua, a man of his age should have regular visits and tests then his problem would have been diagnosed years ago and his problem would have been under control by now. Tara bua would make me understand that old people are too vain to go to a doctor unless something terrible happens to them and then they are a nuisance to everyone. This is a normal reaction we have to accept it sooner or later. To show how strong her influence was over me I will observe that when everybody else's "stop complaining about the old man" had ceased to affect me in the slightest degree, Tara bua could still stir my conscience with signs of life when she touched upon the matter. The moment she opened the subject I became a calm, peaceful, contended creature. She would tell me he was not like that; he was a pleasure to talk to and then a memory came to her that made her smile.

It made Pratik feel good, that smile as if he had recognized it from his childhood, as if they were part of an understanding, of something the two of them knew that no one else there did. It was the way he looked who had seen places and done things in life and like someone who had known freedom. He could never bear disrespect all his life.

Life at home was stormy with all sorts of scenes and upsets that happen when two people who are married do not get on together. Suddenly in the middle of the conversation he would say, "Father has dogged, dogged me, all the days of my life, that was misery enough now also he was tagging after me like another shadow in my illness, it is intolerable."

Then he would ask Tara why it had happened like this; he was fine all his life then one day suddenly everything descends on you. He thought he would probably never get better. Tara tried to pacify him, "There doesn't seem to be anything in them now yet they nearly break my heart when you say them Pratik, if you stop struggling hard against it, life could be tolerable. You should rather look about your health, think about your diet and be charitable to people, it is our duty to God."

Tara was a cheerful and hearty soul; it was easy for her to narrate the happy events of his life. Pratik's earliest happy memories were of those times when Tara lived with them and they shared the room. He would linger near her and she would take him to bed telling stories till he was awake enough to listen. She had a trick of saying things and would get his obedience easily as water slips on the oil; her mild words would make him jump faster out of the bed than all the shouts of his father. They went on a lot of outings. When Sunday mornings came, they cleaned, got dressed as if they were going to far off places, and mother would pack cheese sandwiches, chips, crisps, thermos of milky coffee, lemonade and bunch of soft drinks and cut fruits. They visited ornamental gardens, animal parks, old churches, market shows and caravans. Tara always drew his attention to the sheep in the fields, windmills and to the march of deer crossing the road. They made faces at each other and had fun anyway.

Sometimes when they recalled, a new detail appeared, a face he had forgotten for so many years, or an incident whose significance he had suddenly recognized after all this time. Tara was always telling him things when he was small. He marvelled at everything she told him. She loved to tell him stories and he looked in her eyes to believe they were true. He heard her with attention, reading and reciting softly to him it was the sound that made him smile and this was the happiness he would like to remember forever. She was an enlightened woman who wanted to change things for him and wanted to make people think about their life. She loved reading books about history, novels, stories, religion, philosophy and poetry.

She told him the stories of laughing elephants when they raided the battalion storehouse in Mongpong in Siliguri east that made him laugh too when she told about their trunks sounding laughter and big bellies swinging off as they trotted in troop.

And it was Tara who told him the story of his life and its beginnings; how the mahatma had organized the *kirtan* in their house at his birth and asked the children if the new born could have mother's milk because their mother had refused to breast feed him. She was afraid she had lost the older boy because she had breast fed him. She was not certain if she could feed again.

After kirtan the children said in unison he should have mother's milk. That mahatma became his saviour. The look of surprise Pratik had given had stayed with her yet. Tara preferred to stay over those memories for while, to linger over the image of Pratik before the illness, and times she visited him on *Rakhi* and *Bhaiya dooz,* the way he looked was how she would like to remember him till the memory lasted. It was the happiest time of his life he yearned for that time always.

She wanted him to forgive his father in this old age when illness afflicted him. Tara said, "Don't distress yourself anymore Pratik; at times I think that we had been unkind to father in what we thought of him all those days. After all, he struggled to make us live the lives we lived. We could understand now how difficult it must have been for father to be unable to share in the enthusiasm of his children and run the house with a meagre salary. What do the parents always expect? To make their parents shine with pride. I know how painful the death of that hope could have been for him, but he was a tough and stubborn man who had somehow kept his balance and advanced further." She stood still for a long time, thinking of him.

At that time silence ensued in which I felt him moving deep among his memories. Pratik's silences were sometimes dark and his solitariness had a feeling of menace, as if he had gone somewhere where it was difficult to reach him. At times she had to be patient, sometimes he was not himself, pained by the memories or just distraught he was not well.

Then somehow the collected wisdom of friends, family, doctors, nurses and internet advice emboldened us to ignore everything and get along through everything about parenting. Tara bua would read to him from the *Bhagwad Gita* and the *Puranas*. Pratik was growing increasingly unhappy with his mundane life. Tara saw him in the early hours of the morning, deep in self-pitying anguish and hopelessness and sobbing uncontrollably.

She would tell him, "Life is uncontrollable and incomprehensible that we barely make sense and what difficult is like living in this world at this time of life but we have to do something with this absurdity of life that swarms us daily and drives us to despair".

She was fond of poetry and read Mary Oliver's *The Fourth Sign of The Zodiac* (Part 3)

I know, you never intended to be in this world.

But you're in it all the same.

So why not get started immediately.

I mean, belonging to it.
There is so much to admire, to weep over.
And to write music or poems about.
Bless the feet that take you to and fro.
Bless the eyes and the listening ears.
Ked after
Bless touching.
You could live a hundred years, it's happened.
Or not.
I am speaking from the fortunate platform
of many years,
none of which, I think, I ever wasted.
Do you need a prod?
Do you need a little darkness to get you going?
Let me be as urgent as a knife, then,
and remind you of Keats,
so single of purpose and thinking, for a while,
he had a lifetime."

Tara bua helped him in his exercises, in his walks and in the therapy sessions. As the days passed he grew stronger and could sleep peacefully. The rest was doing him good along with the physiotherapy and the medicine. She had no idea the miracles physiotherapy could do. Tara was really looking after him very well. She was doing everything for him. She brought him audio books from the library and read poems from the poetry book he had in his personal library. She cleaned him, medicated him and kept reading and reciting softly to him; it was the sound that made him smile

Otherwise illness was wearing him down and he was unable to keep himself busy or distract himself, lying in the dark only waiting for the pain to subside. Actually the stoke had finished him. It was sad to see his shoulders droop, legs tremble, his belly sink into itself. He would lie there voiceless and incontinent, groaning for sympathy, there was no one else to turn to in times of trouble except Tara. His pain was thick as the winter mists. At least Tara's presence seemed to distract him, pull him out of despair. But Tara dwelt a cold eternity of eternal grief. Human beings are incalculable and he is a fool who tells himself that he knows what a man is capable of.

Tara bua spent hours in managing his tempers, his sulks and his silences. It was as difficult a feat as balancing fire-fighting bulls. His face was empty of all thoughts, he sat beside her gazing up, fatuous and empty. She found satisfaction in watching his worst of tempers ebb like seeing the garden well-tended.

Leaving that alone, I was aware when Tara bua talked she was a lawyer and a bard at once, arguing, entertaining, pulling back the veil to show Pratik the secrets of the world. It was not just words, though they were clever enough. It was everything together: her face, her gestures, her sliding tone of voice, I would say it, was like the spell she cast, but there was no spell I knew that could equal it. The gift was hers alone.

I was rapt, my face struck with wonder; I worshipped her with awe. I closed my eyes and spun fantasies and wished for strength. It was strange how comforting the idea was to me. Sometimes I would see her watching me. After scanning my face with intense interest for a while, an intentness would come on her face, she would begin to ask me casual and sideways questions. At that time my father wore the serious look as he always wore and I did not answer her. The world was full of mysteries and Pratik was another riddle among the millions. When I did not answer her it pleased him in some strange way. His looks slid into me smooth as a polished knife. I wondered what my father expected of me and felt the weight of his hopes. I imagined his weariness, his inward grief before he went to sleep each night.

The sensation of being with her was always luxurious and I wrought my days with unflagging pleasures. Her cheery voice and ringing laugh not only drew me closer to her but also emboldened me to ask Tara bua for favours when I found her alone. In my childhood she alone had persuaded my father to increase my pocket money and allowed me to play video games once a month when I was in school. Even now it gave me sharp pleasure to see her come in our room with plates full of baked cookies and cakes. She had learnt domestic niceties early in her life and she soon learnt my favourite food and smiled to see my pleasures in eating them. Sometimes she would bring baskets full of mangoes plucked from the backyard mango trees. At times I also joined her in the garden plucking them. Sometimes she gave me gifts. At night we stayed together and talked over the gay things. Somehow I found a way to keep her happy and I was doing her errands and strove hard to stay in her good books.

I still remember the look that she used to give me was pure, unmixed wine. The closing weeks of her memorable visits would melt away as pleasantly as a dream.

It is three years my father passed away and consequently the enjoyment of Tara bua's company was also gone and I know what it feels like to lose someone and not want to put those things away. Now I am sifting his things to give in charity. It's very hard to pack them away. The grief was climbing into my throat threatening to swallow me when I happened to find that brown sweater my Tara bua had gifted my father.

It almost gave me a crumb of comfort and I could not part with this brown bond of love she had knitted for him long-long ago. It still wafts of that perfume of her love and warmth, of her feelings and understanding. I remembered all the hours I had spent in her company. The reminder of her company was in every way a delight.

At that time something shifted in me like the releasing of tension I never realized existed. There are people you just cannot forget and the things they do always stay in your heart. Every person needs to know his roots and there is no better way to learn than by looking at this marvel of love yarn. And I cradled that brown sweater he had left behind; that knowledge brought its own sort of pain and I hugged it to my chest and felt her overwhelming presence all around me. A grateful sense of rest and peace descended on me.

For the first time I was overcome by the sudden feeling of hope, a living breath that might grow in future to keep my spirits high anytime. And again I was smooth as oil and calm as windless water.

5

Confessions of a Mother

I was in Curzon Road apartments in 1996 looking on as my son played cricket with his friends in that big compound. Watching them I found myself thinking of my daughter, Aabha whom my husband Sanjay had taken to Safdarjung Hospital Delhi for a check-up. Sanjay told me in a deep voice that the doctor had announced his judgment that she could not make it to matric because she had problems with her organizational skills. I was uneasy. My first reaction to his verdict was that the doctor was wrong. This won't happen to my child. It couldn't be. I winced and shook my head. The more I thought about it, the faster my disappointment turned to anger. I dreaded thinking of her future. Nobody can imagine my fears and the upsurge of emotions I experienced. I found myself indulging in self-accusation. The list was unending for not being a perceptive mother. Why couldn't I see it happening? My focus was always on my work and household chores. Why wasn't my husband, Sanjay with me when I was raising my elder daughter 18, younger daughter 15 and my son six? Why had I not put my teaching career on the backburner in order to run my household? Why had God singled me out to be a target of social ridicule? Why me alone to suffer the stigma of having a daughter, who won't be able to make it to matric even. Would she be a social embarrassment to me? For the first time in my life, I was at a loss to understand all these complexities that life is. I shouted, screamed and wanted to hurl blame at anyone who would come near me. I was inconsolable. I thought I had lost hold of life. I was sinking under the pressures of these questions.

By sitting there with that report in my hand, all of a sudden, the prospect of her passing the 10th standard seemed bleak and hollow. Exactly at that time Sanjay confronted me, "Why don't you quit acting like you are the victim. Get off your high horse; start acting like a normal person. But do mothers have obligations only to intelligent children. Give her a break. She's to live with this the rest of life". It took me a while to realize that my husband was saying that the child needed my help not the doctor's judgement or our guilt. I apologized to him for not being more understanding. It was too late to get her 10th standard certificate but could we still get her a life. Today for the first time I realized that the most important part of learning takes place outside the school/ college. I wondered if from all the truths I had learnt in teaching could this be the toughest to ignore. I kept waiting for my husband to tell me what I needed to do. How long it would take, I didn't know but I had work to do.

I realized that what she needed from me was not just my work but knowing that I cared about her. It was not just about teaching her sums anymore that what we were doing but about realigning her life. I got up thinking, "You are a fool. You have missed the boat". I had let my work become automatic forgetting the essence of what a mother is called to do. Others knew how to show a child that someone cared. When had I stopped noticing things like that, when had I become so impatient to deliver lectures and be off? I had learnt a valuable lesson that day. There was someone I needed to thank. I must believe myself, our skills as teachers.

As I looked at Aabha, I found she was so beautiful, her big innocent eyes seemed to implore me, "Please help me mother." If I messed up, horrible things could actually happen. I could hurt someone. A thought came to my mind; abnormality was a big bully so was her classmate forcing herself on this beautiful daughter of mine. If I won't be there for her who was going to stop it. Much water had already flowed under the bridge and now I must prepare a repair kit equipped with different set of tools for mending and rebuilding trust in one another. I wasn't the one who was going to leave the things lying down. Now the foundation of parenting is going to rest on trust and not power play. Before expecting her to give her best shot, she must be made to feel secure and good about herself. I was not all about her and it was about me too. I must deal with my insecurities and feel worthy of this child.

That night Sanjay and me decided that I would take one-year leave of absence from my job and assume my duties as a stay-at-home-teacher mother. I studied the case histories of suitable examples, made ways-to-do-it lists, took into account all the factors in the expected problems, acknowledged certain and special needs (physical, psychological, emotional and intellectual) of my child, planned a big list of special efforts to deal with them. In fact, I was ready with a repair knit. After setting aside my own career, I flung myself into helping her. These duties daunted me more than others. If I had to pinpoint the defining characteristics of my first few weeks at home, it would be exasperation. This was the near collapse feeling I would sink by 10:30 PM only to realize with despair that I was sitting on her homework copies and my daughter had dozed off in my lap.

After all, schoolwork was the toughest, than pleading with her to have little pasta or sandwiches, begging her not to mess up the room was much more difficult. In the past if I had noticed her with unwashed hair and school uniform on, I would feel a little sad. Now I knew she had given up upon herself. At times she would not answer me or even look at me. She just shrank deeper into her friendless world. I grew impatient; finding her moody and unfriendly would put me off. I lost my temper at times, but I had to remind myself again and again that I was the adult in her life's play. I could not afford to show my fears. Nothing would come between us. I didn't feel belittled even if I had to say sorry or seek a compromise. If I lost my temper at times, I would apologize to her for not being an understanding mother. I haunted her central school, pleaded with teachers, explained her problems, prayed to be more patient and understanding to her, went on my knees before the teachers to take her tuitions, expended thousands of rupees, sat on the benches outside their homes, spent all those hours of waiting to walk home with her when it would grow dark. Everyone seemed to help in his or her measured ways. They were marvellous. I appreciated them for what they were doing for her. The caring was surely there. Paulo Coelho's words "When you want something all the universe conspires in helping you to achieve it," kept echoing in my ears but I had miles to go on this less-travelled road.

I was somehow coming to terms with the situation when suddenly she would sometimes show no enthusiasm to learn anything and spent all her time watching TV slyly when I would go to sleep. I emphasized. I reasoned if I loved my child, my mood would improve drastically the instant when she would be able to complete her arithmetic sums, but I was seething, changing her wrong answers in cold fury. Sanjay who was transferred to Srinagar encouraged me in his letters: "Your job is inherently frustrating because so much of single parenting of this type of child is exasperating." He gave me credit for setting aside my own career.

Sometimes fantasy also releases lots of energy in facing the problems. I kept envisioning her arms around me, her wet tears on my neck, as she would thank me for making her a graduate that kept me going. Sometimes I would read books to reassure me that I could do it. "The mind is like a house -- thoughts which the owner no longer wishes to display, or those which arouse painful memories are thrust out of sight and consigned to an attic or cellar and in forgetting as in the storage of broken furniture there is surely an element of will at work," remarks Margaret Atwood. (Alias Grace, p.435). Sometimes I urged myself to be a compassionate human being, "Carry on teacher/ mother," with kindness and generosity.

At night I would read mythological stories which offer a fresh perceptive on mother-daughter/guru-shishya relationship and read Tolstoy, Shakespeare, Margaret Atwood, Bertrand Russell, Krishnamurthy, Camus, underlined their words, would keep repeating them to myself when I found myself in the dumps. I laid more emphasis on nurturing her self-esteem and would not let anything affect her negatively. I also worked on myself, my self-esteem and to leave the victim status, devoted more attention to who she was and to do it her way. There was a lot under the surface of this life (new resolution) everyone knew that: A lot of dread, guilt, fears of failure and so much of loneliness. Sometimes I would strongly believe that my plan was impossible to follow through. My journey was tedious and laboured, it required my intensive involvement at every stage. I was not following through my plans so much as I was reacting to her tantrums and lack of interest. Recognizing that my attitude needed some transformation I began a concerted search for joy in this journey on this road. Tolstoy's words urged me on, "Men are like rivers: the water is the same in one and all, but every river is narrow here, mere rapid there, here slower, there broader, now clear, now dull, now cold, now warm. It is the same with men. Every man bears in himself the germs of every human quality, but sometimes one quality manifests itself sometimes another, and the man often becomes unlike himself while remaining the same man," (Resurrection, p.252). Step by step this led me towards positive and committed parenting and helped me to build a loving and special relationship with my child.

I was beginning to understand that there are some things - hope, optimism, unfailing trust in your child - no handicaps can ever take them away. I adhered to the guideline and do-it-yourself list and reminded myself again and again. I stuck to my own version of her -- she is a slow learner and has all the traits of a self-effacing individual. Our words of approval kept her going. Any disapproval or raising of voices would make her sulk and not participate in discussion. Her retention was proper, but she took longer to grasp a concept; once it was done, she wouldn't forget. Being busy with raising children I had to split time among them; might be such a child needs extra attention and more time. She was marvellous; she kept thanking us for all we were doing. She hugged me and thanked me for teaching her. Now that the actual moment was here, the one I'd dreamed of. I didn't know what to say.

The same year I registered her in Govt. College Shimla and even volunteered to teach the same class she was in. I watched her struggling to improve her grade, develop new relationships; her sociology & psychology lecturers also walked extra-miles to reach her. In the meantime, my elder daughter and son moved to Delhi to pursue their studies and she moved in to fill the void. She tried to do the same odd jobs they were doing. One day, during our walks to the college, I discovered she was giving me the canteen gossips in bits and pieces and what all that happened there. I could feel my daughter's all-encompassing love for humanity, qualities that every mother wants to cultivate in her daughter, manifesting very gently. She started having her own profound philosophy of life what was emanating from her own experience and events that unfolded around her. After graduation she decided to do B.Ed. from IGNOU, but the proudest moment was yet to come. She got married, got a good, loving husband and caring in-laws. Hence, she picked up life beautifully and within two years of marriage, she was blessed with a daughter.

This summer she visited me with her baby girl, I was overwhelmed to see the way Aabha was taking care of her daughter Asmi. She was doing laundry, folding the clothes, bathing and cooking for the baby and even instructing her maid how to keep her clean and stay alert when she would take her for walks. It was simply amazing to see she had gained so much not only in speed but in wisdom too. She would meditate and do Buddhist chanting and play with the little Asmi. Before going to her in-laws, she shared with me her decision to remain a housewife now and devote full time to her child and not to beat her and to compare her with other siblings and to help her grow in a home free of rivalry and tension. At once I read between the lines and regretted my comparing her with other children and the damage, I had done to her. No matter what happened to her in life now I knew she would find a purpose/way to stay happy and lead a fulfilling life. That much Aabha had taught me.

6

Covid Sage

Life was running full throttle then it skidded to a halt at the Corona milestone. With OPDs closed, OTs closed for routine surgeries due to the pandemic lock down and medical facilities almost turned into COVID hospitals, what amazed Shikha was the sudden change of heart of the public towards doctors. Overnight doctors became 'Corona warriors,' 'Front Liners', 'Soldiers in white' risking their lives to save others. There were cheers and national wide clapping for them.

Shikha, a senior consultant and head of cardiology in PGI, was not convinced of this sudden change of heart. She was tall and striking and of terrifying intelligence with bright blue eyes and strong features, with sun bleached hair and long eyelashes. She looked twenty years younger than her sixty-two years. She was a natural, dynamic and did emit a kind of raw and blistering energy.

After having worked for a few days in constricting kits and suffocating masks, when she got hard-earned offs she visited her waiting family. During her visit her son asserted, "Mama, look at your condition, you look so exhausted, almost on the verge of dehydration due to excessive sweating. You should take a break from your profession. You are a senior citizen with diabetes and hypertension, though these two terrors you've reigned for years but I fear if they find strong ally in the Corona virus, they could overthrow you and prove fatal. Mama your age is also a big factor."

The thought of leaving the job made her wretchedly miserable, as if all of the life was lost somehow, all that she had dreamt of and now she would have a life that would be different from the one she had planned and thought of. She could never go back to PGI, the doors would be shut forever and she didn't even know if this would lead to anything good. It was as if the giant black mouth of the volcano was before her and she was about to fall into it with no idea of what all was there at the bottom.

The trouble with the friends, with the family and with the world is that they think the things had to be a certain way. They think you have to feel something for them and it has to be the same thing that everybody felt or else you are doing something wrong. In Shikha's case it was not the fear that she would be thought doing wrong if she did not agree, nor was she succumbing to pressure of the family to please them or to avoid unpleasantness in the family. Instead, she felt Ramit was so far ahead of her in the ways of the world and above all, she loved her son more than anything else and she did not want to stress him more as he was already over worked at the COVID hospital. She resigned from PGI. It was not the worst thing they said, she could always get a job after COVID.

For a while the enforced holiday was a dream come true; it felt like a vacation for Shikha. She transformed from full time doctor to full time housewife and was not even a part-time doctor. As soon as she settled in the downstairs room, everything brightened in the house as if a new glass had been fixed into the windows. Icon lamps were lit, the tables were covered with snow-white table clothes, red eyed flowers appeared on windowsills and the front garden gave a fresh look. For dinner they no longer ate one dish but she cooked their favourite food. Shikha smiled pleasantly and gently and it seemed as if everything in the house was smiling. Since she stayed at home she could talk with her son and daughter-in-law in leisure moments about various things and ways and could give quality time to her growing grandson. She could hear the noise of the rooks in the garden and singing of the starlings. At night she could sleep for as long as she wanted, sure in knowledge that there would be no night calls, no early morning surgeries, no threats of court cases and no fear of violence by belligerent patients. She watched movies, ate food that was not healthy for her and read books that she had meant to read when she got time.

Novelty soon wore off and now something that had previously seemed simple had turned messy, difficult and complicated. The only thing that kept her going in those stay-at-home days was her regular communication with her friends and colleagues with whom she still remained in touch and who updated her every day. Things moved through the group in this way: information sliding around as if through an invisible circulatory system, carried on veins made of text messages, e-mail and whispered conversation in hospital. Looking back, she realized how the generosity of these young doctors and the emotional support of her son Ramit who was a doctor in Chandigarh Medical College kept her away from sinking into depression and helped her to heal through the trauma of pandemic. These doctors always knew just what to say when she was feeling lost, confused or just downright sad.

One night when Ramit sat at the dining table to grab a quick bite she said she was distressed to read in the Times of India, that a senior doctor was dragged into the streets and stripped and beaten for complaining that they were not being given N95 masks, leave alone PPE kits to protect themselves against the virus! In her dismayed voice she asked, "How are these warriors going to fight? How was the infantry expected to fight the enemy merely with batons? Where was the ammunition, the protective gear?" Ramit said, "Mama, it would hearten you to know that despite being demoralized by the futility of their sacrifices, surrounded by death and decay, they toil on without pay, precariously holding on to their sanity. They work for days in constricting kits and suffocating masks, when they are released from the double prison of hospital wards and PPE kits, and visit their family, for doctors are offspring and spouses too, to their horror they are shunned as leper's and barred entry into their own colony gates while off duty as they are regarded as hazards to society. Mama I will talk some other time, I am getting late for night duty."

She was training her mind to the difficult task of making sense of an uncertain world when she received a WhatsApp message from Dr. Ramesh who had worked in her team at PGI: 'Some of our dear friends have fallen ill. The saviours have become victims while serving the sick, and were asked to pay for the hotel rooms where they were shifted for quarantine.'

Reading these gruesome details, she felt repentance, lost inner peace, and at night when she lay in the bed her thoughts carried her to the distant past, into her childhood and youth. Now the past appeared alive, beautiful and joyful but she remembered the sacrifices of her parents who struggled hard to make her a doctor. The memories now burnt brighter than flames. As she thought of her late father, her mother and her native village Chile, where she studied till matriculation. She screamed in that room, "Papa I miss you". The image of her father came vividly to her -- a placid, good natured and tall man who worked as a Manager in Palace Hotel Chile and whose only wish was that Shikha become a doctor. After formidable difficulties her father got the recommendations of the local minister to get himself transferred to headquarters of tourism in Shimla so that she could study in IGMC Shimla. How his wish became her goal that she pursued with naïve faith, naïve smile and was infinitely happy. Of course, her father was filled with pride when she did her MBBS from IGMC Shimla and got admission in AIIMS New Delhi for her MS and later completed her specialization in cardiothoracic surgery. When she married an engineer, she had to move to Chandigarh where he was posted and joined PGI Chandigarh as a cardiothoracic surgeon.

She was forty when she was promoted to professorship and her son Ramit passed his ICSE examination from Saint John School and joined DAV College, Chandigarh for his senior secondary classes. Life was so easy and pleasant and it seemed there would be no end to it. Then her husband fell ill and succumbed to cancer and her life turned 180 degrees. After the death of her husband, she felt it was her responsibility to build a magnificent future for her son. She braced herself for whatever lay ahead and saved by cutting her living expenses to bones to meet the rising expenses of his college.

Eight years passed and she was made the Head of Department of Cardiothoracic and Ramit also got admission in a Medical College in Chandigarh. The past had withdrawn all into the distance, she asked, "Why did it return to her now after all these years when it was cut away like cataract. Discarded; why was it stuck to the bottom of her mind like garbage?" She jumped at the fright of it, the wholeness of memory.

She now understood that stepping out of the normal job of a doctor into the role of a "jobless" doctor was not as easy as moving through the open door into another house. She had totally immersed in trifles, had forgotten everything. Everything she did, every single thing was meaningless when she was not able to do her work in the hospital for patients. It had been so long since every part of her mind was set alight with new ideas (to help the sick). It was not that she was vain or arrogant. The years of expertise, experience and loyalty could end this way was beyond her comprehension.

The change of sitting at home soon wore off. How long had it been since Shikha had slept well and easily? How long had it been since she had felt beyond world's grasp? She who slept soundly after long working hours began to have disturbed sleep. The disciplined eater began to feel her stomach revolt against all the unhealthy food she ate. She missed getting up four in the morning when her children had curled up in bed and to reach hospital early finding the peon still cleaning her office and giving new excuses feeling sorry for being late again. She missed her meals with her colleagues during lunch break and remembered how in an almost angry way Prakash her colleague ate his meals. She began to miss the OPD hustle, the thrill of OT, even the corporate politics she had so detested She missed may be, other things, the weight of the unnamed feelings moving through her. She suffered from withdrawal symptoms besides the monetary pinch. Once she was earning a handsome salary and had a contingency B plan in place -- a rental income that would stand her in good stead once her working days were over but now, they were severed at the source and she had to draw on her savings for substance. If this was her state, she thought, what would be the state of migrant labourers who had no means to live or leave.

Her son was busy in hospital and daughter-in-law was working from home plus attending to her son's homework that was assigned online. Poor girl had no time for herself what to say of spending with her mother-in-law. At times she longed for them to notice her and come and sit with her but they always had other things to do. Some of her young colleagues acted as if she had been a candle which had burnt down leaving no trace not even a blob of dried wax. Even though the music in her room was going on, she could hear her son arguing with her daughter-in-law about their son Raman. It was not the outside world she wanted to drown out but the world inside which had always seemed so much wilder and stranger to her than anything else. She decidedly did not have a single moment free and her soul trembled, she found peace only when she was in the hospital. As soon as she entered the office, she was active, vigorous and happy. Retirement comes with its own burden, besides the risk of being redundant.

She could not bring herself to look at her white doctor's coat, though she knew she must, so finally she lifted her head and forced herself to look, to really look, to see. She texted to her friend Dr Asha that night: I sit by the open window in the evening alone and the neighbours start playing the music and hospital sickness exactly like home sickness comes over me, and I think I would give everything to go to hospitals and be with you.

For Shikha Facebook became the biggest social media platform, She posted messages and received messages and saw posts with articles in which doctors are praised. She inspired them as she used to do in PGI. It felt amazing when she talked about their work or something she felt strongly about.

Asha called her and said, "Shikha, oh, I wish we were talking together in your room instead of on the phone." Shikha replied, "You give me all the news; I feel I am with you all. Half of me is still with you." Asha reminded her how the entire day used to pass without her leaving the operation theatre or hospital and how as head of department she helped many junior doctors with the preparation of case studies and their thesis and guided them wisely and they were very open and frank with her, shared their personal problems and sought advice. In fact, her unit worked as a team. Asha asked if they were in touch with her even after she gave up practicing in COVID times.

"Yes Asha, they share every news and keep me updated whenever they get time. They text messages to me or WhatsApp me; off duty they phone me. Meeting those energetic and enthusiastic doctors was one of my greatest pleasures. They would arrive early to greet me cheerfully. It was my small endeavour to instruct and educate the young doctors deeply who also worked with seamless teamwork." "Yes, I remember they could come to your office after the class. A warm and friendly atmosphere pervaded in your office as they sat with you to discuss the cases. I recall you telling the students: "My greatest desire is that you develop into outstanding doctors who work actively to relieve the sufferings in the real world and it is my source of joy to prepare the way for you with all of my strength. Can't do it alone. My life is limited. Even if something should happen to me, I want you to carry on this spirit. You study, work hard and develop yourself to become the very best you can be in your chosen fields while you also enjoy your life to the fullest. When you join the work force, apply yourselves seriously to your jobs. Marriage is not simply a guarantee of easy life, it entails a host of new responsibilities. Therefore, master the art of living, find meaning in each struggle, rise eagerly to life's challenges, and make each moment meaningful and enjoyable. We don't need magic to transform the world; we carry all the power we need inside ourselves already." They listened to her with the kind of stillness that came from suspending everything, even breath. She realized later when she understood that her being their professor was not the reason they were listening to her; they knew she lived every word she said to them and that had a momentous impact on them.

She had a big network of friends, therefore, she never felt lonely for a long time. However, on some days it appeared to her as if her time on earth had gone like an inconsequential scene rushed through the moving window. Locked in confined spaces, assailed by fear of the unknown, raw emotions and beliefs swung like a pendulum from end to end. Old memories came to her as images, feelings, glimpses, sometimes fleshed out, sometimes in outlines. Time solidifies as well as dissolves yet many things she wanted to forget remained painfully vivid.

She had lived through phases so painful that it was not easy for her to revisit pain, nor the idea of telling people about her life. As our feet shape new shoes for themselves so that in time they stop hurting, she had also shaped her past for herself. She understood that there are things in us and in our life, we cannot fight, however hard we might try. There was one thing that the experience of Shikha taught her was to keep her own counsel. She would watch, hear, discuss and debate but hold her judgment. She refused to be swayed and defeated by Corona. What are you doing with your life, she asked herself.

What everything she lived through and no matter what the outer atmosphere of circumstance, she must lift the inner cloudscape by her own efforts or perish under it. Like Viktor Frankl, she would say 'yes to life, in spite of everything.'

She wanted to live. "I do not want to be wasting time sitting at home when I can live. To be right in the middle of life, living each minute intensely."

When she was mulling over life, Ramit came from the hospital and told her, "Mama, COVID has unmasked a very ugly face of society. It has shown us how uncaring and dismissive we can be towards our fellow human beings. Today four dead bodies were sent back from graveyards as people protested their last rites for fear, they might contract the disease." At once she reminded him, "Even amidst the gloom there have also been shining examples of fearless, selfless service by members of the medical fraternity, many unreported and away from the public glare. Only today I read in the Times of India, what Dr Salem (who had become a COVID patient) wrote when he lay in the ICU, 'I could see a nursing station with about ten nurses dressed in white PPEs bustling about collecting samples, giving injections and scheduling tests from the patients. One of the nurses walks into the cubicle at 6:30 am and asks whether I had a peaceful sleep. She checks my vitals, does a blood draw for the day's tests and leaves only to reappear moments later to make me get out of bed, helps me brush my teeth and freshen up. Then, with help from another nurse changes my bed sheets and gets a dress change for me… Housekeeping, steam inhalation, dietitians, physiotherapists, nurses and doctors came to do their bit, all clad in oppressive PPEs but doing their job.' We are very proud of these warriors, Ramit. Haven't you seen when the COVID positive is detected in the neighbourhood and the municipality sanitizes the area and pastes a notice saying the house is COVID infected; how the fear grips the society and gated community. They shun their citizens and age-old neighbours have turned hostile. But this fear is missing in hospitals as the soldiers are brave on the frontlines. These healthcare workers help the patients, hold and calm them."

Ramit said, "Mama. Thousands of healthcare workers including doctors have died while treating patients. Do they not have family, parents, children and spouse? Even then they don't ignore the patients to stay safe; they are warriors but state does not take responsibility for their family. If a soldier dies fighting a war, he is aware his family is the state's responsibility; if dead he is glorified as a martyr. Only reward we will get shall be in the form of prayers by the survivors. The only acclaim would be a thank you by the indebted patient or a superior for doing our job."

Shikha said, "You are right my son. There will be no 21-gun salute for their bravado, no bodies will be wrapped in the Tricolour if they die in the line of duty. No state honours, no medals, no movies or books written on them, but still one feels humanity which exists in their spirit and their arms now. That is the real meaning and purpose of life. Have you forgotten the Hippocratic Oath the doctors take on becoming doctors?

The world is in turmoil, our people are fighting COVID. How can we think only about ourselves? There is a time for everything. Now is not the time to think of your needs and entitlements. We have on our hands a monumental battle.

Our members have displayed invincible and dauntless spirit. I can say with pride what Arnold J. Toynbee said, those living in the age of crisis must become pioneers of a better age, striving to find positive solutions and thereby turning the age into one of achievements.

Whenever she heard the extraordinary acts of the brave warriors, she sent messages in WhatsApp, "My colleagues, l know no matter how long the winters of hardships and adversity might persist our team members would bravely weather them and would spread that hope-filled message that winter always turns into spring."

The more intense the emotions, the stronger the wall of reticence she built around it. For Shikha each day was a tremendous struggle. It was not that she was feeling miserable at being cooped up in her house for months on nor was she raging like school children that they will suffer psychological damage if they do not socialize with other children for much longer. It was also not that she was not able to tolerate the slightest inconvenience. It was the lost time that was precious to Shikha. Of course, she was youthful still retained the enthusiasm and vigour of youth as sap of life still surged in abundance. She had thought that age mattered only if it was cheese wine or scotch but now, she knew better.

Until now she was thinking that she had achieved everything possible for a woman in her position, yet not everything was clear; there was something still lacking. She did not want to die and it still seemed that there was something most important which she did not have, of which she had vaguely dreamed and in the present, she was stirred by the same hope for the future. She wanted to do something for the suffering humanity in this pandemic-stricken society where patients with heart problems, diabetes, and hypertension were deprived of the best health care as COVID had become their primary concern. Shikha was deeply troubled by the misery around her and gave a long and measured thought to how this living hell -- the anguish, pain and despair of these patients, could be transformed. She pictured herself responding to the sight of people so suffering, sharing in their pain and agony and acting on their behalf. She wanted to open her doors to the sick and suffering. She felt despair that in spite of her having time and an intense wish to do something she was not able to do anything.

Now with her motto of, "Never blame others for your difficulties. "Try not to complain," and "Have confidence in yourself," she turned everything into part of her personal drama of human revolution. She wanted to make something of her life. She recalled what Buddha who had apparently said that there were two mistakes one could make on the road to truth -- not going all the way, and not starting. Shikha resolved not to make either of them.

Despite her firm determination it took her a long while to come to this decision. She had always looked truth in the face, however hard its glare hurt her eyes. She realized then her decision depended upon her son's acquiescence. However, one Sunday afternoon as Ramit got a day off, she told him, "Ramit there are so many things I can't say still, even to you. I am afraid if I don't tell you today, I would lose all that is myself. There is a bird trapped in me, beating its wings. It makes me bleed and it hurts, I have to let it free. I wish to give consultancy on the phone. Future is elusive, I have to adapt to the present and live it as if it were celebration." She declared with the conviction of the young who have no reason to believe life usually turns out different from everything they planned. The air around her was charged with a spirit of sacrifice and service. If you sat in her presence for a couple of hours you would also come out feeling charged. After she had the consent of Ramit, she had the confidence in the depths of her life that everything will be fine, come what may. She realized that it was the best thing that could have happened to her. It seemed her sense of self had been restored to her. As if all of life's possibilities had been locked away behind a door which had opened again. She had already earned the reputation in PGI of being an extraordinary doctor with the gentleness of a woman. Being a popular doctor and very compassionate towards patients who thronged her unit in OPD days in PGI, now lock down was lifted and life was coming to a new normal, she threw her basement office open to patients. Besides she talked to the founding director of Max hospital, he was so impressed that he asked her to join immediately as head of the panel of consultants on telemedicine in Max Hospital. Eventually she became a consultant at the prestigious website of Max Hospital. She took this project, perhaps fully aware how she was going to complete it to her satisfaction and raise the common standard of excellence. It was instant success drawing attention from the entire trinity that included the warm messages from old patients who were feeling neglected in the COVID period that she valued far more than fame or anything else. It gave her patients a great deal of relief that they could consult her now. Success for her was never measured in terms of money. It was the gratitude of her patients, the respect of her colleagues and the undisturbed sleep at night that only a clear conscience can ensure. She was charged with a new zest for life. She could read, write, swim, and enjoy the beauty of nature and love of her family besides finding pleasure in her work.

She had chosen the austerity and sacrifice of the fight for the common cause. Happiness somehow came back to her, she felt as if she had accomplished the most useful work. It not only gave a strong stimulus to telemedicine, it enlarged the very idea or conception of telemedicine. Her work made her forget everything else for a while.

After all, Arjuna saw all of the Universe, past and present in the opened mouth of Sri Krishna. She also saw the same way in her work. Work was her worship it was her life. Her favourite from *Bhagawad Gita* was verse 47 from Chapter 2 that said "Work for work's sake, not for yourself. Act but do not be attached to your actions. Be in the world but not of it." She felt fulfilled by doing her task but did not seek fruit of her actions.

Above all, she possessed the defining mark of the great human being -- the ability to hold one's opinions while remaining receptive to novel theories and willing to change one's mind in light of new evidence or inventions. She hailed joyfully any new idea or theory, medicine, any new technology or any research in heart surgery and gave it honest attention in her practice.

Very often, she was engaged in attending to -- what Hermann Hesse called, "the little joys" that are the slender threads of which we weave the lifeline that saves us. She had begun gathering a few grains of happiness as she thought often of this verse from Jane Hirshfield's splendid poem "The Weighing":

So, few grains of happiness
measured against all the dark
and still the scales balance.

In short, all was cheerful, all was well, just as it had been the year before, and as it would also be, in all probability, the year after.

7

Daughter of a Late Captain

Rita's father Shaksham was a modest and honourable Captain in the Indian Army. He was a decorated soldier of the Indo-Pak War of 1965 and the Bangladesh War of 1971. When he wore his medals, his chest would swell with pride. His acquaintances were mostly of those who were from the army, in his service. There was not a single brave solider with whom he was not closely acquainted. He was popular, richly endowed and unquestionably useful. Besides he was also staunch and hardworking. Never had he dabbled in politics or sought popularity or given speeches either during dinner gatherings or at the graves of his colleagues. Owing to his wife's early death, the house was left without a woman to look after it and that's the same as a man without an eye. So, the Captain took premature retirement and after serving for about twenty years or so, he returned to Ambala, his hometown to look after his family. Now he had no one to be friends with but if you speak of the past there was a long list of glorious heroes who offered him their warmest and sincere friendship.

The Captain was receiving a meagre pension so he applied for re-employment, got a Himachal Government job and moved to Shimla along with his family. He was earning rupees 700/- a month. He had two daughters and a son. No extra penny was coming to him from anywhere, and there was no chance of his income increasing for at least another three-four years. He could not think of one blessed thing in his favour. Nobody to look after his children. He had no money to afford a servant. Of course, the whole responsibility fell on his elder daughter Rita as his younger daughter's health had always been delicate and a son though promising and clever was still only a little boy.

Rita was strong and bright, she had beauty and cleverness, and her father believed that there was nothing she could not do. Had it been feasible, she would have been a genius at anything. She adored her father as he adored her and so intense was her love for him that she was willing to look after him, taking all his responsibilities, of making it her job that he had everything he wanted and nothing came near him that was not perfect. How she loved her father! But there was no denying that he was rather a stern and grim parent. He meant well, he had no end of grit and so on.

At times she was convinced that to be a widower's eldest daughter was the greatest responsibility a girl could have. What made it difficult was rather he was positively all she had. He was the combined parent, her only vision of her father was tall and stout rustling through the house with Renu and Ajay at his heels.

After all she had learned to be mother to her siblings and a home maker to her father. She was very exacting. She never just wiped the kitchen counters but scourged them. She scrubbed the bathrooms floors, vacuumed rooms, made beds, cooked food, and wiped mirrors. She baked, washed, ironed and cleaned. She polished the rims of the burners of the gas stove after every use, polished the taps, cleaned the bay window panes till the stains disappeared and people were in danger of smashing against it and then there was the business of putting everything perfectly in place. Now that her mother was dead, she felt this work was her responsibility. Besides that, there was men's work and there was women's work. She believed in this and so did everybody else she knew. Moreover, the work kept her occupied to a certain extent and tired her out so that she could sleep at night. She was content to do what she did. She studied in her spare time for her graduation.

She often remembered the time she had come to this house, how she crept out of her bed in her nightgown when the moon was full and laid on the floor with her outstretched hands. The big pale moon always reminded her how she felt exultant whenever they were on the sea side, she had gone off by herself, she had got as close to the sea as she could and gazed at the restless water. Of course, now there had been this other life, running out, getting things home in bags, getting things on approval, discussing them with Renu and going to get more things, arranging father's tray and trying not to annoy him.

Even now whenever she sat in the room and saw the moonlight thieving its way through the window and flashed on the mother's photo, she missed her mom. Why did the photographs of the dead fade so soon? wondered Rita. Would everything have been different if mother had not died young? She did not understand why aunt Meeta didn't live with them until they had left school and during holidays as well. She didn't understand why her queer little heart was grieving for her mother.

If mother had lived, perhaps, Rita would have been married. Certainly, now she knew she had no ghost of a chance. The very idea of such a thing was preposterous if she perfectly could understand her father. In fact, it was nothing short of desperation, whenever her mother said something about her marriage, her father passed no opinion, and he didn't say whether he approved or disapproved. He maintained his air of discipline and privacy. This made her mother angry at him for his abdication, sick of his self-absorption, which seemed so flagrant and improper in a father. And for the rest of life as well he was orderly and quiet.

The conversations she remembered most were the ones that were interrupted. What could her mother do? There had been no boys of marriageable age in her acquaintance, nobody for her to marry. Her father had few friends in the previous station. Since he moved to Shimla to take up a new job in Himachal Government, Rita had not met even a single man. How did one meet men? Even if she had met them how could she have got to know men well enough to be more than strangers. One read of people having adventures, being followed and so on. But no one had ever followed her. Yes, there had been one in the college who had slipped a note in her chest of drawers but by the time she found it was too torn to read, they could not even find out to whom it was addressed.

Raj was the only one who was serious about Rita. She was almost eighteen years old and used to go to visit her mother in the hospital who was recovering from the operation of her back which was said to be serious. Raj was an intern at the hospital. He was stocky, broad shouldered and authoritative and had sensitive skin, light hair and bold eyes. Every day from morning nine o'clock till late in the evening he received patients and was busy in the ward. When her mother complained of pain, Raj sat day or night watching at her bedside. So much self-sacrifice and genuine sympathy! Whenever he had free time he came to chat with Rita; they talked about concerts, protest marches, drugs and the outrageous people. He recited poems and she appreciated him. Besides he was popular with the patients because of his jokes and deep concern. Raj also stayed up nights, sitting by her mother. Suddenly the fine fellow was conquered! Raj was smitten and head over heels in love. One fine evening Raj confessed, "Rita I have not known anyone

I like as much as I like you. I have never felt so happy with anyone. But I am sure it is not like what people and what books mean when they talk about love. Do you understand? Oh! if you only knew how horrid I feel without you." He was letting out more secrets than she could handle.

One night her mother died suddenly of embolism and the affair also breathed its last. After her mother's death he met her once at the supermarket where she had gone to buy groceries, "Why do you look so awful? Why are you so unhappy?" Raj asked. "Oh Raj, please don't be dreadfully stuffy and tragic. You are always saying or looking, or hinting that I have changed. Just being the eldest I have responsibility of looking after this house, these siblings and my bereaved father. You don't seem to understand my compulsion." "Yes, it is true your compulsion has killed my love. It is absurd, it is maddening." Rita could not help but have a grim look as she knew the full extent of Raj's sentimentality. She said goodbye and he silently left.

After a few days she received his letter, "My precious darling Rita... God forbid, my darling, that I should be a drag on your happiness." As she read her feeling of astonishment changed to a stifled feeling. She felt confused and frightened. "Oh Raj!" She pressed her face into the pillow. But she felt that even the grave bedroom knew her what she was, forlorn and lonely.

After this her philosophy of life also changed. In all these years since her mother died, any thought of marriage had been something she had to get rid of, pull out immediately like a knife in her throat. If she heard that name she had to pull it out too. Now such an idea had to be banished by a sort of gate that she could slam down behind her ears that was all. The rest of her life now involved looking after her father and at the same time keeping out of his way.

She felt no remorse, only a sense of destiny and submission. She had felt that she was born on this earth for no reason other than to be with her father and to try to understand him and his needs. She once said to Renu, "Do you know the feeling that overtakes me when I am in the presence of father? The fact that he exists in the world at all, this alone makes this world, and a life in it, meaningful."

It was in the later years after her mother had died leaving her (18), sister (12) and brother (10) that her father had no time to occupy himself with their upbringing. He had taken up a job in Shimla. He observed them only in snatches and therefore could say very little about their childhood. Rita was now used to working alone and she had been doing it, since her mother died. It was hard for her to imagine having somebody else around all the time. But the strange thing was that she didn't consider those times as unhappy. There wasn't a particularly despairing mood around the house. At first, she and her father were extraordinary polite and very glad to talk to each other. They both laughed though they hadn't said anything funny nor could they help laughing if one of them produced some witticism, even an unfortunate one. She was inquisitive and would sit on the desk facing him, following his movements and asking questions. She was interested in knowing what he read and what he did in the office. She was meek, patient and a kind girl. For few years or so everything seemed to prosper. Rita believed in work and was happy. There were gaiety, unconstrained conversation, jokes, laughter, mutual tenderness and joy that animated them when they used to come together in the dining room. For a busy person like him, dinner was the time to see his children and for them it was the festive time that belonged to them and no one else. They would laugh at the very triviality and silliness of things they (siblings) were telling or at the revelation of some appalling selfishness, deceptions, meanness and sheer badness. This lasted till Renu got married and Ajay got a job in Saudi Arabia.

After the marriage of Renu, Captain's day began with the coming of Rita in his room. After anxious inquiries about his welfare she would suddenly remember about her brother Ajay in Saudi Arabia and said, "Of course, it is difficult for us but until he finally gets on his feet, it's our duty to support him. The boy is in a foreign country and was drawing less pay." She told him regularly how Renu was happy in her house and her son was growing up well and how the prices of sugar, *atta and dal* had gone up. He listened mechanically saying yes. Otherwise, he sat motionless, not thinking of anything and not feeling any desires. Rita said to herself, "If I were a son in my brother's place I would have left the job and ran to him. What is the point of saying? To harbour spiteful feelings against ordinary people for not being heroes is possible for narrow-minded or embittered people; enough of that."

The imbecile thing, the absolutely extraordinary thing was that her father had not the slightest idea that Rita was not happy as others. That this stout ungainly woman with the dull expression of petty care and fear over a crust of bread, with eyes clouded by constant thought of poverty and debt and capable only of talking of expenses was his slender and beautiful Rita whom he loved for her good, clear mind, pure soul and beauty. Nothing had survived from the past except her fear of his health. What blindness! He had not the remotest notion in those days that she really hated that inconvenient little house and that she was desperately lonely. Her large, kind impersonal sobriety had taken out all cheerfulness out of her life. The clothes did not make her look as if she really cared what she put on. She had worked like a horse and never heard a kind word. Her sweetness soured, her mind was narrowed by the society of the small town in which she lived, her friends were married and had children, but she remained a prisoner to duty. There was nothing for her to do but have patience. What did it mean? What was it she was really wanting? Where did it all lead to?

After Renu was settled and her brother had gone to Saudi Arabia, she knew something was coming that she should watch for but didn't know what. She wanted something badly. Was it a nice friend? Not quite, no hope of that anyway. (Something in her was turning traitorous though she didn't know what). Her father, for instance, was not reconciled to the idea of her wedding. It aroused some perplexity in him. For all these years he had played a strange and unenviable role in regard to her. When she had earlier announced to him that she was going to be a professor and when she told him she loved music and theatre. He was at a loss each time and all his concern for her fate expressed itself in thinking a lot and doing nothing. Why it ended this way? Was it that he believed that daughter cannot look after the father's responsibilities after marriage? Was it either sacrifice or marriage? Were these apprehensions true? He said nothing as if he had not heard anything. Indifference is the paralysis of the soul, a premature death. But Rita had the dual courage of facing the broken reality while refusing to cease cherishing the beautiful world.

However, Rita's strength had taken a slump that seemed to bring about a profound change in her personality. The visitors of her father made her nervous. She felt too tired for conversation. She didn't want to go out. She kept up the house adequately but she rested between the chores. She lost most of her interest in television though she would watch when father turned it on. She lost her rounded, jolly figure becoming thin and shapeless. The warmth and the glow -- whatever had made her nice looking were drained out of her face and black eyes. She thought to herself, "There is something unbearable in my soul. Something is going on inside me: the spiteful thoughts wander through my mind and feelings such as I have never known before are nesting in my soul. I hate, I despise, I feel outraged, indignant and afraid. I have become excessively severe, irritable, ungracious and suspicious. Even something that before would have given me the occasion for one more quip and a good natured laughter now produces a heavy feeling in me. There are moments when I long to forget everything and just collapse on the bed and sleep."

"Why is it that amidst great joys man cannot forget his own grief?" she asked Renu who had come to visit them. She wanted to say something to Renu, something frightfully important. She would not have said it a few years back, she would have been more cautious knowing how her father would have revolted at the idea.

Rita was a person who questioned her wants and did question if she was right in whatever she said or felt or did. Often, she had been saying to people more or less what they think they would like to hear. Now she knew Renu was married and would just take it as a way of trying to understand her. "I wrote the scripts of others' lives, but my own was already inside me. I wanted to remain ignorant and unknowing in this house where I ate and slept but the door, that blind hinged door, kept opening elsewhere," Rita continued. "I am afraid I am feeling rather upset today, more likely father would see my interest in things that has nothing to do with work as an act of impudence, unnecessary," said Rita. The thought of being truly understood, stirred up an alarm in Rita just as much as being taken no notice stirred up resentment. For the moment Rita was conscious of an immense effort it was taking to tear her secret out of herself and offer it to her sister.

"Do you think you care for it?" she faced her sister Renu and said

"Don't take me wrong, I see myself as a middle aged daughter who did her duty, stayed at home thinking that someday her chance would come until she woke up and knew it wouldn't see myself not like you and Ajay who to some extent have flourished in life; or father who has adjusted himself to it but more like the one of those misfits or captives-nearly useless celibate, rusting-who should have left but didn't and could not and are now misfit for any place, have lived life whose choices had not been plentiful and whose luck had not been in good supply..."

Suddenly Renu interrupted, "You mean it is lonely," said Renu who knew her sister would never admit. Rita wanted to say, "I have at times wanted to be happy and married like you," But stopped at once. Instead she said "Oh yes! It is loneliness. It is not that I am not awfully fond of father as I am fond of you." At that moment Rita became so solemn, "Please forgive me for being so horrid, please." "There is no question of forgiving you. How could there be?" replied Renu. Then Rita said guiltily, "Sometimes we say something that cannot be forgiven or that we cannot forgive ourselves. But we do it, we do it all the time." No, no. "You are marvellously kind and simple. You have performed your duties rather than follow your heart. You have given up your dreams for the good of the family. You are blameless in your dealings with the family because you are so selfless, you have the grace and fortitude. Your selfless love has entered our lives like the stirred in honey goes into tea. You have embraced grief and gladness, comic, glum, the dead and living. But nobody has truly appreciated your sacrifices. Don't question your right to pry to bring it to the surface. The society we come from, these things are buried for good and horror/pain like badges mostly women wear throughout their lives," said Renu and folded her in a warm embrace. Rita was old enough to see that a lot of things you might have wanted out of life you would never get. It was hard to explain how you could be happy in such a situation, but sometimes she thought, you were.

Something had come upon them that was more unexpected and would become more devastating than the loss of income. It was an early onslaught of Parkinson's disease which showed up when her father was in his fifties.

For almost four years now Captain had not taken notice of the things that generally made people happy like nice weather, flowers in bloom, and the smell of the bakery. He didn't have that spontaneous sense of happiness, but he had a reminder of what it was like. He had transformed into a small, skinny old fellow from an eternally smiling face and sparkling eyes. She began to notice clear signs of decline. As his condition deteriorated, he became dull and irritable. Misfortunes never come singly. She did not have what you could call conversation with her father. She asked some simple and ordinary questions. How was he feeling? Did he get enough sleep? What did he want to eat for dinner? Did he want her to walk him to the park in the evening? She said, "You have to get some fresh air." "That's true," he said. "Do you want me to invite your friends in the park?" She asked, the way you ask your kid after school. It cost her such effort to look at him, to get him in the chair, this thin and grey mechanically moving, uncoordinated man. What was she here for, if not to listen to him and at least serve him?

To take off his shoes or to put them on was a great agony for him and it had been an agony for years. In fact, he was so accustomed to pain that his face was drawn and screwed of the twinge before he could even untie the laces. She felt unbearably pained for him. Now he was an old man with a bald head and front teeth gone. His chest was shrunk and shoulders narrow. There was nothing imposing in this pathetic figure.

She liked her father the way he was, so she didn't reproach or apologize for him. Out of old habit he would get dressed and sleep at his regular time. Back then, despite all the changes that happened to him, she had not to mother him, to wipe, to wash and feed lying in the bed. He lived boldly like a brave soldier. This Parkinson's disease had been overtaking him for some time with erratic symptoms but recently had been diagnosed and pronounced incurable. Towards the end, he had become so feeble and helpless, his memory had weakened, his thoughts lacked consistency and he forgot ordinary things. His tone with her was still firm and slightly irritable but that was with everyone else. His blustering was almost about the things he had misplaced or dropped or bumped into. "Where the hell is this ...?" He would say or "You did not happen to see the…?" So it seemed he failed to grasp the name of the thing he was looking for. Someday he said, "I know who you are. You are the new girl helping Asha (his dead wife) in the kitchen. Can you tell me where your mother is! I have not seen her running around for a long time?" His air of sullenness and complaint also seemed glamorous to Rita. This disease's progress took more and more of her attention. She embraced him, stroked his head and said tender words as if he was a little child. She would close the door, made him sit on the bed and start reading to him with his half closed and lazy-looking eyes.

The warm, the cosy atmosphere and the presence of a sympathetic person did not make him contented as before but instead there was a strong urge to complain and grumble. Gone were the former gaiety, unconstrained conversations. It was years since their relations became strained and he did not treat her benignly. Many a time he told her, "You obviously have neither the desire nor the vocation to be my nurse," and silence ensued between them. Not seldom she happened to see how she was punished for no reason, how her curiosity was unsatisfied. There was no one to see her sadness, to draw her to him and pity her in the tone of an old nanny: "My dear, little orphan!" She regretted that no one had either the desire or the wish to follow the beginning and development of her passion that already filled Rita when she was eighteen years old. Her father didn't listen to her, he was the only one who lacked the courage to pay her any attention. Whenever she used to come to his room to share feelings, he would point out to the clock and said he had no time. And she would leave each time more disappointed than before she entered it. Still she would say to herself, "I always loved you as my father and a friend. Forgive me". It is said that the way in which you accept your sufferings under such restrictions and how you deal with difficulties truly shows who you are. She had neither minded nor bemoaned her responsibilities, so many anxieties, demands and complications. Yes she was the modern version of Cordelia of King Lear, loving, committed, concerned and devoted daughter of the Captain.

She would mechanically ask him some question and he gave her a very brief answer. Then she noticed that his face didn't have that trustful expression. His expression was cold now, indifferent, distracted, as with the passengers who had to wait a long while enough for the train. She dressed carelessly and was not as curious as she used to be.

She looked at him and it became perfectly clear to her that her inner life had escaped his observation a long time ago. She had a feeling that once upon a time she lived at home with her real family and now with someone who was not her real father. She could be exasperated but tolerant with him as if he was her younger son. She still believed that a father was the most important, the most beautiful, the most necessary person in a child's life and that her father had been and always would be the highest manifestation of love.

Then her father breathed his last peacefully in bed one night. "If it was I that died or someone else, it wouldn't be so noticeable but it was father who had died. Nobody else but father. It's hard to believe that he's no longer in the world and can't stand it. It is simply killing me, I can't see but I hear him moaning and rolling on the bed in pain, While in the kitchen, I would keep thinking that his voice would come from the bedroom anytime. He used to get out of the bed and call out to me in the middle of the night if he needed anything. As a result of intense struggle against mounting weakness, a strange thing was happening to him; he would start pacing up the room at night and howl, 'For a moment, for a moment! Sit down! Just a couple of words!' He was a kind and loving soul. Some people's mothers are not to them as he was to me. Lord save his soul!" she said to herself.

The pain was so intense that she could not utter a single word, only sucked in air, her teeth chattering like drum roll. No matter how worn out she got with him, he was still the closet person in the world to her. She had told him after her mother's death, "When you will grow old I will feed you, I won't let anyone hurt or harm you. When you die I will pray for the repose of your soul as I do for mama. To concentrate on prayer is out of question now. There are no prayers but only the unabashed swaying and jostling of people." What a restless night, she thought but she didn't see the same restlessness and sleeplessness in all of nature, in the darkness of the night and the trees under which the people bustled out. Now she was so sick and tired of it that she wanted to run out of the house.

Her father had a certain way of looking at things; she was used to it than any other person would understand. The truth of the things between them, the bond, was not something that anybody could understand, it was not anybody else's business. If Rita could watch her devotion! After his death, what other use could she be now in this world? She was asking herself. "Now I am like an orphan. Now I too am forty plus, there is no other life." It was not easy to live through such terrible moments. That's God's will. We all must die. You should be glad because whoever dies on Ekadshi day in the month of November will surely go to heaven," she heard people saying.

What makes the soul to grieve and refuse to listen to reason?

Why did she have to suffer? She could not understand. It was too much. She had too much in her to bear. She had borne it till now; she had kept herself to herself and never once had she been seen to cry. Never by a living soul. Not even her siblings had seen her break down. She had kept a proud face always. What with father gone, what had she? She said nothing. He was all she had got from life, now he was taken too. Why did all this had to happen to her? She wondered. What have I done said Rita. What have I done?"

Her misery was so terrible that she put on her jersey and walked out of the house like a person in a dream. She didn't know what she was doing. She was like a person so dazed by the horror of what had happened that he walks away-anywhere as though by walking away he could escape. Nobody knew, nobody cared even if she broke down after all these years. If she could only cry now, cry for a long time, over anything. Beginning with her mother's death, leaving of her brother to Saudi Arabia, departure of her sister for their in-laws house after marriage, all the years of struggle of his illness and misery that led up to his death. She must cry. She could not put it off any longer. She had a hard life.

Where could she go? She could not go home. Renu was there and it would frighten Renu out of life. She could not sit on the bench anywhere, people would come asking her questions. She could not go to anybody's house, she had no right to cry in strangers' house. If she sat on the steps the police would catch her. Was not there any place where she could hide and keep herself to herself, not disturbing anybody and nobody worrying her? Wasn't there any place in the world where she could cry out? Yes there was nowhere and she was left alone to get over it.

Rita stood looking up and down, darkness came imperceptibly and it began to rain. She looked up at the empty bed in her father's room with her meek and dull eyes and then rested her gaze on the rosy and black browned face of her young brother who had come from Saudi Arabia and stood next to her and respected her pretence (as she always did) that she was not unhappy but preoccupied. It seemed that in her brother's face she was seeking the soft and tender features of her deceased father and hearing her father's voice, "Life cannot be repeated it must be cherished."

8

Epiphany

Neeru, in the morning session, joined Olympus-a six-week Guided Meditation programme organized by Buddha CEO, Quantum Foundation. On Sunday morning she woke with a strange feeling. She felt like running to the park.

As she walked to the park, there was a spring to her feet and she was humming a tune. When she turned the corner of the park she was suddenly overcome by a feeling of sheer joy, it felt as though she had swallowed the morning sun and the spark of delights were filling her entire body.

Somehow she felt interconnected with everything-the trees, the firs, the pines, the blue sky, the garden, revived, warmed and caressed by the sun and dew drops sparkling like diamonds on the leaves.

"What a heavenly morning-so young, fresh and festive! How joyful, sweet and gracious is the atmosphere. Everything is good at this happy time of the morning. Sun is sublime, formidable and full of wonder-working miracles. All is well with me; I am immeasurably and unreasonably happy. My soul is brimming with exultation, joy and hope!" she exclaimed.

There was so much beauty and richness in nature that what we need is the courage to feel it and make it our own. In that jubilant mood she returned from the walk-the chirping of the grasshoppers, corncrake's cry, the calling of quails enhancing tranquillity and revitalization restored her energy and filled her with vigour to face the new day.

Back at home she asked Raj her maid, "Have the flowers come?"

"Yes madam, fruits have also come."

"Ok bring them here I will make the arrangements before I go to wake up Shurbhi."

As she turned towards the dining room, she happened to look into the cold mirror that reflected a radiant, smiling woman with dark eyes and long eyelashes who was waiting for something divine to happen. Again, those sparks came back to her with such a surge of deep happiness, it was unbearable. It was difficult to breathe but she tried to.

At that time Raj came with two glass vases and flowers. Neeru made the ikebana style flower arrangements in two Japanese vases and placed them on the centre and side tables.

When she finished arranging the flower vases, she stood away to see the effect; it was just wonderful. She began to laugh. It was not that she was drunk or disorderly or hysterical but simply blissful to be alive that morning.

She picked up her jersey and went to the bedroom to wake up her three-year-old daughter Shurbhi. She woke up, looked at her mother with a disarming, chubby smile and Neeru could not help saying, "Raj, today I will give her a bath and ready her for school, you prepare her tiffin box and bring her school bag downwards.

Shurbhi kept holding her doll and playing with it but she would open her mouth to take a spoonful of porridge and omelette and ate delightfully. Neeru hugged her baby girl passionately and very smilingly said, "What a lovely baby doll you are! Mama loves you. I am very fond of you."

Raj also came with the school bag and their Peter also walked with her. Neeru allowed her to play with the dog before going to school which she usually did not permit.

"Your phone, madam," said Raj from the lobby. Picking up the phone Neeru said "Oh it is you Dharam darling?".

"Yes dear. You do remember I told you that I have called friends for dinner? I will be late in the evening, suddenly a meeting has come up, you get the dinner ready by 9pm."

"We are making the preparations. Is it not a divine day…?" she had not completed the sentence before Dharam snapped the phone down.

They had people coming for dinner The Thakurs were coming. Ramesh Thakur was an art connoisseur and his wife Richa was an interior decorator. Harish Bande was a writer who had just published his novel and his poems Love in Digital World, and I went to woods after break-up. Both were instant successes and were talked about in all literary circles.

Preity was a gifted and exceptional actress and her friend Rupanshi was accompanying her. Neeru had met Rupanshi in the club, sitting in the corner with an iced glass of coffee. She had a sunny appearance, fair complexion, dark hair, blue eyes and pouted lips. Neeru had fallen in love with her instantly as she always did with intelligent women who had something 'weird' about them.

Rupanshi was quiet by nature, up to a certain point she was quite frank but beyond that point she would not go. Neeru didn't know much about her except that she was a corporate litigation lawyer before she won the much-coveted education award from the British Government, the Chevening Scholarship and did her master's at a top university for Gender and Development in UK. There she was elected as a Fellow at Royal Society of Arts, London to work on women representation in global leadership. She was visiting India in that connection.

Neeru found her to be a wonderful person but Dharam didn't agree with her and found her dull. "Like almost all single women she is cold and arrogant and has a frozen heart," he said. Neeru was excited to be meeting her in the evening.

She went to the guest room and picked black and golden cushions from the cupboard and threw them one by one on to the backs of chairs and sofas. They added colour and warmth to her drawing room and that made all the difference and the room came alive at once. She played ball with her pet and hugged him but the fire in her bosom wouldn't go away.

The window of the drawing room looked out into the garden and she saw chrysanthemums in yellow and white in full bloom and there was an apple tree in pale pink blossoms, the song of the thrush and the bloom of the magnolia and the lush optimism of that first blade of grass. How happy I am! How happy I am! she murmured.

She had everything. She was young. Dharam and she were in love and loyal to each other. They looked wonderful as a couple; she had a splendid house of her own at this young age. They had an adorable daughter. They had beautiful friends, artists, writers, painters, intellectuals and poets. They had no worry about money and they went abroad every summer. They had books, music, garden rare collections of artifacts, a wonderful cook and a loyal servant.

In that joyful mood Neeru dressed herself in a green gown, embroidered with sequins and wore an emerald string of beads and golden shoes and carried a Michel Kores green purse and was ready to receive the guests. The guests began to arrive and the sound of laughter and voices and soft rustling came from the main door.

Neeru kissed Mrs Thakur, the sweet smelling and elegant lady and ushered her into the drawing room followed by her husband in a grey suit. Harish Bande came in a dismal mood. Right upon entering he complained about the terrible experience he had had while locating their house. The taxi driver was vile and malevolent and kept circling the ISCON temple for almost half an hour. It felt like an eternity before they would reach the house.

Neeru tried to calm him down. When he saw the Thakurs already in, he settled down quickly and Preity came looking fragile and beautiful in a pearl white crepe dress. Pleasant and polite conversation followed. Harish asked Preity how the theatre was doing. It was showing the adaptation of his novel My Daughter's Father these days. They talked at ease and laughed for a while when Dorthy who had come with Preity asked what he was writing for Preity this time. He told them it was called Virgin Queen and discussed the set, the costume, the stage setting and other nuances in minute details. They talked and laughed while Neeru kept them engaged in conversation until Dharam came.

When Dharam dramatically entered the drawing room Neeru blurted out that Rupanshi had not come. "I wonder if she has forgotten." "Why don't you ring her up? You have her phone number," said Dharam.

As Neeru turned to make the phone call she heard a taxi stop and saw Rupanshi alighting from it. She was dressed in a black gown with a long string of black onyx beads and golden shoes and smilingly entered the gate.

"Sorry for being late," she said. "It is ok. Come along," said Neeru and took her arm and they moved to the drawing room. The touch of her arm fired the same shafts of joy in her body that Neeru did not know what to do with.

Suddenly an intimate look passed between them that told Neeru that Rupanshi was also feeling what she was feeling.

It was such a delightful group with everyone intimately talking to each other. Neeru was feeling magnanimous to the world and everyone around.

When the dinner was laid, they all moved to the dining room. While enjoying Indian food, they talked about movies they had recently seen. They reminded others of Uncle Vanya-the play of Anton Chekhov that was staged last month and were full of praise for the actors who played the roles of Uncle Vanya and the retired professor Alexander Vladimirovich.

Delhi was overflowing with new plays but this was different. They discussed recent happenings in the society, the intolerance towards free speech and mentioned about the journalist writer who was arrested for voicing his views.

Draconian 'Love Jihad' laws will rob our young of the glory of youth, the very essence and purpose of life, Preity said. "Right to live with a person of his or her choice, irrespective of religion professed by them, is intrinsic to right to life and personal liberty. Interference in personal relationships would constitute a serious encroachment into the right to freedom of choice of two individuals."

Dharam said, "Sorry to interfere but why don't we move to my 'collection' room? I want to show you my latest collection of artifacts and books." Ramesh readily agreed and they moved to his library.

Rupanshi asked Neeru if they could go to see the garden in the moonlight. As they walked to the balcony overlooking the garden they stepped in a new, wonderful more thrilling and exciting world than the daylight one. Behind the hills the afterglow of the evening sunset was fading from the sky. Only a single strip of the pale crimson remained. Already night was enfolding nature in its tender and soothing embrace.

Neeru was so charmed by the beauty of the moon that she wanted to hold it all her life in her hands as a new mother holds her unblanketed child, not thinking at all.

"Moon so proximate and unassailable, this radiant orb of primeval scar tissue; silent witness to countless human heartaches What a beauty, an oasis of tranquillity," said Rupanshi.

That's the way to live, carelessly, recklessly and spending one self. To take things easy, not to fight against the ebb and flow of the life but to give way to it that what is needed. To live and to let live."

"Yes," said Neeru, "surrender to what you watch, abandon yourself to this mood, let it float on, carrying you in its placid ecstasy."

As both the women stood together looking at the blooming apple tree which looked like a flame, they moved into the silence and quietude of the garden. Neeru looked at the immense tree, its whiteness, its softness and felt her breathing die away as she became part of the silence. It seemed to grow, it seemed to expand in the silvery light of the moon. Deep, deep, she sank into silence, staring at the tree until it grew slowly and then rapidly it grew taller and taller and reached the edge of the silvery moon and she felt enfolded. So great was her heavenly happiness as she stood there, she wished she might live forever.

Both were caught in the aura of unearthly/celestial light, understanding each other perfectly. They looked like the creatures of another world wondering what to do with that treasure of bliss in their hearts. They were lost in breathing this pure joy and true inner peace when suddenly they heard Dharam calling them inside for coffee which he was fond of making in the coffee machine for the guests after dinner.

Dharam went to Rupanshi and asked coffee latte or cappuccino? "No thank you, I don't drink after dinner," she said.

Neeru wanted to say to Dharam, "Please, don't dislike her. She is such a wonderful person. How could you just think so differently about a person who means such a lot to me. Come to me in the bed I will tell you things we shared. How I love you. Soon these people would be gone and we will be alone in the warm bed. What splendid things I would confide in you, she murmured. For the first time she desired her husband. She felt strange. The beast that had slumbered so long within her body had finally stirred and fixed its longing hungry stare at her husband. But all she murmured was, "How I love you and wish to confide in you."

She was in love with him; they were great pals. She knew he was different. He was so understanding and trustworthy. In the beginning it worried her awfully to discover that she was cold and frigid but then after a while it didn't not matter.

We talked; we were frank with each other that was the benefit of being modern. But now she wanted him intensely. Was this what that feeling of bliss was leading up to?

When she was overflowing with joy Romesh announced "We must leave now. You know it would take us another hour to reach Gurugram". Dharam insisted, "Take one small peg of whisky for the road."

No thanks we have thoroughly enjoyed the dinner and whisky, your hospitality. Now we beg your leave," said Romesh.

"You must not miss your last metro, it would be awful. I will walk with you to the gate," Neeru said.

When she came back to the drawing room the others too were ready to move. Preity told Harish, "You can come with me your house is on our way." Harish felt relieved to hear it. "I am simply thankful to you, you saved me the pain of another drive after that dreadful experience."

Rupanshi said, "I will get my coat from the dining hall." Neeru wanted to follow her but Dharam pushed past her. "Let me help you," Dharam said and they moved to the dining hall.

Neeru thought Dharam was repenting his rudeness to Rupanshi throughout the evening. "He wants to make up for it. He is such an impulsive and simple man If he believed in people, it was with his whole heart. He could not be disloyal; he couldn't tell lies. I like him for this."

Now Harish and Neeru and Preity were left alone. Preity said, "I wonder if you have read Neeru's Wheel of Life, latest anthology of poems. I like it, especially The darkest night in Panchkula.

"You must read my poem before you leave," Neeru cajoled Harish. Quickly she went to the bedroom to bring the book. He read it and said, "It is incredible. You are a superb poet."

Preity and Richa bid goodbye and Neeru said goodnight to them. As she turned back and looked towards the hall she saw Dharam holding Rupanshi's stole in his hand and her back turned to him and head bent. He put the stole on the dinning chair and placed his hands on her shoulder and then turned her aggressively towards him. She placed her hands on her cheeks and smiled slyly.

Dharam seemed to say, "I like you. Don't be afraid to say you also like me," and planted a kiss on her lips. "Tomorrow" "he whispered and she said "Yes". "If you prefer, I can book you an Ola.."

When Neeru heard this the waves of happiness suddenly ebbed. Rupanshi came back to say, "Thank you, it was a memorable evening. Apple tree was awesome." "Good bye," said Neeru as she was taking leave of her forever.

"What is going to happen now?" Neeru said in a voice that was exactly how miserable and inconsolable she felt.

She ran towards the window of the drawing room and saw the apple tree was as lovely as before and full of flowers.

And life... it is always sad and all the excitement has a way of leaving you in silence.

9

Kashmiri Shawl

One evening Anu went to visit Mrs. Sahdev who had come back after her knee joint replacement surgery from Max hospital in Delhi. As Anu's husband Ravi turned his car towards the gate of sector 20 of Panchkula he saw old men and women as well as young married women all engaged in conversations.

He said, "These societies are so noisy and chaotic; residents seem to be always sharing joys and troubles in the open compound; celebrating birthdays and promotions. Something is surely going on today as well." As soon as Ravi parked his car he saw his junior colleague Bindra who had returned last week from his posting in J& K, frantically waving at him.

After exchanging formal greetings at the lift gate, they got busy in animated conversation and Anu knew it would continue for a long while now. In the meantime, she adjusted the Kashmiri shawl on her shoulders. She had bought the shawl during Ravi's posting in Srinagar and her friends at the society began admiring it.

Anu liked the way the neighbourhood gathered on such sunny winter days. Now and then in the middle of more casual conversation, there would be a joke or a story or a bit of news to share.

Just then she heard the agitated whisper of some Kashmiri Khan, like the distant flow of a mountain torrent and she saw the open mouths and excited faces of the people who were enjoying his alarming experiences. Suddenly Anu's attention was drawn to a Kashmiri hawker, Abdul (whose name she gathered later and whose story no one really told her but she learnt it from bits and pieces dropped out of conversation she heard while moving in the society and talking to elders.

She learnt what she knew without asking direct questions from Abdul fearing the pain she knew would also surround the story. She along with the elders seemed as curious as little children; probably most of them had either lived there or visited those places in Kashmir.

They listened with rapt attention when Abdul said, "Sir, Kashmir is a peaceful and secluded place and humbling in beauty. I used to earn my living in a *shikara* where with each dawn the light brings life, while other members of my family cultivated *kesar fields* and discovered on their way herbs and roots to make potions and collected almond leaves for keeping the moths away from clothes. Ah, that was the time when it was a heaven for tourist as well.

Nothing they had seen before had made them so happier. They felt more like angels floating on the Dal Lake. What better way than to spend holidays in Kashmir they exclaimed! Then suddenly one night the chinar carried sound of the bullets and the crashes and cries were heard from the gallery. There were the terrorist attacks in Kupwara and the loudest voices that everyone heard was that of terrorists and their guns. In the days that followed they were busy in driving sheep out of our fields, getting extortion in the middle of the night. At first, they were picking only on the innocent, on local women and girls. Then they were looking for houses to stay in and had already evicted some families, even some of the residents were killed while others were anchored to the walls of some dark cell in their basement. They got bruised, bullied setting off that trail of fire and violence. Eventually as if that beating up was not enough, they started cutting the crops to throw them at the mercy of a less forgiving world. They were not only responsible for all the disarrangement of the houses but they staked their claim on common ground and fields and repeated their warnings that the village would be punished for the sins. I had hoped the good times, as deserved with some sweat, to last forever but they blighted our lives; they brought a curse on people and the land called 'heaven on earth'." Abdul sighed as he stopped for a while. The pain in his overall personality was too loud to be ignored. Soon Abdul calmed down and recounted or recalled the progress of his war against terrorism.

An old man in the middle of the compound asked rather innocently, "Why didn't you complain to the Government?" and by his question or probably by accident, had got the Kashmiri going on a spiel like this. "None listened when the complaints were made to authorities, no one hunted for them despite their warnings." The old man agreed, "True, terror threats cannot be countered if security issues are turned into a game of political football or a popularity contest".

Abdul continued, "Soon we felt the properties were not ours anymore and these terrorists won't let us rest till they drive us out to rot away. It was becoming increasingly difficult and much too risky to continue staying there. Some families left immediately, with tearful farewells and hugging their neighbours wondering where they would be scattered.

For others it was not an easier choice either, even though their sons had gone ahead of them and would be reunited on the road (they had set off in fear and trepidation). However, mine was the most reluctant family which would not be easily driven out?

"We are the ancient families," my father said one day, "We have not picked/packed up our apples for marketing. We would take the risk and stay. We have grown these apples since Adam's time and what would happen to the goats and hens?" Father cast a lingering look at trees loaded with raw, green apples.

"But Abba," I said, "An orchard of apples is not worth our life. It is safer to be anywhere else but here. Unless something is done immediately, another torrent of the shells would ruin us completely. We have to think of disappearing to towns or villages where, of course, our names and the names of our families we belong to would not ring a bell of familiarity, nor would there be standing orchards of our future, still it is best to get away before the trouble started again".

The neighbours also persuaded my father to pack the cash and jewellery, burdens and sorrows in shoulder bags and join them in the flight which meant we could not carry our valuable animals, buffalo or goats, or other things we owned. To pack up, move out and save ourselves was unsettling me as my head was bursting with bristling possibilities

"What should I do"? I asked in a voice that sounded helpless. "You must not delay anymore. You must leave fast," my father tried to persuade me. But for himself he was relentless as old people usually are when it comes to leaving home. I stared at tall trees that stood arrogantly on either side of the narrow path, "'How will we cross these hills at night to reach Jammu?"

Kara my wife asked sceptically, "What if we are shot on the way?" It was a question that numbed me. Come to think of it, Jammu is two-three days journey, almost 350 kilometres away but at that moment it seemed impossible to navigate even the narrowest trail through the pitch dark in the hills.

I who took pride in my strong physique, if need be, could level the earth and cultivate the fields for hours, felt helpless when it came to taking the family with me. Would we reach safe? This thought ripped me apart not only my conscience but my parents too. Eventually like everyone else even I got busy with shoving things into bags, tying the bundles and stitching valuables on the clothes to be worn during the journey.

Everything was in a fluid situation; I found my father just staring at my children with that kind of look that says, "I love you with an all-consuming love, the kind of love that envelops you and sustains. I want to see you. Won't I really see you again?" He was beginning to feel the pain in his chest that all parents feel when their children move out.

It was a kind of look that invariably draws your heart out but I left with my wife Kara and Tikku and Abida, my children, leaving my parents behind with lingering, longing looks as I parted. I slipped out of Kupwara (where my parents lived) late at night in the darkness of the mountains (I had fears I won't see them again) by the forest route but that did not guarantee any safety from the terrorists. I found myself silently repeating the *ayt-al-kursi* and others walking quietly beside me, each instinctively aware of the other's fear.

I feared terrorists could do anything to individuals on open roads. A chill ran down my spine; I walked mindlessly as my son continued to talk. How terrifying these places seemed now, these silent canals, the deserted path and whispering groves! Suddenly I was sure someone had slid down the branches and was following me.

I feared one around the bend, ready to strike me. My mouth went dry, I could not breathe, with slow, scared steps I moved on. May be a terrorist was taking aim now to shoot a fire ball on me. I was feverishly reciting the *kalimaed* time and again. If there was a name to be whispered and offerings to be made my family members willingly did that, just to be away from this place and their nightmares.

Despite the fear of being noticed by these terrorists who might come back with their pack armed for battle or to catch or hunt us down like deer, fleeing still made sense as staying in the village won't be secure anyway.

When people flee from their homes they are at least, driven by the hope, who knows, within a day or two they might reach another land, someone else's land; they could put up their hut, four rough and ready walls, a bit of grass roof and light up their hearths. I knew what's ahead of us was not predictable but surely life beyond their land could not be as sinister, dangerous and as fearsome as some of our neighbours had predicted.

I took the slower, deeper forest route without the certainty of the moon or any other light. From Kupwara to Handwara, Sopore, Pattan and Srinagar we came through the forest and reached Baramulla after leaving far behind those rows of dwellings that we had built from timber felled from our trees to share them with poultry and pigs and then hitched and hiked covering the route of almost 500 kilometres. I was relieved I could get my family away before they were caught and reached the border of Jammu.

Now being on familiar road with the rattling of vehicles on the national highway, the distant horizon shimmered in the brightest of distant lights and hope ensued that Amritsar too would come about. All of sudden I felt I was homeless.

Now the other questions raised their ugly heads: where and how to live, what job to do, what to do with the little money we carried? There isn't a way in this world to know what a human creature is going to do next," Abdul said. He was standing on the strata of history that would go down through the known past into the unknown future.

By the time Abdul reached this part of his story, he realized that he had attracted not only the old man's attention but also that of the residents walking that way. A huge crowd had gathered in which a few older ladies were present, but mostly the crowd comprised the young women of the society.

At that moment Anu who had got out of the car suddenly heard one lady, (after losing her patience,) saying, "Is your tete-a-tete with him not as yet over? Are you interested in selling this black Kashmiri shawl or are you wasting our time in just recounting your troubles?"

Her outburst interrupted the flow of talk among the bystanders. Immediately Abdul replied, "Of course, memsahibs, our ancient livelihoods in Kashmir have already been snatched away from us. We have lost everything--apple trees, loaded with royal delicious, the milching cows, gleaming golden yellow kesar fields and able-bodied goats--in the flicker of a moment. Now we have come all the way from Amritsar only to sell shawls. Without selling these shawls and Kashmiri suits our fate would be far too cruel to contemplate. They are our unrealized dreams and hopes.

Look at this red cashmere shawl also, memsahib, it is a fine Kashmiri shawl," he said spreading it before her. As she started examining it carefully, he sat in tongue hushed silence throttling the thousand words midway: "Do you know the price of losing things like the brick house I was born in, and trees around it, air and water, silence and soil all twined with my childhood, my youth, the birth of my Tikku and Abida? You don't think what a little plot of land means till someone takes it and you can't go back. How could you know, memsahib?"

Instead, he said, "Look at this shawl with intricate and elegant designs. My family members embellish clothes with their roughened hands and gritty eyes; embroider them in Kashmiri patterns, colours and threads. I sell them by carrying on my back though they do not smell our hearths and country odours and do not wave away my anxieties and allow me any peace. Still, it is the product of our relentless hard work".

Without encouraging him to talk any more she asked him to show other pieces. Abdul thought, "Life here taxes us from dawn to dusk and torments us at night. My great task each day and week, each month, each year is to defend against hunger and defeat. No one wants to hear my grievances, what happened not just to him but to his entire family, or have me list the details of my life these days--where the best reeds are for our thatching, from where the wood for firing can be garnered, what walls and fences need attending to and where holes can be dug for latrines. Besides, there is the suspicion of anyone who is not born within these boundaries. What can you expect from these people when my own country has dished out scars and bruises?"

Then Abdul struggled to pull himself away from painful thoughts and said to himself, "Forget about this humiliation at their hands, shrug off the insults if you want to sell these shawls. Abdul, the only important thought, that should hold your attention at this time and persuade you to tolerate even their unreasonable bargaining, should be that they are your prospective customers and you should not trifle with them. How could you dare risk losing them?"

And Abdul got busy in taking out from his bundles more shawls and matching Kashmiri ladies-suits to display to the ever-increasing number of ladies at the society.

Their conversation had left Anu uneasy as one thing that shone out clearly in the course of all the conversation she heard between Abdul and others was that a fine Kashmiri shawl, though once considered, a buyer's pride worth thousands had ended up as a shabby thing in a hawker's sack worth haggling and an act of piety/charity even if bought for 500 bucks.

It is not given to some people to understand the meaning of these shawls and sashes where the unrealized dreams and hopes, sighs and sadness were irretrievably entangled. For Abdul it seems to symbolize the destiny of a Kashmiri, destiny filled with difficulties and hardships."

While Anu was busy thinking, Ravi called her and apologized for taking so long. Then they moved towards the lift that took them to the sixth floor where the Sahdevs lived.

After making inquiries about Mrs. Sahdev's health and hearing the detailed description of the surgery and the care she had received in the hospital, Mrs Sahdev's glance turned to Anu's shawl and she hurriedly said in an excited tone that they also bought shawls from Kashmiri vendor.

"Yes, last week we got a good bargain." Her sister, Mahak who had come from Delhi with her to take care of her convalescent sister, went inside and returned with two Kashmiri shawls and announced happily, "Last month I got a similar one for my mother-in-law for 1300 rupees from Sarojini market. Today just for the price of one, we got these two.

These Kashmiris have no other way of earning money. They are scattered all over the country. Last summer I got one suit in Shimla where I had gone to visit my parents' in-laws. One day when a Kashmiri vendor came, I shut the door but my mother-in law came out and this fellow touched her feet and asked if she remembered Zahir Khan who lived in *khanno-ka-dera* near Negi's building and used to bring gas cylinders. I am his son Khureshi.

After the terrorist attack in our village, I came to Shimla and accompanied my father wherever he went. You used to give me apple and something to eat whenever I came here. You being a teacher always wanted me to study in school and on Sundays you used to teach me in the evenings. You won't be able to realize what all you have done for me."

These khans are a common sight in Shimla; they work as coolies and carry heavy loads which locals cannot carry. She had taught so many children in their *basti* but couldn't place him. Anyway, *Mummy jee* was happy to see him big and grown up and asked him to come in. He brought the bundle and started showing her shawls and suits of different material, colour and designs of Kashmiri embroidery.

"Where did you get them from?" she asked. "By your blessing now I am married, have started a small industry in Hoshiarpur where my wife engaged a few Kashmiri women to do this embroidery and I market them." *Mummy jee* also selected one beige suit with pink and brown Kashmiri embroidery. He packed that dress in some transparent packet and offered it to her. When she tried to give him money, he said, 'This is my small gift to you. I had come here year after year searching for you, I learnt that sahib had undergone bye-pass surgery and you had gone to your daughter in Delhi."

It was very overwhelming for *mummy jee*. She brought 1100 hundred and gave him *sagun* on his new venture along with a hot cup of tea and bakery biscuits. "God bless you, my son", she said.

Hearing this, Anu said, "I don't think people here treat Abdul like Khureshi there in the hills." Mrs. Sahdev replied, "It may be true of small places like Shimla but people in Chandigarh, Punjab and Haryana are not so keen to have these Kashmiris in their company and sharing anything with them. Here relationships are private and impersonal."

Even Abdul had told my mother-in-law: An excessive preoccupation with themselves and an irrational dislike of others is the general trait of this place. This is the town which runs like smooth machines, dictated by computers, the beep of electronic tool and never-ending sound of traffic of those sedans and SUVs–luxurious cars and music produced by latest gadgets but there is not a soul around who could share his anguish.

Mummy jee felt very sad because she was also a refugee from Pakistan and told me that back then the government gave them land in lieu of their possession, none discriminated against them and eventually the whole business was taken over by refugees in these parts of the country. "Why do people treat these Abduls so indifferently now?" she asked me.

Anu said, "You mom-in law is absolutely right. This is an incontestable truth that people haven't been kind, they could never offer to share his burden of bereavement, a crust or a glass of tea or a greeting. Instead, they ask themselves questions: whether it is sensible or stupid to trust him these days."

While enjoying Mahak's hospitality (she had come with a tray of tea and snacks) Anu continued, "For Abdul, it is natural to miss his land because he leads a solitary existence and those who lead a solitary life always have something in their hearts which they are eager to talk about.

As you know I go to America every year to be with my children. I tell you when we live in America for two or three months without break, we begin at last to pine for India. In foreign countries at least you can hang around the bars, tell strangers most interesting and intimate things of your lives at night and might not recognize them in the morning.

In India, we open ourselves to our guests but as far as these Kashmiris are concerned why do we have apathy? Perhaps it is our apathy that does not allow people like Abdul and Khureshi to forget their village as well as their memories that are like an etching on stone. Otherwise, it is the characteristic of twentieth century that people believe they would be greatly improved if they were someplace else, hence these migrations to big cities. This is not true in their case."

Mrs. Sahdev was quick to remark: "Since they have been away all these years, their memories must have disappeared or they have obliterated them from the timeframe of their consciousness like a song being accidently erased from a cassette by a new one taped over it".

Anu said, "This is possible, as my mother used to say, when a tree has been transplanted, if it has a firm stake to hold it up, it will not topple even though fierce winds may blow, but for Abdul or for that matter Kashmiris like him, there is not a soul around who could share their anguish and there is no willing soul within their bonds who entirely belonged to those common people."

Looking at Mrs. Sahdev, Anu asked in a gloomy voice, "Is it Abdul's fault to have been exiled from the land he owned and lose the last vestige of possibility of redeeming his forfeited land that could provide him happiness? Is there any chance he would ever return to his land?" Mrs. Sahdev replied in a matter-of-fact way. "From what I have heard from the news and seen it appears that his happiness would elude him for many more years."

After bidding goodbye to the Sahdevs, Anu came down in the lift and found Abdul still sitting there. Suddenly she heard children shouting, "Go back where you belong?"

But is there a place he belonged to? Can such a thing ever happen? Even if they succeeded, would it be as peaceful as it was before? Abdul wondered.

Or perhaps there would be locks on the doors of his friends--Arif, Sameer, Faiz, or no trace of their living; the houses completely ruined where Mushaffar and he studied under the light of the lantern and those walnut trees they would climb when his grandfather would abandon his game of cards and run after them for stealing the apples. His memories of his home kept hurting him continually.

There was no end to his physical suffering. He had to leave behind the playground of his childhood and the pleasure garden of his youth as well of his future.

"Go back to your home" Abdul heard again. Where was his home? He is not at home in his own homeland, he is exiled from the place he belonged. He worked for it and came to own it: now they own it who never worked for it. They have shut the doors of his own home on him. Through all these years of working for it, he had aspired towards it as towards a Promised land. Kashmir had been too much his life.

To have it, he had deprived himself and his wife Kara too had deprived herself. It was what he had transformed his life into--the shadow of his failure and he couldn't bear to look at it. And the only thing he could not understand was why man's destinies are so diverse, why simple things other men receive from God for nothing had cost him such a price. The more he thought the more the force of his failure gathered and shame raged in him.

It was as though each word carried the burden of disrespect, ridicule, and cruelty and sought to expose his helplessness. "Don't they know I also long for the house? For that matter who won't after all this work of selling door to door? Isn't it pleasurable for him to look forward to a square of drying cloth, a roof, a bed and sweet dreams in his bed at home?

His face, neck and shoulders were bathed in perspiration and his neck and forearms burned as black as chimney oak as he thought of home. His eyes dimmed with tears, but still he gazed into the distance (the direction of his home) where the pale lights faintly gleamed and his heart ached with yearning for his (lost) home, (his proud memories, his enduring hopefulness) and he longed to live, to go back home and to save from ruin if only one man, and to live without suffering if only for a day.

10

Migrant Workers Blues in Covid -19

India clamped a nationwide lock down for three weeks on 25th March 2020. Yag Raj's first reaction was -- what after all was this period? A short space, especially as the darkness would dim soon, and soon a bird would sing, a cock crow, day would succeed day and it would be over.

Yag Raj was in his early forties with medium height and of stocky build. He had brown eyes and had been prematurely balding for years. He had strong solid hands like that of a farmer, for which he was grateful.

For almost four days, he cooked, watched TV and heard the news and was relaxed. But each time he did the household chores, he remembered his children and his wife, he had the guilt burning inside, knowing that he had not done enough for them. He had left them in the village all alone to fend for themselves in lock down.

How could he have brought them after a week of his mother's death? He justified to himself his decision of coming alone as he had unfinished work of painting to be done as his employer had to move in the new house during Navratri. A few days back he was working along with other painters in that building, changing the exterior and interiors of the house. Now they were being locked down in their homes and hunted down by the police without even the chance of seeing the faces of their family. How could he forget the evening he had heard the news; he had grabbed his shirt, gone out in the terrace to ring up his contractor, informing him about the lock down. He said they could be in deep trouble. No doubt, lock down was clamped to prevent spread of the COVID virus -- the disease that spreads on contact like wildfire and ensure the safety of the citizens. But it was bound to have side effects, such as leaving migrants stranded. Yes, the contractor was right. He did not get milk in the morning and he was stuck in a situation he had not chosen.

During the lock down, people who had family, a job to go back to, and were healthy in mind and body, also lost all sense of proportion. Raj rarely lost his composure, nor did he complain, and when he did, it was only for God's ears. He was religious, a believer through and through. He prayed every morning and evening, didn't touch alcohol. He fasted for nine days during entire Navratri. He followed the old customs and traditions with a mix of superstition and folklore. Suddenly a thought upset him; "Perhaps I have not said the right prayers otherwise I wouldn't have ended up in such a situation." He thought, "A person of faith is also a responsible citizen. He upholds the law of land and follows what is good for his fellow human beings, complying with the government's rule of lock down is his essential obligation. He knows lock down entails stringent restrictions and cessation of movement".

After a few days of lock down, he didn't know what to do in this crisis. The question was how to meet the basic needs, how to survive when the lock down was adversely impacting his livelihood and there was no possibility of any earning of his daily wages as he was forced to stay indoors and away from outdoor work. He was becoming aware of his powerlessness to survive or do anything for his family. There was no option but to flout this lock down and move to the village where he had a small piece of land. But he shuddered even to think this option.

However, it was one of those moments when everyone wanted to protest but, no one wanted to be the first. Raj was poor and did not have the courage to stand up against the lock down and for this he probably hated himself and would do so for the rest of his life. He broke into terrible sweat and silence swept across the room when he heard curfew had been clamped in Chandigarh, and no movement of people and vehicles was allowed, and essential commodities were also delivered at the doorstep. In such a situation if anyone developed symptoms of COVID and cowered in their home, did not report their illness, they would be forcefully hauled into isolation hospitals, strictly quarantined in dedicated facilities, till they recovered. In case he did not recover, or he died due to shortage of testing kits, health infrastructure like ventilators, beds and personal protective equipment, nobody would know about his sudden death. "Have you wondered what will happen to your family if you die here, he said to himself; you have run away from your duty, abandoning your wife and children in village, shaming your family and tribe. They won't understand your constraints. Do not expect sympathy from them. Do not say all have baggage. It is life. If COVID doesn't kill me, losing my job and hunger will. Do something before it is too late".

That night he preferred to take chances with COVID because he feared harm to his family. Who would provide them food and supplies, take them to hospital if they fall ill? Everyone panics in a disaster. When fear grips elites and rich, they overreact with all the resources and power at their command. The poor can only react by running to their villages. He also thought of going to his village. He called his nephew and brother-in-law,"I do not want to force you or anyone. If you don't want to come, I will understand. I will do this alone; I have to do it ". When he heard his nephew was evicted in the middle of night in the most horrific and cruel way, he got irritated. Ever since childhood his blood had boiled to witness anyone being treated brutally and unfairly. It hurt him to see the cruelty human beings are capable of inflicting on other human beings. He was not naive enough to expect fairness from a world so crooked, but he believed that everyone had a right to a certain share of dignity. Life was unfair but now he knew people were more so. He could not sleep that night as the thought of how he used to lie on this charpoy near the window, thinking one day his son would go to college and work for him, kept troubling him. Now this city would be memories, and longings and forever elusive.

Desperate times call for desperate measures. Faced with a grim choice of being stranded far away from home and no earning, no work and little money after a nationwide lock down, he decided to cycle 2000 kms all the way from Panchkula to reach his home in Sartal in UP.

On 4th April he embarked on the journey with his sneakers and lugging bags on his cycle. That day no cars passed him, honking horns with abandon, no street hawkers shouted their wares, no school children sang the national anthem on the loud speakers, no construction worker was sighted on the building sites, no bulldozer rumbled, no newspaper vendor, no babble of sounds reached the sky but only a crow sat with its blackened limbs and talked about what's gone. He was alone cycling the road that led to his home which was miles and miles away. Next day he found himself among few other people to whom life had been unfairly harsh. Nobody could give the other person hope or cheer as they themselves were constantly assailed by fears and worries. There was endless commotion in his mind which was clouded by dark forebodings in these unsettled times.

With no food available on the roads and highways, he managed with the food he had carried with him. He slept on the roadside and quenched his thirst with water from tube wells saving his water bottle for a rainy day. The thought, "My family must be in dire need. I should be with them", kept him moving. Even on third day the road was almost empty. Very few *dhabas* were open but he could not still eat there as people thrashed him for fear of contracting the COVID virus infection. At check points cops allowed him passage after checking his Aadhar card. Thus, he completed in four days his journey to Delhi which was normally a few hours, braving heat and hunger on the way.

On the fifth day when he got up from his fitful sleep in Delhi, he gazed upon the right, upon the left, all the way along, far away in the distance, he saw migrants like him confused and lost but moving. Taking up his collar against the wind, he also disappeared in the sea of people -- the migrant workers were returning to their villages. They had come from small towns and big cities where they suffered from a fear of an uncertain future and imminent starvation. All of them were thinking the same thoughts, sharing the same fears and battling the same enemy. Frustrated like him they had decided to leave their houses and protest or plead on roads to send them home. Many workers were doing this now as though it held the answer to all their troubles. Police had no desire to learn who they were, from where they had come, or whether they were new to the job. The story of the victims was of no concern to them. For them they were an unwelcome faceless horde of migrants. What police was interested in was how to stop their movement to their villages.

Seeing these multitudes of people Raj said to himself: Banaras is a city of burning pyres; Hardwar, a city of devotees; Punjab a city of bhangra; Delhi has become the city of moving multitudes. Many of them were expert masons, skilled artisans, carpenters, tailors, drivers and delivery men who kept the engines of the city moving. Now they were moving on India's scorching highways, hungry, jobless and dog tired. He recognized his fellow villagers walking with bundles on their heads. Eighteen years back, he had also migrated to the city of Chandigarh in search of employment with his brother-in- law and nephew who worked as security guard and a construction worker and he started working as a painter.

Their women had stayed back to look after the family as the cost of living in cities was higher and also living conditions were not suitable for migrants' family to move into the city. They used to go back to their villages in May and June for the sowing season. Ten years back Raj brought his family and stayed in Mauli Jagran in Chandigarh in a dilapidated building that housed migrant workers like him. After two years he shifted to Sector 21 in Panchkula and his good times began. He settled into a passable life -- as a good citizen, a good employee and a good father. His piddling wages required him to work the night shifts as a chowkidar in an industrialist's home in an adjoining sector. And at no stage in his journey of life did he give up on any chance of enhancing his source of income. He started taking contract jobs of painting. He wisely invested in the education of his children. His son Brijesh went to an English-medium school in Panchkula and daughter Meenakshi was sent to a government school where Haryana government provided free education. The family income also increased when Rajvati, his wife, got work as a domestic help and one room set free accommodation in the house of the landlord. For a while his economic condition progressed rapidly. He bought beds, steel utensils, a cooker, a fridge, a TV, and two cycles. He was satisfied with whatever he got and now his son was in tenth class and daughter in ninth and his life had changed.

Suddenly all economic activity had come to a halt and he could not work. If he ran short of money, which he surely would, he would have no cash to buy food on the road. At least in his village he would get something to eat. He remembered how at his father's death, people had gone overboard in helping them in their village. Our neighbour's house had turned into a community kitchen where people were organizing help. The whole village had spontaneously stepped in much before the relatives had moved in. In times of misfortune, villagers are generally kind. Fellow feeling is natural especially in moments when we see how fragile our lives are. One feels about the pain of others. He stretched and arched his back and wondered how many more days of starvation and exhaustion he would have to bear before he got to his village.

In normal times Delhi to Muradabad then Bilari to Chandausi is not a long journey by train, but he didn't know how long it would take him on the cycle. As he advanced towards Muradabad, huge luxurious mansions came into view and behind the solid bungalows of the rich and middle class, there were rows after rows of ramshackle sheds. Scattered between the buildings were old shrines, small restaurants and hotels. Raj longed to be in his home with a hot cup of tea and *makki ki roti*. The reality was he was alone in that dark night and had not eaten anything throughout the day. No one had warned him of these dangers, nor did he have the slightest idea. He feared he would die of exhaustion and hunger before reaching home.

The pangs of hunger were so excruciating that he couldn't endure them. No one watched him cycling a little unsteadily, his gaze firmly fixed on the road, as if he could not trust the firmness of the ground. He tried to dispel his drowsiness by rubbing the inner corners of his eyes with his fingertips. His shoulders stooped and his head bent at a painful angle. He seemed drained of all vitality. The bag fell from his shivering hands. He could not stand, speak, walk, feel and think. He fell unconscious.

However, when he opened his eyes, he found himself surrounded by two three people, who were pressing him to eat food. He seemed so weak and his face more gaunt than usual. Talking, like eating, was too much of an effort. No one wished to talk, but when they did talk, it was in hushed tones. He recovered quickly -- perhaps his body was fighting against all unexpected complications.

Eventually, like many others before and after him, he was again cycling on the road that was going to Muradabad. It was exhausting and dangerous. Every person that stopped him left an imprint on his soul as he watched every detail and thought a lot. Insulted by people (he was given food as if he was a beggar) abused and arbitrarily stopped by police, he felt one humiliation after another.

After a week of cycling, Moradabad was within sight. Looking on the path, he thought many have come, many have gone, not a soul remembered anything now. Time has covered and erased everything. In few days no remnant of his journey would also be there. He had worked for years, saved money, put up with the whims of the landlord, bosses, restrained his anger, swallowed his pride in moments of despair, dreamt of good lazy days in the sun with his family in the village in the harvesting season. Now he was a migrant worker unworthy, unwanted, who had become an unwelcome person in his own country in times of hardship. He belonged neither to BPL (below the poverty line) families to whom the government had promised direct transfer benefits, that would allow needy households to see through the next few months, nor did he live in slums or camps where combinations of public and NGO provisions of food, healthcare and shelter could reach. He was a daily wage earner in a private accommodation where a community enforced ban on eviction did not exist.

He couldn't concentrate on the road. The road at this hour was anything but empty. When he shifted to Sector 21, he had told his wife that the worst part of his life was over. Most of all, he told himself, he would never be on the road again. He was happy and he had all he needed. Then unexpectedly his mother died leaving a hole in his heart that would never heal. Slowly it all came back to him -- his childhood in his cramped little thatched house in village, room overlooking his small field, with sound of the swallows over the window. Shutting the memory out, he focused on cycling. The most important thought now occurred to him, "Raj hang on for a few more days without water and food, and you will be able to reach the village." He rolled his eyes to the heavens. But he did not believe in the heavens now, as he did in the past when confronted with a difficult situation.

Still he managed in daytime. Time and again a police car would lurk behind thick clumps of bushes and catch unsuspecting migrants racing on the road. Sometimes the road was unmanned for hours -- everything was so unpredictable. One policeman saw a look of hurt and helplessness on his face and felt sorry for him. He offered him a glass of tea with sugar and a packet of food which some NGO had left with the police in Bilari.

In normal times from Muradabad to Bilari is not a long journey by train, but on cycle he reached Bilari on ninth day of his journey. This lonely sight in Bilari could have been anywhere in the world. Night-time on the lonely road is not like night-time in the village or in the city. Around here, darkness was less the absence of light but the presence of something fearful. But now he was seized by a raw and primordial fear, in the middle of night and finally came melancholy. He tried to stay calm, but he couldn't, he could not see how he could possibly shake off the fear.

With the moon hiding momentarily behind the clouds, the darkness plunged the entire landscape into shades of black. Something told him it was not going to be easy -- this night venture as he had hoped in the beginning. When making that crazy plan and hopping on to the cycle had felt like an adventure, the right thing to do for his family but it was not so now. The shadow of an animal scurried past the road, a rat perhaps or the hedgehog running for shelter in the dark. At first, he moved briskly, with eagerness sparked by discomfort, if not plain fear.

He saw rocks, tree trunks, with their leaf like scales bright and ghostly in the dark. In places mist hovered before his eyes. Once he heard a rustle that sounded as if it rose from below the earth. A dog had materialized out of nowhere and started chasing him. A large black mongrel, ears flattened, eyes flashing yellow, teeth bared. He told himself, "Stay calm. If you do not make a move, he won't attack." There was no traffic at this hour, so he raced the cycle and the dog stopped chasing him.

The ferns and thistles brushed against his legs and his cycle got stuck. He dismounted it and crisp yellow leaves scrunched. He soon realized the path had disappeared. He found himself trudging a trackless area, and in the anaemic light of the moon everything looked scary.

His nerves -- they were all frayed by now. He thought he was going to have a heart attack. In his father's side, all men had died before 48 years of age. His own father had died before he was forty-two. Blood pounded in his ears and he closed his ears to shut out the sound. Grabbing the water bottle from the bag he guzzled an impressive gulp. Of course, death is scary for everyone but more for the one who has led a life of obligation and whose life had been shaped by the needs and demands of others. He had reached the age of his father when he had died, leaving him and his brothers alone in this cruel world. What would become of his wife and children if he was gone? He had already known that miserable life without parents.

When in pain you remember your mother, and when in fear you invoke the power of God to save you. He heard his mother saying, "Do not panic, do not run, just chant the Hanuman Chalisa". Eventually Raj halted; with eyes closed and palms turned upward he recited the Hanuman Chalisa which his mother had made him learn by rote. The prayer is the courage to persevere. Prayer for him had always been the source of hope and resilience, a lift that carried him from the bottom of darkness to light above. "All right it is time to move", he thought. He moved with such renewed courage that it belied his surroundings. There was something elusive in his expression, defying time and place.

The hush of silence had descended on the path in absence of traffic horns and other noise, birdsongs abounded like a winged opera. The pall of gloom surrounded everything as all motorized transport had come to a standstill. Normally he felt sweaty and irritable from all the time spent in traffic, fuming at the stupidity of the drivers and pedestrians alike but now he just felt drained in their absence. He kept moving on.

In the background of the setting sun the road extended as far as his eyes could see. He watched the last ray of light disappear from the skyline and the day came to an end. He was filled with a sense of abandonment. At such time he remembered his children and thought that he had to reach his village otherwise his family wouldn't survive. Busy with these thoughts he reached Chandausi.

By the time he reached Chandausi he was completely exhausted, and he quickly tumbled into slumber. How strange, comforting sleep is! It rocks the people around the world in the arms of the loved ones even in moments of distress. He saw himself as a child in Sartal, scooped by his mother's arms. Then his two older siblings joined him and now they were whirling and laughing. In the distance the half-reaped fields stretched, and the windows of the temple caught the sunshine. He ran to the old house and fell, he sobbed.

He had got a packet of food which some NGO had offered him on the road. He ate and drank water from a tube well. When he glanced up at the sky the rain clouds rolled down the northeast area around his village. Inhaling a lungful of air, he glanced over his shoulder and announced, "Finally I am nearing my village Sartal." His eyes that had been doleful and pensive throughout the evening now acquired a determined gleam. Far away on all sides, cluttered and chaotic but beautiful, was his old village itself. He cycled the complete length of the street like a general inspecting his troops before the final battle. He felt light and content. With every pedal of the cycle, he shed off negative feelings: anger, sadness, pain, longing, regret, resentment and their biggest cousin fear. He jettisoned them all, one by one and his world came alive. It was unlike anything he had experienced before. He cycled slowly and clumsily at first braving the heat and exertion, then smoothly and assuredly, gradually increasing the tempo. There was no reason to rush anymore and nothing to run away from. There was not any pain, he was relieved to have left Panchkula.

"Thanks to God I am alive. I have at least arrived safe and sound while there are over 6,00,000 migrant workers stranded in India right now. There are daily wagers in the 21000 camps which the government has set up. How he wished the government had anticipated this and organized their return path with provision of tracking them! He prayed to God to let these workers go back home where they could have access to rationed food, oil and welfare schemes. He envisioned he would be busy with harvesting for a few months and thereafter there would be no dearth of work for labourers in Rabi procurement, movement of goods and perishables from the farms to warehouses and from factories to the markets and vendors.

Now this journey was a race he had to finish at full speed. After twelve days one bright morning Raj reached his village. "Nice to see you all, finally!" he exclaimed! When asked how his journey had been, he was slightly distracted and unusually quiet, but said it was ok. At many places, locals, social workers and policemen provided him with food. He was immediately sent to the quarantine centre upon arrival at his village but for him the joy of reaching his village was worth the pain. The sun was rising above the horizon and houses in the street seemed aflame. Above him was the clear sky, beaming an apology for the storm of the previous night. He was happy to be part of this vibrant realm, these golden ready to reap wheat fields, bright as the birth of a new flame.

11

Mushroom Pickle

After five years Reena saw him in the restaurant. He was seated on the chair and a vase of artificial roses was placed in front of him. The restaurant was hot and not so clean. The motion of her eyebrow indicated that she was trying to recognize. She noticed his tanned face, the long strands of his shinning hair; his eyes were attentive and severe, he was contemplating something.

Bright sunlight poured through the aperture of the door. Inside beyond the tables, a violin wrung its sounds as if they were human hands, accompanied by full bodied resonance of the rippling harp. "He looks like Rajan, doesn't he?" she thought. She got a little closer and from the special way he was eating the *dosas* with his hands and enjoying the mushroom pickle she was certain it was Rajan. He was making smacking and sucking noises as he drank the coffee. She made her way among the tables and swinging her thin arms approached him, smiled and said, "Hello Rajan."

He lifted his heavy eyelids. Looked at her appearance and the movement of her open arms but didn't take her proffered hand, nor did he give her a look of recognition. Certainly, he didn't know her. She came near him, he looked up, closed his eyes and opened as if someone had withdrawn the curtain and room was lit.

"Reena!" he exclaimed. "Sorry, for a moment I did not recognize you; it was not that I had forgotten you. It was more than five years and I had to take such a leap in time with you; I had to take a leap over my whole life to recognize you today. Shifting the chair to make room for her, he said, "Why don't you sit? Would you like some coffee?"

"Yes, I would like some. I am feeling so cold." He pounded the palms on the table. Now the restaurant was more crowded than before, but the waiter came quickly. "Two cups of hot coffee and cream," he ordered. "Sure, you won't have anything else to eat with it. Some cookies or cake?" Rajan asked Reena. "No thanks," she said laughingly. After making the normal inquiries about health, she told him, "How many frantic inquires I made of your whereabouts! Your friends wouldn't tell anything; I begged them for news, a phone number or anything. Not so much as a postcard to say where or how, no note from you either, no apologizing? You didn't tell where you were. Wasn't that cruel? Wasn't your behaviour weird?"

He felt neither guilty nor sorry but simply told her he had gone abroad and was back this week only and now they had met. When old friends meet after a long time, they forget about their grudges easily and try to catch up on missed times. After a while they were busy sharing their memories while little sounds around them made themselves heard -- people entering the restaurant, doors opening and shutting, murmur of voices. But it didn't matter, they were reminiscing about old days. Rajan said, "You have changed a lot, Reena. You are looking good. However, there is one thing that is not changed; your ringing laughter, I can recognize it even among the crowd. Remember when we went to the Mughal gardens in Pinjore; you wore that lilac dress you laughed so much because I did not know anything about the plants. I was the person who couldn't tell an oak from the pine; I did not know the name of trees and flowers or how to care for them; I did not know one green thing from another. I knew only roses but couldn't distinguish their colours either. I still hear your voice saying fuchsia, hydrangeas, geranium, the dahlia, chrysanthemum, arum lilies, hyacinths..."

Reena did not remember these names but her thoughts moved swiftly to that time and she remembered how he kept batting the dragon flies with the newspaper and was furious. She suffered silently at his maniac behaviour but it delighted the onlookers who went into peals of laughter and kept laughing at them.

Rajan said, "I was such a kid those days; I wanted to become your magical flying saucer for you to travel on without hurting yourself. I wanted to fly you on that saucer to many places you longed to visit. When I think of that day now, I perfectly understand that you were right when you laughed at me. How could anyone love a person who behaved like that?"

Reena said, "I also remember the other time when you had brought two big and juicy mangoes; I refused to eat it, you took big bites and juice ran down your fingers and I laughed saying -- Such a perfect picture out of the comic books!"

Rajan remembered how she had laughed at him, unlike a person who simply knew him couldn't have. He felt ridiculed and out of shame he ran away and hid himself under the mango tree throughout the evening in case she changed her mind and when she did not, he was quite upset.

This memory faded and another floated in Reena's mind. There were sipping coffee in Coffee Day when he suddenly burst into tears. "How I wish I were dead here in the warmth of the sun." She felt shocked and asked him the reason of this emotional upheaval, "Why do you say so?" she asked.

He said, "You know I love you so much. You won't believe me but I treasure your every delicate thought and feeling. Yes, laugh; I don't care what people say but I adore all of you. I know you better than you know yourself but you should take me seriously. If you wouldn't love me so I will suffer terribly. It is better not to live to see that day." He said these words as if he was putting forward the case of his existence in front of her.

Reena did not understand why he was behaving like a sentimental fool when she had never felt these emotions for him herself. She never realised it before but now it was clear that he had changed a lot. She looked at him and he gave such a hearty, creaking laugh and his teeth flashed like a flame. There was aura; it felt he was having fun in this small restaurant.

Now he looked cool and competent. Clear forehead, blue eyed, had a walrus moustache, overall appearance was decent and placid. Now Rajan was more self-assured and a man of confidence who had achieved a place in life. He was happy to relax and have a peaceful chat.

He was looking impressive; he must have made good money. He wore smart trendy clothes and took out a watch to look at time, Reena thought. "It is such a priceless watch. Where did you buy it?" she asked. "Yes, I picked it up in Lucerne while on a visit to see the ice caves in Switzerland. Yes, I had been in Europe for a year.

Do you remember we'd always talk of going to these countries? I went to Italy, Paris, London, Germany, Belgium, Austria, and Venice and the Vatican City. Paris was such a wonderful city. It has one of the world's oldest art museums -- the 13th century Louvre with its radical primary modernist geometry -- the glass pyramid. Pictures, galleries, theatres, restaurants, fine pink buildings, shops, theatres, all are in it. I have travelled all over Europe but it is Paris I would always return to.

The Eiffel Tower, the insertion of an untested vertical wrought iron structure in the midst of a horizontally spreading city -- a city built almost entirely in 19th century Neo classical mode required an act of cultural courage that willingly accepted a future technology. You would enjoy yourself there while exploring the city and having a cruise on the river Seine. You ought to take a little holiday yourself, especially when it is Christmas."

By some miraculous, secret association of thoughts, the world appeared grander to him. Rajan pensively tapped a cigarette out of the case; a golden eagle was etched on its wooden case.

Reena smiled and listened attentively when he narrated the pleasant memories of Paris and how it had reinvented itself. Now she was able to read every muscle around his mouth, eyes, tell with perfect accuracy that he was not lying. She quite understood and she became silent. Something was happening to her, something heavy, huge and slow, coming from outside that she did not understand. The silent desire of visiting places that had been lying dormant in Reena's bosom for such a long time stirred and raised its head with longing heart and she murmured, "How I envy you! I have always pictured myself alone in Paris. Paris is a city of love, romance and passion, food and wine; I am really obsessed with it."

He felt encouraged to describe the amazing gondola experience in Venice while crossing the city. On both sides were clumps of white houses, looking like mushrooms, whose lower parts were submerged in water with people on both sides of the Grand Canal looking perfect picture. Women waving from the windows and doors of houses and beautiful flowers on their window sills -- geranium and roses, boatman singing in their own language transported us to another world and out-of-the-world experiences.

You need not know the language; it created a bond with people who were waving from their balconies and windows. How pretty it was! How pretty and different! We were happy and we sang. Everything was so lovely only if you were there. You were so fond of these places; I still remember you longing for them."

"Even now I am crazy about them, but tell me more about Venice, I am hungry for the knowledge of these worlds," she said. He continued, "You would like the life of these people, they are so spontaneous, so free, informal and impulsive. They are such amazing people, such good human beings that the boatman who sails you has a part in what is happening in your life. I remember that our group of four friends went for a picnic after the boat ride. We were having champagne with fish and French fries; the boatman came with a bottle of wine and offered us fish and mushroom pickle his mother made that morning. He wanted to sit and share with us, it seemed so right."

When Rajan was narrating his European adventures, Reena was already away somewhere in Paris, in all those places she had seen in the movies -- *Moulin Rouge, Paris, I love you, Amelie, Before Sunset, Funny Face* and in the web series *Emily in Paris.* Even while hearing, Reena was imagining herself traveling abroad in the foreign land, looking and reading the foreign advertisement boards, eating their delicacies and asking guides to tell her about the places and famous statues, their history and legacies and talking to beautifully dressed ladies with open pink and yellow umbrellas in the sun. At the time of visualising those places she felt a strange deep thrill unlike anything she had ever felt before. She wanted to cry, "Oh How frightfully happy I am while imagining them! What true bliss it would be to be there in person!".

In that silence Rajan looked at her and said, "You are such a wonderful listener. When you look at me like this, I feel I can tell you everything that I could not think of sharing with anyone else. Back those days you had no friends nor had you made friends with other girls either. You were as alone as I was," he went on talking.

"Yes, I am alone even now," she said. He said, "I am also alone. Listen we have known each other for such a long time so why not speak our heart out. Really and truly, this has been the happiest day of my life. I would have never imagined such a meeting! Such a beautiful day! I want to be with you forever, you know that that's why I keep saying I love you."

In spite of her silence his heart glowed with the love for this girl. She did not know quite what to say. "Do you think we're going somewhere?" he heard her and said, "Look, I want to marry you." These words in his mouth turned baroque and alien. "I can't get married. I always treated you as my friend. I don't have those feelings for you," Reena said.

He started laughing, shaking his head, "You are joking. You aren't joking. What the hell is that supposed to mean? You are lying to me for the first time. But you do love me." Reena said, "I always had this feeling that you understood me, my real self far better than any other person as I am also my real self with you. We talk quite intimately together. Yes Rajan, I am really fond of you but I don't love you the way a girl loves a boy and gets married. I cannot commit to you without feeling any love for you; I cannot think of marriage, I want to be single and free. You know me from childhood, I am different from other girls. I never played with dolls or girls; I went to parks and gardens with you. I never wanted to be the archetypical Indian woman who finds sanctuary within the narrow confines of marriage, who marries and breeds children, spends her life rearing them and looking after the husband. I don't want to be imprisoned. I am an independent woman who wants to make her own decisions and have always dreamed of an independent life. What had seemed an overwhelming task had come, finally, to fruition?"

She continued, "I don't understand why you who are utterly and endlessly brilliant fail to understand the simplest thing that I do not love you. How complex the human mind is! You are fast and fantastic in knowing people and places of far-off countries, but do not see the nearest being and my state of mind, do not see the truth that is just before your eyes. However, I am indebted to you. You have given me a thing I could never have imagined before I met you by chance: It's like I have the life and I can choose.

You came along and said, "Oh, you can reinvent yourself like Paris did by incorporating the Eiffel Tower. Yes, you are right. Individuals have to reinvent themselves like nations. Of course, one of the real challenges faced by individuals in this age is the dilemma of balancing a stagnant work life with the need to reinvent oneself – to move into new unexplored arenas so as to stay relevant, alive and always fresh. Your words awakened something in me though the awakening has come, perhaps, too late. You gave me a chance to reinvent myself, gave me the promise of a new life. Almost in a few hours, my world has grown larger with possibilities. I had to relearn everything -- myself, my likes and dislikes, the width, the height and depth of my passions and what I want to do with my life. It is true life is what it is, what it has always been, what it will continue to be but we will have to adapt and change. What is imperative for me is to think anew." The look on his face was one of surprise, as if she'd slapped him.

"Why don't you love me as I love you? I love you. I adore you. Tell me you're lying, say that you do," Rajan said frantically.

"I doubt now how well I really know you," she said. "Enough has been said about true love that sustains us and nurtures life but I do not love you. All this talk about love and romance is fine for other girls but not for me. I had been your friend for so many years and you had been in my mind when you were away for so many years. I have never encouraged you to have these sentiments. Neither have I promised you nor have I led you on -- offering you nothing and nothing at all I have always been your friend and will stay your friend for ever. I certainly understand your difficulty in accepting my decision but with time you would also learn to accept what you couldn't change. I had been indifferent, felt contemptuous, full of hate or pity, not once I believed you incapable of change. But if I could change, why couldn't you?

With time, you would get over it. I want to tell you frankly that I don't want to live -- to find food, find partners, mate and reproduce. I do not want to scurry about in my restricted space. I am confident that I would make to the other side. I shall go forth from this point onwards, stronger, wiser, healthier, the journey has begun. I always had a fancy to sail up a river in Paris. I always see the river covered with rafts and boats and boatmen with yellow hats speaking in high voices. I always had a dream of an independent life and making my own decisions. That was what I wanted! A life that could fulfil me in a way that marriage or children wouldn't.

They say the person who has found a way to turn his innermost hopes and dreams into active processes is a happy person. Today I am, certainly, feeling like a blessed being, I must go." He had not fully grasped how much of a secret fantasy life she had. How little he understood her feelings! How little he wanted to understand them, she thought.

There was a tugging feeling at her heart as if her happiness was trying to get free. "I will go I will not stay." She wished if he had read her mind, he would be saved of the trouble of running around and chasing her still. She caught him gazing at her, dared him with a glance to own up that she was leaving.

She said, "No reason. A lark. A whim. Freedom. There is of course freedom. How blessed it is to be young and free and doing what I always wanted to do!" She felt lighter and righter than she had since he had disappeared. She had just to show him that she wanted to be alone. The mere idea that human behaviour possesses hidden and knowable patterns as beautiful as anything she had witnessed made her insides sing.

She tried to take her coat. He stopped her, but she looked at him like a nun. "Is something the matter? Has something happened? Why are you going? Have I hurt you; I find so few people to talk to I have become loner? I have always confided in you; I remember a day before Diwali I had confided in you everything about my miserable childhood, you had shown such indifference as you are showing now. Why are you throwing our happiness when you knew I was the only person who understood you? I want to be with you. You know that and that's why I keep repeating it."

Of that evening she did not seem to remember anything only that they were not compatible that time even. She mused what we lose as we plunge into adulthood and pursue pragmatism. What is essential is invisible to the eye.

Something had happened. Real silence. Silence came drifting like snowflakes, she shivered. The tugging feeling of happiness seemed to rise in her throat, it ached and ached. Gathering up her coat, she got up as if in a hurry to reach somewhere. She was conscious of the vast world out there waiting for her and she knew instinctively that she would feel at home there as in this city. It expectantly awaited her arrival. She saw herself walking along Seine. She even carried herself differently -- shoulders back, neck long, she walked with surer steps. Her life as she had imagined it, was about to begin. Plans meticulously made were about to unravel.

He wanted to follow her as she turned into a dark and glistening allay but he was afraid for some reason to overtake her. Instead, he felt a void as wide and as deep as the river Ganges. An instant later he heard rapid footfalls behind him, breathing, the rustle of dress, he looked back and there was none. It was not a dream! It was reality.

Rajan's eyes were tearful. If one person has loved another truly and wholly, then it is more than love that collapses when another person turns away with a goodbye.

Something stirred in his breast. Something dark, something unbearable and dreadful pushed into his bosom, he floated like a leaf. He was whirling, it was like the whirling of leaves nobody knows and nobody cares where they fall and where in the dark ocean/river they float. He couldn't bear anymore. He sat there so dumbfounded and astonished.

"Now I have no one to hold on to. What do I do with myself?" (He considers the human condition, the isolation of our times, love, loss, pain and solitude and the fragility of all relationships.) He heaved a sigh, thrust his fists deep into his pockets and began descending seaward.

12

My Baby Girl

When Neelu came to meet her parents in Panchkula in January, she was pregnant and looked broad. Otherwise, she was of a small built, brown eyed and dark haired like her mother Uma. Her face was round and fairish. She was a quiet child with eyes that seemed to listen. She was so conscious of what other people feel, particularly her mother. Uma adored her and she was always attentive to her. One evening when they were walking around the park, Uma said, "Neelu, it would be great if you stay here for your delivery. Meerut does not have good medical facilities. The Chakravati Nursing Home in Panchkula is reputed and its gynecologist -- Dr Suman is also very efficient..." Interrupting her mid-sentence Neelu said, "Mama, why don't you speak to my mother-in-law?" Uma wanted to say "Why? Do you really have any serious problem asking her yourself?" but quickly said, "Surely, I will do." Uma wondered when would Neelu start to decide for herself and thought it would be better if she called Neelu's husband Rakesh as he was the most sensible person in that family.

Uma's mind flashbacked to the Sunday evening when Rakesh's family had come to see Neelu. She was about 25 years of age; no good match was coming her way. And that day Neelu was in a hurry to approve of Rakesh the first boy who said yes. Uma implored to her, "Neelu, for God's sake, don't take any hasty decision; you will miss out the best that life has yet to offer you. Take your time to think about it. We have worked and worked so that you could have a better future," but Neelu said quickly in contempt, "Wait? What I wait for can never come," her voice rang with defiance, her eyes full of reproach. Her 'yes' was actually more of a surrender to her fate by one too tired to wait any more. It was but natural for parents to be upset when their children ignored their advice. The saner voice within Uma said that her daughter had the right to choose the kind of life she wanted to lead. Still forlornness descended on Uma like a shroud then and she hoped it to lift when she would visit Neelu in her in-laws' house in Meerut.

Finding Uma in her Meerut house one Sunday morning, Neelu exclaimed, "What a surprise! I wasn't expecting to see you so soon." Holding Neelu tightly in her arms Uma said "I missed you. Are you alright?" And noticed that Neelu's face had become more thoughtful, more solemn than what it was in Panchkula. They had lunch and retired to her room. It is every mother's wish to see her children well settled in life and after a while Uma whispered to Neelu gently, "I have been meaning to ask you something for a long time. See, you are looking so pale. Are you happy?" she asked struggling to keep the misery out of her voice. Neelu understood that her mother needed to see her happily settled. Looking in Uma's eyes but speaking from a distance almost beyond the memory of hurt or anger, Neelu said "Don't worry, mom, I am just fine. Really mom, I am happy with what I have." Uma really wanted to believe what Neelu was saying but she needed no sixth sense to discern when the signs were all over there to see otherwise. She saw that Neelu had turned into a calm, pensive *bahu* with a demeanour that to Uma seemed appropriate for a dutiful daughter-in-law. She marvelled at her manner of speech, her action, the way she wore saris, had long plait instead of short hair she always wore before marriage. She was making efforts to do all the cleaning and cooking. Though there were complaints that vegetables were too salty, too greasy or too bland for taste; the floors were either too wet or too unclean but she didn't say anything. Uma wanted to ask Neelu, "How do you do this every day? How quietly you endure all that! Doesn't it drive you crazy?" but Uma did not say anything thinking it was always best not to interfere in a married daughter's life. It was Neelu's life, she thought, and she was trying to get ahead with it.

What worried Uma was that Neelu was not doing those normal things that she always did before her marriage. She didn't read as there were no English magazines in their house; never spoke in English as it offended her Hindi-speaking relatives and watched only Hindi serials which everyone else did in their family. Her enthusiasm for English music had also died down. She didn't step out of the house even to go for walks. Uma remembered how Neelu used to throw tantrums when her demands were not met, got her father to buy her English videos when she was back at home in Panchkula. Her time with her parents always felt natural, effortless, uncomplicated and Uma remembered how they made small, harmless jokes at each other's expense over meals and conversation always flowed. There were no arguments, no open discussions and no loud laughter anymore. And Neelu made no demands on life and would never let others know that she too had sorrows, disappointments and that her dreams had been ridiculed. Uma realized how hard it was for her to do all this. Uma asked herself if it was not natural for a mother to know whether her daughter's relations with her in-laws were cordial, strained or neutral. Had her marriage, their family and time changed her, or was she making concessions to her marriage in order to sail through life smoothly? Neelu wouldn't say anything about them. Uma had no other means of knowing the truth. It had got Uma worried.

Uma was feeling an odd sense of compulsion; there was something she must do. Her thoughts were interrupted by a phone call. Who could be at this hour, she thought. The phone rang more than a dozen times before she answered:

'Hello? Mama, are you there?' said Rakesh's voice.

'Yes! Yes!' she said trying to pull herself together.

'Rakesh, here.

Fine! Mama. fine! Well, I spoke to my parents and grandmother.'

'What did they say?' Uma asked

'They are fine with Neelu staying with you for delivery.'

'It is good to hear that. Thank you.' Uma put down the phone and heaved a sigh of relief.

When Neelu appeared from the inside room, Uma told her quickly, "I talked to Rakesh, they have no objection." "Are you sure?" Neelu asked in surprise. "Of course," Uma said. "Well! That is absolutely amazing!" said Neelu and her face lit up and her head nodded slightly. She looked pleased. After all, she also needed the change. But Uma was surprised at her grandmother-in-law consenting to Neelu's stay with her in Panchkula. Uma recalled her conversation with Rakesh's grandmother when she was in Meerut for the delivery of the first child -- Abha. Her grandmother-in-law had told Uma, "We don't send *bahus* to their parents for child birth. I have all my grandchildren delivered in my presence in my own house."

Now Neelu was with her mother for her delivery. But she had become quite reserved and had resorted to excessive TV viewing. Last night after putting Abha to bed, Neelu came to view her favourite serial *Balika Badhu* in her mother's room. Uma knew that it was not a good time to talk but in between the serial ads she couldn't help asking Neelu about her pregnancy, "Neelu, weren't you using copper-tee? How did you conceive?" Neelu said nothing and Uma also didn't press the question. After a longish pause Neelu blurted out what had exactly happened: "Mama, for the last one year my grandmother-in-law was pestering my mother-in-law, 'Subha, what are you waiting for? Why don't you tell Rakesh to complete his family? Now he has Abha and she is three years old. It is the right time to plan for the second child. My mother-in-law told her that they are not planning the family so soon. You know, Rakesh has just started a small business. Let him settle down in his new work in Bangalore. You have seen what happened to Neelu. She virtually collapsed after her first baby. She is too weak to bear another child." Somehow, last September, the grandmother-in-law took Subha and Neelu with her to visit the Bala Triputi shrine, and they all stayed with Rakesh in Bangalore after visiting the Bala Triputi shrine. She believed this time with the blessing of Bala Triputi, the child would surely be a boy. Neelu wished they should not hitch their hopes to the new born being a boy because their expectations weighed heavily on her.

Time and again Uma thought of what Neelu talked yesterday about this preference for male child. "Well! Yes, she is right. In our culture it doesn't really matter which part of India you are from, this desire for male child cuts across all states and castes also." Rest of the days passed uneventfully but happily -- leisurely breakfast in the morning, meals at home, sometimes late dinner at the army club after *tambola,* visits to Chandigarh for shopping and evenings listening to music or walks in the park surrounded by children and babies in prams and their chattering mothers.

Neelu had come in January and it was now the month of May and she was finally at the Chakravati Nursing Home for delivery. And the nurse, a rather young woman of twenty came, "Well, it is baby girl," she announced coldly. Uma followed her into the labour room with the clothes of the baby. Leaving the new-born baby in Uma's lap, they wheeled Neelu into the room without even saying congratulations. Neelu's eyes were closed; she seemed to be in shock. "Neelu, congratulations!" said Uma, her face clearly showing the elation which rose within her. Uma held her hand and stroked Neelu's forehead. After a while Neelu opened her eyes but looked bitterly disappointed. Her face quivered as she looked at her mother. Seeing something through and beyond her, Neelu asked her mother "Did you tell my mother-in-law? What did she say? They were so sure of a boy". "Do not worry, I will tell everyone," said Uma and sent an SMS to everyone.

Within few hours of delivery Renu, Sushma, Rajni, Asha, Praveen and many other friends came to the hospital with the gifts.

"Congratulations Neelu!"

"Thank you, aunty."

"Neelu, cheer up. Nowadays there is no difference between boys and girls," said Renu with no noticeable cheer in her voice.

Uma expected them to congratulate her with a hug. She wanted them to ask, "Uma, when are you celebrating her birth? Where is our party? *Laddos* won't do." Nothing of that sort happened, Uma was upset. Sometimes what people say upsets you and sometimes what they don't say also upsets you. But Uma was hiding her feelings and struggling not to express her strange sense of outrage at their remarks. "They are my friends with whom I spend most of my time every day, why are they asking Neelu to be cheerful when they are feigning happiness?" she said to herself. For the first time she understood that they only pretended to be modern by speaking impeccable English, but in reality, their conservative nature was deep rooted. Even the tones of congratulations were low, subdued, that told a different story.

Hiding the sense of disappointment from showing in her voice Uma said to her friends, "It has been a pleasure to have you here so soon." They grinned, she hugged them. Uma was busy gazing upon them while they talked politely. She listened deferentially but without understanding. Strangely enough, she was enjoying little of what they were saying. Rather, she was attentive to the delirious cacophony that busted upon her from the other room. And she peered into the other room and witnessed families eating sweets on the birth of the baby boy and heard them chatting excitedly, laughing amidst noisy and animated conversations. But nothing like that was happening in her room. This killed her efforts at fine conversation. She didn't want to hurt those whom she loved and only thanked them for their visit. "Please let us know if there is anything we can do for you," they asked out of courtesy before leaving the clinic. "I will surely do that," Uma said and could breathe freely when they were gone out of the room.

Neelu followed her gaze to the baby in the crib; her eyes also showed hatred for their false sentiments. She did not seem to like their remarks either, thought Uma. After a minute or so Neelu asked hesitantly, "Are the girls so unequal children in our society?" Without waiting for answer she continued, "It is usual for the ayahs and sweepers to come for *baksheesh.* When they didn't come, you had to call them. Mama, did you hear what they said pocketing the tips? 'If it were a boy, we would have asked for it. There was no need for that,' Mama, you noticed Papa didn't like it either as he had kept enough money in change for giving them." Uma kept quiet but warmth radiated through her eyes.

They brought the baby home, neighbours visited them, repeated the benefits of having a girl child as if to console them on the birth of the baby girl in the family. One neighbour even narrated, "Uma, you know Puneet Verma has thrown his parents out and rented out that annexe they were living in. Now Malika, their daughter has brought them to live with her in Panchkula. What a shame on boys!" and Sharan narrated what she had read in the newspaper that day. It was getting very difficult for Uma to hear this girl child thing but she was keeping her cool as Neelu's mother-in-law Subha had come.

One day Uma was busy making preparations for *Chathi* in the *puja* room; Subha came to the room and said sarcastically, "*Chathi Puja* is done only for the boys." Even after seeing hurt in Uma's eyes, she said "I am surprised how Neelu got a daughter while we had given her sex selection medicine. My elder sister-in-law also gave the same medicine to her daughter-in-law and she gave birth to a baby boy." Uma was a bit taken aback. Human reactions are so unpredictable and difficult to handle. Uma had taken the flak from others but she could not bear Neelu's mother-in-law's remarks. They were making her furious. However, some things become clearer after a lapse of time. After a while, when Uma could see things in their true sense, she understood that this simple woman from a small town shared the same biases of modern urban middle class educated women against the baby girl. She no longer expected any understanding from Subha while her own friends failed to show that.

It was not an easy thing to keep silent. Mothers instinctively sense when their daughters are not happy but they buy excuses and pretend that everything is well with their lives till confronted with these glaring evidences. Uma was no different. She had felt things those past few days that she never felt before. After Neelu's mother-in-law left for Meerut, Uma went to Neelu's room. Locking her arms tightly around her neck she said in disconcerted tone, "Now I understand why these people who denied you your honeymoon, had taken you for this trip to Mysore and Triputi." For the first time since her marriage, Neelu cried bitterly and amongst her sobs said, "Mama, I have no idea what I have got myself into but I am feeling exhausted," and at once became quiet.

At that time Uma saw that Neelu rested her baby's head on her arm and for the first time had a real close look at the baby, her dark hair, thick lashed brown eyes, dimples on her red cheeks. Her love came up hot, in spite of everything; this child seemed to draw her innermost resentments out of her. "I love you darling. With all my force, with all my soul, I would make up for having brought you into the world," she said and held her close to her breast. Looking at Neelu smiling at her child, one could have a glimpse of the mother Neelu would be -- a mother who would stand like a rock shaping her daughter's future. There was something deep in her core that neither her in-laws or the society would be able to break. This budding of her motherly love embedded in the earthly pain would be baby Ashtha's salvation one day. And Neelu's eyes drifted again and again to the child sleeping in her arms. When the child at last sank down in her arms, Neelu put her to bed and dropped off to sleep around midnight.

When Neelu got up Uma sensed from her tone that she was displeased about something. Whether her husband forgot to call her or what happened on *chathi* day was bothering her, Uma couldn't tell. Neelu stopped and turned to her mother unfazed, "What were you talking about motherhood last night? It is the greatest experience a woman has, next to goodliness! It is sheer nonsense, mom. You don't know anything about this, mom", Neelu said, her anger rising. Did not Uma think there was no anger in her daughter? There was a time when Uma would have risen to such remarks and got irritated but that was years ago, before Neelu's marriage. Uma said nothing but her eyes brimmed with tears.

Neelu looked her in the eyes and said boldly, "Please don't look so miserable, Mama, I need to tell you the cruel truth today. Nobody not even you, mom, bothered to notice how I was under pressure during the months of pregnancy, how I lived in fear of their shifting moods, their temperament, their taunts about my inability to run the house on my own, how I coped with the family, what adjustments I had to make, and now after the delivery, this girl issue." Neelu continued, "You did not prepare me for this. Mom, you never did. It is unfair, Mom. All those years I was alone, and you did not care what I thought and how I lived. Now suddenly what right have you got to talk about gender inequality when you failed to pay equal attention to me -- your second daughter? What a terrible thing it was for me to know that my mother doesn't love me; and to suffer the pain of not being loved. Why did you have me when you have given all your love to other children? What an unnatural thing for a mother! Being an average girl in a family of two other intelligent siblings, I suppressed this urge a long time back to say anything about myself. Now I am not sure if this was right," her words came clear and ringing. When Neelu finished speaking, her heart was pounding and her mouth was parched. It took Uma a moment to register what Neelu had just said. Neelu had never before spoken in that manner. After a while, Uma leaned forward and said, "I can't understand why you talk like that…" she touched her shoulder but Neelu flinched and drew away. Uma dropped her hand too.

There was in Uma's eyes a look of disbelief that lasted for a moment or two, before it was replaced by shock. Uma's lips trembled, her face broke into a frown, and she buried her face in her hands, dread filled her chest, ripping something out of her. Uma was too stunned to understand Neelu's boldness and then her look of apprehension turned into anger. It was not her daughter's face she saw but a face of unspoken grievances that found a target to focus all her simmering anger on and Uma saw no trace of respect in Neelu's eyes for her.

Uma sighed and slumped in her chair. Uma remembered how she had shaped her entire life round this thankless task of raising Neelu and, in her own way, of loving her. And this was the reward for everything she had endured. Uma made an effort to open her mouth to say to Neelu, "You are such a huge part of my life. We have seen each other pass through both good times and bad. I will never stop loving you. Please don't taint my joy of this baby," but she could say nothing. She knew that children these days blame their parents if something went amiss in their life but never give a thought to all the sacrifices, all the self-denial and all the trouble they endure in raising them. No matter what Uma did to please them, no matter how thoroughly she fulfilled all their demands, it was not enough. Neelu was a mother now. How strange she was unable to see the sacrifices her own mother had to make for all these years.

The next day Uma saw Neelu coming with her husband towards her before leaving for Merrut. There was no locking of her arms around Uma's neck, no tears, no smiles, and no whispered promises of her coming soon. Uma's eyes threatened to well up and she knew how hard she was struggling to be brave. Her knees weakened, Uma wanted to grope for Neelu's arm, her shoulder, something to lean on. But she did not; she stood perfectly still and looked at Neelu. In silence Neelu left with that unforgiving look in her eyes. Uma watched them walk away, a shudder passed through her, a current of something sad and forlorn, and she looked shaken. Even then Uma wished she could see Neelu and wished to hear the sound of her daughter's laugh again. She wished Neelu to visit her with her husband to see Aastha growing up. She would have liked that very much, to be old and play with them She feared she would never see her again and would never play with Neelu's children.

Now all sorts of questions raced through Uma's mind. Had she been a complacent mother, she asked herself? Had she been such a dreadful mother unmindful of the pain of Neelu? Had she taken out her guilt of having the second girl on Neelu and then tried to forget it all? What harmful things had she unwittingly done to this daughter that she was not forgiven? These unanswered questions and the silence were all too painful for Uma. There were days when Uma believed she was being punished for what she had done to Neelu and she could not forgive herself. She had laughed at her friends and now she was the one who was under the microscope of her daughter, she was the one having to prove her motherhood. In the darkness of her room, she lay awake with the demons of her own but had no courage to confront them and live life again. The mere thought of resuming her old pattern of life seemed so exhausting to Uma. She had to make enormous efforts to get out of bed, to do the laundry, to make meals and to do her prayers and found it difficult to sleep at nights. Other days a voice inside her tried to soothe her with consolation that *life is* very complicated to understand but it goes on moving forward, unmindful of these crises. Mechanically Uma would go over and over again on this scene and found herself thinking of Neelu. She feared she might lose her nerve if she let her mind wander.

One day when Uma got up in the morning, there was a message from Aruna, her friend in Bombay on the cell phone, a card from her brother in Europe. The phone rang, Uma picked it and heard the voice of her son -- Lucky who was calling from USA, "Mama, I was trying to reach you for so many days, you were not picking the phone, are you alright?" Questions of how she was were met with vague but cheerless replies, "Doing fine, I am fine. Yes, I am. Yes, Neelu has gone. I will move on. Oh! I will be fine," said Uma to Lucky, laughing nervously, to fill the melancholy with aimless banter. By instinct she kept the phone clasped long after Lucky had hung up and looked at her house. When Uma found the house empty, her disquiet heart began to beat quickly and her mind got lost in their childhood memories.

13

A Poor Boy Falls Down

As I read 'The Simple Life' of Sudha Murthy in an interview with Naorem Anuja in *Reader's Digest* of February 2021 in which Sudha said, "Studying was not *rajamarga* -- a smooth sailing highway -- for me. It was the road less travelled and I accepted it. Anyone who makes the choice undergoes [difficulty] but there is also an advantage -- their efforts are recognized."

I was reminded of Raju, an eleven or twelve-year-old thin boy with squeezed cheeks and starved looks who could not make this choice and had to drop out of the school when his family, after the death of his grandfather, moved from the village to a jhuggi in Railla village, which is part of Sector 12 in Panchkula. His parents could not afford his education even in a government school as they had three daughters, four, six and seven years old and the father was a daily wager who could get only irregular and odd jobs. They lived in a small shabby place where there was no furniture except a rickety and fraying bed and a few mats on the mud-plastered floor with a couple of hole-ridden blankets which some proprietor of the bungalow gave his mother on Diwali where she worked at the time of marriage; now, they were tattered and still protected her children when they huddled under them in winter. His father had an income of approximately 800 rupees a month and they lived on this and what his wife earned working as charwoman.

Finding work for his son Raju in Panchkula was much more difficult as well. His father ran from pillar to post in search of work for his boy. Raju was either too small to work as a factory hand or inexperienced to work as a domestic help. With the help of some driver from his village he found a job for him in a big bungalow. From that time onward Raju's life became a never-ending war against the tedium of monotonous tasks. He did not like this. Whenever he was sent on some errand to the market he would start playing with stray dogs and talk to urchins and came late; he was scolded. He felt lonely. He kept crying and his soul craved the freedom of the village. There he was free not only to ramble at will and at large when he was beyond family supervision or had not been put to work. He would go into open fields on the ridges, or down into the woods on the steeper land along the creeks. Raju was wandering in woods or working in fields and drank from wet weather springs, the water, cool and tasting of ground, with no thought of chemical contamination. It was a pleasing and desirable world of lasting values. These eight or nine years of his boyhood were most active and carefree. He was sufficiently free in the village in the company of elders who were not much inclined to worry about him and who treated him as a child when he was in a way, in danger, or in need of correction. They spoke to him as they spoke to each other. He sometimes tried their patience but he liked their company. Now, he missed his grandfather who was up long before day light and would go with him to the field, recline there upon nature's breast, listening to the whistle of birds in the grove. He lived in the clean air and ate the sweet bread of contentment and had given his heart entirely to his older place of his grandfather that he always called his "home place." It was a motorless world of stones, streams and soil, plants and animals, woods and fields, footpaths and its native silence. It was only rarely disturbed by the sound of a machine, its darkness after bedtime unbroken by human light, its daylight as yet unsmudged, its springs and streams still drinkable. This fine loveliness of earth held him with its witchery and grace. The perfume from her woods and meadows stirred him strangely. It was a creaturely world, substantial and alive. He simply lived in it and loved it.

Here he was always uneasy, could not get adjusted to their urban ways of living. He and his grandfather walked through the fields, talking endlessly and never tiring. He learnt from his grandfather the names of all the grasses in the fields, and all the animals and stones. He knew which herbs were used to cure the diseases and had no difficulty telling the age of a horse or a cow; he learnt the significance of drying roots and leaves -- walnut leaves for treating anaemia, chamomile for fainting spells, thyme and rosemary for muscular cramps. By looking at the sunset, or the moon, or the birds, he could tell what the weather would be like tomorrow, ways of the livestock, of handwork, of all the life of farming that would make him a countryman. He was being shaped as a creature of his home place, a son of the soil. He was untrained at any trade that is practiced in the city. Anyway, here this knowledge was futile to him but these were the only things he passionately knew. He was a misfit in this city; the village life loomed large in his mind. He, with disgust in his heart, sat in the corner of the servant quarters of this bungalow of *Lalajee.* Silence was mostly the thing required of him and for hours he would be left alone, disturbed and his mind full of troubling thoughts. Never before had he hated their world as he did then -- the exhaustion in his limbs lying down on the floor and shivering uncontrollably. How could one forget such things? He could recall many details: sandwiched between many siblings and feeling neglected by parents, ignored by elderly servants of this house who had seen him crying. He leaned against the cold metal door, the loneliness he had to live with, all of a sudden, unbearable. He viewed with swift horror the pit into which he had tumbled, the degraded days, unworthy comments, dead hopes, no words of affection and no trace of compassion. At the beginning, Raju did not understand what was said or what they expected.

He failed to understand these people in the bungalow and wondered how could they be so glad in a city so great, so complex and diversified and how could they savour this life and stroll so leisurely with a heart expanding at the thought that they were citizens of this city, sharer in its magnificence and pleasures, partaker in its glory and prestige.

For Raju, life was cruel and unforgiving as there was no comradeship and sympathy in any member of the household to make life bearable. He was lonely in his box room which was at the back of the house. While the house was heated, scrupulously clean and full of conveniences, his room was not. He was cold, the air chilled his bones and made his teeth chatter. He wanted to tell someone everything he was now imagining in the darkness, everything that's making his thoughts race but there was none. Other servants were either too big or wouldn't understand. To tell the truth, their behaviour seemed to say to him, "You are not our concern. You could suffer the most horrible thing, we wouldn't give a damn." Raju felt pain upon hearing their remarks that they made thoughtlessly. He did not know what waited him in this house, it was full of unexpectedness. On weekend nights there were sounds of revelry in a big drawing room and sometimes he was caught in a web of their ravishing music and dazzled by a panorama of lights and colours -- the new coloured, new shaped life in their enchanting late-night parties, then with strong voice in the hall they would *shoo* him out those places and call him 'uncouth, disagreeable and ill-mannered,' the bad names whose meaning he did not know. He knew they were so different in dress, habits, manners, provincialism, in their charming insolence and sophisticated crassness and irritating completeness. These parties that sent them to cheers brought Raju nothing but despair and at times beatings. He muttered, "They treat me as if I am a scum, intruder there. When tired I doze off, they shout choking and gurgling curses at me. Helpless, ridiculous, confined, bobbing like a toy mandarin, I sit like a rat in a trap." It was a terrible thing to be alone and he had known nothing except suffering and solitude. Tears from the depth of some despair rose in his heart and gathered in his eyes. But how could they understand other people's pain, these city people, full of themselves, he thought.

They are the people who have been granted happiness as their birth right and who believe that every mystery in life can be solved and every pain salved with the power of money. There is nothing we can't achieve."

Like a good soldier who was about to invade the enemy's territory, Raju was seeking to guard every point against possible failure was still not noticed. "They do not reach out to me, offer help, pity or stay by my side to help me smile and laugh." He became sad thinking of his grandfather who was very gentle. He had never smacked him nor did he shout at him. He would say nothing, just open his arms and he would wrap him up and would stay like that for ages.

Here in this big bungalow as well, he was always looking up to Lalajee the elder in their family who would be his advisor, a counsellor and a mentor. "It is their kindness that would have made me indebted to them for life. Kindness binds as obstinately as love does. A stranger's kindness, like time itself heals our wounds in the end but they fail to give me even a momentary hope. They hadn't had much to offer me. If I had got a little bit of their attention, perhaps I would have subjected myself completely to their will. Why would they, when life to them was a simple transaction between those who owe and those who own."

Fortunately, Raju did not mind work, even if it was drudgery, and considered work even pleasure -- its own reward -- well enough to afford a meal to his family. He wanted to work and work well, to be a good hand long before he was capable. He had learnt quite early that good work was worthy. In the village there were hours and hours when he hung about the men at work, to watch, to listen, hoping to be given some bit of real work to do. Sometimes he was assigned to some drudgery that men preferred to avoid: go to spring or well to bring back a fresh jug of water and in the afternoon helped grandpa with the fields. He stacked hay in the evenings. He picked mushroom in the woods. He grew big and strong to cut swiftly and accurately with axe, to lift hay. The difficulty of his work was relieved by some sort of talk that people do for pleasure, telling of jokes and stories --meals at noon. There was just barely a note of hope; he could neither escape by aping them nor could he adapt himself. He was finding himself cut off from the people from whom he had sprung. How difficult readjustment is!

What an irony of fate! He had to leave this world of harvest dinners, capable mules or horses, hounds or dogs, days and nights of jokes and stories in which was the recognition and acceptance of the human lot. He had to leave such settled and decided people and familiar world known by people he knew who were either at work or at rest in it.

Here he was alien in these surroundings. It was a city where the mentality, the sound of language, the hopes, the possibility, even the appearance of the people in the streets were as strange as anything. He did not understand their continuous speaking of alternatives or alternative lifestyles, of technology, progress or mobility or upward mobility nor their talk of infinite, of choices endlessly available to everybody. He had not heard 'just a farmer' or 'just a housewife' as people in the village did not call themselves these things nor was there nothing to suggest the possibility always elsewhere of something better, and to make people long to give up whatever they had for the promise of something they might have -- at whatever cost, at whatever loss. No talk of changing jobs. His choice in coming here had not been deliberate either. Neither had he succeeded in adapting himself quickly nor had he the speech and movements and the very expressions on his face of seedy Haryanvi. If his grandfather had not died and there was not a certain passiveness (in father) as though everything had been dealt in advance, they would not have been here in Panchkula at all. Poverty is not a goad but a paralysis, he thought.

Almost every night he had the same dream. He could see his mother father, grandpa and grandma, and other people from the village with their eyes on his face and he wandering in woods or working in fields and was assisting people with picking their plums, peaches and grapes, countryside -- limitlessly self-revealing and interesting, limitlessly to be known and loved. It was precisely in this limitlessness that he was free, free from the litter of alternatives, free of fear that has grown greater in every year he has lived in the city…

Raju missed everything, often thought back to the times. The old voices of the soil spoke to him. Leaf and bud and blossoms conversed with him in the vocabulary of his careless youth -- the inanimate things, the familiar stones and the furrows, turns of footpaths had an eloquence. The twilight pixies and pucks plunged poignant shafts of memory into the heart of Raju. When his grandfather died of pneumonia, and within months of his grandma's demise, he thought the whole of his world had collapsed. He thought these deaths were meant to punish him for something. He was chained to the village and it was impossible to escape its pull. He remembered the evening that turned his life upside down -- he came home for supper, he discovered the whole family quiet in the bedroom his grandpa saying to his father at death bed, "I have finally figured it out. Here is my paternal advice: go away. You can't have a life here now on such a small holding. You must forget about your mother and me. Go North, get a job in Panchkula and start from scratch. Break each chain with this land, you cannot expect any good from it after I'm gone." He took his hand and kissed it. This was the last link of the chain falling. With him, the last connection to the past was gone. He lost his grip, the earth below his feet. It felt then like everything was over. Who binds a man to land or water, he wondered, if not that man himself?

Raju thought: Now I see that these links in a chain snapping one after the other -- these deaths were meant to set me free, to get me moving. How much he wanted to be like a river, which had no memory, and how little like the earth, which could never forget. After the death of his grandfather impoverishment had followed. What a disgrace! At night there had been tears and haunting dread that soon, very soon and they would be forced to move out of the village in search of a job as his grandfather had predicted.

It was terrible to feel lonely and out of place. How wearisome and alien it all was to him. Apart from this, it is this irrelevance that makes it hard for Raju to stay with them. His heart mourned for the passing of time as it has never mourned the death of his grandparents. Now he wanted to slip back to a life he was sure of. He left the bungalow, moved through the gate, his head down and his gait slow, but his soul charged ahead, sparkling through the gloom. Would he forget for the rest of his life these years? What would stay with him, would be his frustration, his failure or the misery of it? What Raju considered picking berries minor work, turned out to be the only work he knew. Anyway, he was happy to run away from the bungalow and beatings to fulfil his childhood dream of living by trees.

He had never been able to wean himself from trees, if he had ever tried to do. Now in the city he was alive only when he was with the trees. Raju started earning doing some errands or selling *jamuns, mulberry* and *amlas, red and black berries* whatever he plucked seasonally from roadside trees. His aim was to sell in the neighbourhood and that, he thought, would be attained by making acquaintances with local inhabitants. When he visited them, he spoke sometimes with animation, sometimes with melancholy. At times he would appeal to their moral sense while exciting their indignation to the corruption of morals now a days but he spoke always with feeling and earnestness. He was always in excellent spirits and pleasant acquaintances were formed. What streets with fruit trees, charming parks and delightful society! And he was lucky he thought that women bought his fresh picks? Oh, such happiness! Never before, never again. It was just like a job for him, a work to make ends meet. It didn't mean that he did not want more nor was it an another rung on some endless career ladder, but like some waiter, field hand, or Uber driver or any underserving of any large consideration. The street corner became his playground, park was his drawing room and the street was his garden walk, yet most part he was as inviolate master of himself in them. He would find a bench, tree shadowed and secluded and sat there or move in the park like earth with infinite leisure, with all eternity at his disposal.

Raju was maybe better than an average climber as he had spent a fair portion of his life in trees. He was undoubtedly ignorant, fearless, curious, happy in the secret altitudes of the treetops and little branches, not at all intimidated by the blank blue sky above the highest branches He was small for his age and was secure on branches too filmy for a bigger boy. Sometimes he could step from one thick limb to another up the trunk. Sometimes he had to make his way out to smaller branches of one limb from there into smaller branches of one above. He climbed silently slowly from one handhold and foothold to another, up and out the little branches until he was within an easy arm's reach of those fruits. He leaped from one branch to another like a squirrel. Finally, he was at the top of the tree, a hundred or so feet from the ground. He had an ache in his inward skin of his hands and fingers to catch those lovely fruits. Thus, he collected fruits and washed them and carried them in a basket and sold them to the women in their homes. They talked to him and bargained and bought at rates cheaper than market. This bolstered his moral courage to continue it as a job. When the season of *jamun* was over he would go to 21 Sector where government horticulture orchard is. They would hire him to pick the mangoes and sell them from door to door. He was happy when he was picking up berries and mulberries from the roadside trees. He was never without work; when the season of berries was over, he would shift to plucking *amlas.* For red wild berries and golden *baer* he would visit the woods in nearby villages and thus could feed his family the night meal.

One day he was picking *jamun* in Sanik Welfare Centre near the park. He lost his balance and fell down with a thud from the park side of branch on the park pavement. He was sweating, his hands and arms and legs bark-burnt and stinging.

After a few minutes, my maid rushed in the house crying with rage and hate; she said, "Do you know what happened to Raju who comes to sell jamun? He has fallen down the tree in the park. Raju lay on his face, surrounded by so many people that one could not see the cobblestones. The spectators seemed to have arrived, as they do at street accidents, from nowhere, panting from running, pale with fear that something had been missed. Immediately, heads had appeared at all windows from houses on all sides and balconies were filled with people and people hung out of windows on the upper floors to see him." How could you think anything as terrible as this! It gave me unexpected and indignant shock, when I realized what it had meant for Raju? I was sort of jolted I thought about the things, everything about Raju. He was too easily amused, too loud in his laughter and talked in his local accent, which sometimes sounded comical.

Rajvati the maid also informed that many residents crowded the place but none helped to take him to hospital. The spectacle went to my heart everything tortured me with misgivings. I could not say what was taking place in his life that afternoon. I saw him pleading to me. "Help me: you owe me help. I plucked berries for you. Nobody is coming to help me. Please don't desert me."

I would never have believed myself capable of leaving the child like that unattended after ringing up the police. I wanted to help but felt helpless at that time because my husband a retired Colonel who had undergone surgery couldn't drive. I thought of other spectators and wondered about these people what was wrong with them, why they could not feel those things I was feeling for crestfallen Raju. But my thoughts were overtaken by the yells and screams of Raju. I could not explain what was happening to me.

These events of past few minutes which looked like eternity had been so tragic, unspeakably ugly that only rational response was to feel sorry. It revealed these rich people's ineptitude but also exposed their insensitivity, their pretence that it was not happening. For me, more damning than everything was the reminder that my neighbourhood had started resembling Gilbraith's new class -- all rich businessmen who display a patient inquisitiveness that imparts a sense of moral perspicacity. They know nothing about the lives of the poor nor seek to understand the lives of those who suffer on their behalf. George Orwell in *The Road to Wigan Pier* says "Ignorance is undoubtedly bliss, but it is always morally unbecoming." Just in my thoughts I was thinking about my neighbours. These past few years of limitless prosperity and look at how frivolous, how charged with mean vanities, how selfish, how empty, how ignoble, how indifferent to human suffering! To earn hundreds of thousands of rupees from the hard labour of poor people whom they do not understand and cannot like -- how strange it is!

They do not think of other people but only of themselves. It may be due to their cradle to grave comforts that distances them from an empathetic appreciation of, or even exposure to a workday consisting of drudgery or something like this falling-from-tree accident.

Nor can you expect people (rich) to feel compassion for the poor, to feel their pain or to be empathetic. Did you ever see the rich the epitome/embodiment of concern and care and sympathy for the marginalized? They settle into comfortable disregard for those excluded from (affluent society's) its benefits and culture and they develop a doctrine to justify the neglect. Wilful neglect of the working poor is odious, but the far greater danger is a mere oblivion -- the invisibility of the poor to the economic superior. Poverty for them is a kind of academic phenomenon, something they can identify or even opine on but hardly understand.

I felt depressed again and said to Rajvati -- my maid, "I don't understand why we discuss other people; oh! I am not criticising you." (In my pain and shame) I would have given worlds to have those unkind words back. But the possibility of Raju being delayed for first aid presented itself to my mind and extended its depressing influence over my spirit. Another hour of silence, sadness, hopelessly watching for succour that could not come. All I knew was what was coming.

I was feeling sorry for the boy, sorry for myself, sorry for these people (I respect and esteem these people as much as any neighbour possibly can) who were too unfortunate to help this poor boy. I felt a spasm of annoyance, and at the same time my heart began to beat so quickly that I felt its movement must surely be visible. What is the matter with me I thought and slid in my seat, my hands over my forehead? Am I really feeling sorry for him or cheating my conscience? Am I externalizing my anger or feeling like a prig? I do not understand human behaviour but I had harboured a rigid belief that anyone could help who sincerely wanted to. I could not tell anyone how hurt and humiliated I was. It gave me an unexpected and indignant shock, when I realized what it had meant for him what a ruin this afternoon had been; he could have been killed. Poor Raju does not belong to their world I said. What does it matter? People are supposed to be independent they are supposed to go off their way.

After a few minutes the maid again entered very sorrowful and narrated that in the meanwhile the small boy who was standing in the park and picking those *amlas* had screamed when he saw Raju falling and then all at once others materialised from the park, the drivers and maids, rickshaw pullers vendors all; they stood in a circle around the boy. There is no evidence one way or other that poor were there out of concern for a friend in trouble or there might have been curiosity or anything. How do you know? Meanwhile a driver of the Sharma's came and entangled Raju from the branches wrapped around him with which he fell on the ground; he was covered with scars, scratches, wounds and was bleeding. The message went around and Raju's father arrived. He had to fight through the crowd in the park. At once taking off his shirt he wrapped him up and carried him away. Raju's face looked white and frightened. Apparently, he had not yet begun to experience the pain of his injuries and was simply stunned and shocked. The driver along with his father took Raju on his motor bike to the hospital. After a few moments, Raju's mother, as if she was too distracted to stay indoors or she had to divert her attention to inconsequential things, rushed to the park where she was told he was moved to hospital. Finally, the chatter died down, and even the most persistent observers, with a last look at the blood, the cobbles and now the shuttered windows of the neighbours, sauntered away. They were neither frightened nor hurt. They were talking in loud, matter-of-fact voices about the accident. They spoke of hospitalization and expense and terrible burden.

The mother rushed to the hospital in a hurry. It was a profound shock to parents, they staggered under the blow but Raju was their own, the core of their heart, the blessing of their eyes, their all in all. They struggled day and night to help him recover fast, besides the poor's day-to-day misery to cope with this rotten crisis would remain.

That night I could sense my husband's close attention, his wanting me to say something. Col Gupta could not sleep; he was blaming himself. I should not have left the boy to go on screaming. Instead of the police I should have rung up the ambulance as I was unwell to drive him to the hospital. He reproached himself for indifference to Raju's fate. He told me, it is not a question of right or wrong, is it? Why should it be? It is a question of what one is. He said the whole thing was a mistake, from start to finish. "Sleep you'll feel better," I said. You mean time passing, healing wounds, that sort of thing? He said but if one cannot rely on what one feels, what can one rely on?

Since the fiasco as he called it, he was restless as if he was doing penance for his sins. Given the situation he was in, he had done no harm but he was feeling guilty. For the first time I understood that he began to show his feeling through hints and silences or talking about the wretched and despairing life of the poor boy. Perhaps I had not to persuade him to do something for Raju he already had a new idea. I heard him tell Rajvati to go and tell Raju, "Remember, whatever happened, you will always have a home in 536 Panchkula Sector 12. When he would recover, he wanted him to come and clean his car plant a vegetable garden as he was a farm help before. He wanted him to ground himself again in the irrepressible life of soil and sprout and bud and bloom and make his house his sanctuary of extraordinary peacefulness." He told me it would be a homecoming to his first great love: farming, gardening. He could grow calendula, camomile, poppy, nasturtium, purple iris and his favourite lavender and honeysuckle. In his spare time, he could do some errands; he could learn to iron, make beds, wait on table, wash floors, polish furniture and shine his souvenirs.

I had tried to drive the memory of this accident out of my mind but it would not go, the shame and bitterness of it were poisoning my sleep and dream life but Colonel's offer cheered me up. I said in my thoughts, dear Raju, look forward now, never back, and forget what has happened.

Besides, Rajvati told me he was recovering fast. I wondered how sadness seemed to roll off Raju as raindrops roll off a lotus leaf, without leaving any trace. Raju recalled vividly that faraway time when his grandfather used to say: look at these trees, the cherry blossoms (trees) save energy during the cold winter months to burst into glorious flower in the spring. Similarly the challenging times present you with opportunities to develop strength, depth and resilience." An instantaneous and strong impulse moved Raju to battle with his desperate fate. Surely like them he would pull himself out of the mire, he would make a man of himself again. This was a time, he was comparatively young yet, he would resurrect the old ambitions and pursue them without faltering. As he muttered that weak thing within him seemed to uncoil, to grow tremendously strong, and he recovered fast and now he longed to go to work. He wanted to shut the door as if on dark past and he said to himself: 'I am better and now is the beginning of my life. It is the start of a good life. Everything ugly, corrupt and vicious is behind me.' He had thought of going in the downtown and seek that businessman who had once offered him a job of car cleaner. But now that he was intimated of Colonel's offer, the glimmer of life and its possibility dawned upon Raju. He would be somebody someday, he imagined. In his happiness he sounded almost childlike convinced of the good life ahead to which he would devote his entire life.

14

Progress of Love

Mitchell met Rhea when he was studying MBA in Wharton business school where Rhea had gone to study after IIT. Rhea was a tall, frail, bony girl with brown hair and sensitive skin. Lately she had taken to wearing blue eyeshadow and black mascara which emphasized the watery blue of her eyes. Mitchell saw many remnants of girlishness and thought she was a little above twenty; he loved her fairness and tall fragility. Love is strange. It does strange things to you. Rhea could feel change coming in her life. She had submerged in love for Mitchell who was well fleshed, dignified and fair skinned, freshly groomed and glowing. The unexpected delight in him just as he was, the unusual feeling of being at peace with him, did come to her. A profound revelation came to her that they were bound together after all.

Somehow around the time they finished their MBA, Mitchell had started to talk about their being married. "When we are married," he would say, though this would not happen till he was employed but he spoke of it as something he had taken for granted. And Rhea instead of questioning or contradicting him would listen curiously. She could feel such benevolence towards him. "We have been together for so long why can't we toughen this bond now," said Mitchell and with the blessings of his mother they got married.

Before their marriage, Mitchell and Rhea got jobs in different companies. He worked in Golden Sachs and she got a job in Bank of America. After marriage she moved to his apartment in Philadelphia. The job was difficult and challenging but Rhea was keenly looking in advance for this place and life. They cleaned, papered, painted and furnished, and the house showed the effects of their attention and sociability. Life was real fun, they were inviting their friends and having impromptu parties. She was a charming wife and wonderful person at the party. Her friends were a mixed bag. Some were on verge of retirement while others were younger people of diverse backgrounds and working in varied companies. Therefore conversations tended to be widespread. She was the live wire of the parties. She would come to the party laughing and greeting friends; she brought not only food but all the longed for spirit of the neighbourhood party. With her overwhelming sociability, she gathered everyone in. Mitchell became her good friend and essential companion. She felt the sweetness of his light bones and serious ideas, the vulnerability of his love which she imagined to be much purer and more straightforward than her own. He seemed humble to her as he had taken on such a readymade role of husband, bread winner and devoted son. At home she told him amusing stories at the dinner table about events and about fellow tenants and the French-American landlord whose harsh French and tangled English she imitated. He thought her beautiful.

Every year they were out for three weeks in the month of December and they would go skiing and travel cross country. "I try to keep up my interests I think that keeps me energised," said Mitchell. They would regularly visit his mother in Princeton during long weekends. Mitchell's mother lived in Princeton in an apartment building overlooking the park. Her husband, a doctor died when Mitchell was still too young to go to college. She took a secretarial course, sold her house and moved to an apartment. She came home tired from working all day in the noise and the harsh light of the departmental store office but managed to raise him decently. His life had been sheltered and fussy.

After almost two years of their married life, differences started surfacing in their relationship. Rhea wanted to buy a small car that intrigued Mitchel who disliked her choice of a small European car over a large American car. The real reason behind buying a small car was her thought of saving money for buying a house of her own somewhere on the bank of a river or lake in the countryside. She was already dreaming how she would eat on the green grass, sleep in the sun and spend hours sitting out the gate on the bench gazing at the fields and woods. And in her head she had pictured garden paths, flowers, fruits, birdhouses, pond with ducks and all that stuff. Just to fulfil her dream she lived frugally, ate simple food, dressed God knows how and kept saving money and put it in the bank. She was terribly stingy. Whenever Mitchell gave her money she put that away too. She was also against starting a family soon otherwise, she thought, her dream of having a house of her own would be relegated. When she talked of buying a home, he neither approved nor disapproved of her idea. Once a woman gets herself an idea, there's nothing to be done.

Their relationship was already undergoing a sea change and these differences further intensified the conflict. Since Mitchell was a secret monster of egotism he always thought he knew people and put more stock in his unproven theories and unjustified suspicions. And in the middle of his attention he would slip in a warning, an insult and a reminder of how things stood. He indicated clearly they could be happy only if she would honour his privacy, make no demands upon him and try to alter those things about her person and behaviour which he didn't like. He listed those things precisely. Some of them were very intimate in nature. Her eyes were downcast with shame and she begged him to say no more.

Wiping bead of perspiration from her forehead she sat down thinking, "I am afraid if Mitchell leaves me I don't know what I'll do. I don't want to be alone. I want everybody to think that I have a desirable man. I don't want to be a failure. It would be humiliation." Eventually she made many sacrifices for Mitchell, in living arrangements, in matters of friends, in the rhythms of sex and in her tone of conversation. She even prayed and threw coins in wishing wells. After all she just needed some moments of peace and reconciliation in the house. They are worth having, she thought, even if it meant changing herself. They are more valued in the modern setups than they were in those old marriages, where both love and grudges could grow underground forever.

As Rhea submitted to Mitchell's preferences, his opinions, his dictatorial ways, she felt she had made him such a present of power, that now she had to give up on dignity and cope with ravages. This not only disturbed her sleep but she spent all her waking hours trying to figure out about Mitchell. "He talks intelligently and ironically and in this way covers his indefensible expectations; certainly he has a new idea of love which is ruinous." Rhea thought to herself. She was not prepared for the surprises life was throwing at her. "This guy I thought I knew. He told me things he did not tell anyone I thought that means something. Five years before he told her that he was full of praise for deferential grace of her movement and wistfulness of her voice, overwhelming sociability, vivacious expressions, but these gifts of mine now irritated him. Now whatever I say, he says rubbish; stop overreacting, he tells me, if you wish to be happy. All of a sudden I am not good enough I am trash. At times I think, may be he's right, and may be it is all me. My thoughts change every minute, such a mess my head is. Can it be that that I still love him intensely as I loved when I first met him?" At the same time she was even thinking, "I am stuck in this bad situation and there is too much anguish, too little joy and it drains me emotionally and mentally. He expects me to sacrifice my personal values and change into someone I am really not. My trust is continuously broken, my capability and worth is always questioned. He makes me feel broken, depressed and frustrated." Her marriage, she felt, was like a dangerous swamp sucking in the misdeeds of her partner. But how long could she put up with his misdeeds? That night she tried to reason out in her mind. Why did people exactly do what they should not do? Why did he spend his life abusing me, growling at her, offending his own wife, what need had there been to frighten and insult her? Generally, why do people interfere with each other's life? Why was the world so ordered strangely that life, which is given once only, goes by with so much rancour but she could get no answer. The next morning when she awoke her body was torn into thousand pieces with pain. 'Will I be able to live with it? At this moment it is unbearable to think of his callousness."

She felt like telling him, 'A person does not belong to you just because you are in relationship.' "What you want in a woman is not a mind, an intellect and all you are interested in is finding fault with me. You don't get to decide how someone else's life is run, what is ok for them. What makes you suddenly think you can come here and mock me, my life and my family? You have displaced my life, hardly knowing it existed. You have set up in its places your beliefs, customs, rules and principles which I fear would ruin our life. You think only of yourself. Your feeling, your feelings, no one else's, not mine, anyway. Is this all my life is meant to be, an accumulation of pain? Relationships are not toys for you to play, it is real life. It will have consequences. It is my life it is not game. Think of others too," she said.

Things grew so much worse between Mitchell and her, their grudges, their grievances and their self-justification went on for months. Finally one evening Mitchell very rudely said, "There is no way to have a discussion with you. I hate hysterics, emotional displays, beyond anything."

She replied, "You're on edge with me because you said it. You broke the illusion I always had. I know there is something basically selfish and basically unreasonable/ untrustworthy about you. You are always talking down to me and treating me as if I am beneath you. You walk around like you are so important." Mitchell replied arrogantly, "Yes, I am fed up with you. I know I would be better off without you; you are intolerable. You are incompatible." Suddenly she was overcome with intense anguish and all sorts of thoughts started coming to her mind. Gradually she felt she could see more clearly somehow, what she had been trying not to see for many months but now she could no longer unsee: all the time he was so bitter and offensive. She recalled that he had never been gentle with her nor did he love her. All the five years she had been with him were nothing but a thing like a disregarded, uncared for and unloved house she had lived in so long that she hardly noticed it. He had never thought of her, never had paid any attention to her even when she pined for him. Now she could see his charming irresponsibility, his conviction that the world revolved around him. Of course, she was weary of his self-love. Despite all these musings she said, "How contradictory I am! These civil wars inside me are continuous and exhausting. I am still in love with him and yet I want to be free of him. I have come to these agonising crossroads where each leads to despair." Staying would no longer be that easy and simple like putting the head down in prayer and letting go would just mean to accept the futility of all her efforts to blend in seamlessly and the shutting away the part of her that now throbs and writhes. Hanging on too long was getting too destructive more hazardous than letting go.

She knew there are days in all people's lives when things go wrong, they are forced to ask themselves if they wanted to go on, what sort of life they want and they have to decide it themselves. At once the cold glittering fear rose in her as she had to decide it alone. She had lost her mother to cancer before coming to America and her father had remarried and he was alien to her now. She also thought how much responsibility a parent must take these days for his children's marriage. Above all no parent could do anything about the married life of his children, especially now that matters had reached a point where there seemed no solution. There was no other way of getting advice. One of the miseries of being the only child is there is no one to guide you or hold your hand.

After a few days Mitchell filed for divorce what seemed to him natural and necessary and she believed that the most important thing for that person was to be free, to go ahead. He didn't care. This divorce completely shattered Rhea who had expected to be well settled in a married life, only a little older, a little wealthier, a little better off with a house of her own. She had not foreseen this loss and any of the many ways that life could go wrong. She had thought Mitchell was a ward; an inoculation against the uncertainty of future. There was nothing she could have done to change his mind. There was nothing anyone could have done, she thought.

Nevertheless, this was neither exactly a pleasure as she might have meant it to be nor a deep relief as you feel when the door closes and the house sinks back to normal and you let yourself loose into all the free space around you, but was a huge, unsettling event. It felt heartless and cold at that time. For a few weeks after divorce she was just barely hanging on, raw, sad and spinning down and down, up came all tears, the frustration and the difficulty. It was hard to say if it was pertaining to Mitchell, the strangeness of loss/grief or was it due to everything else that had gone wrong. Everybody is afraid of being left alone, being tossed about, not being good enough, being a monster. This is what I felt when he left, she said to herself.

After the divorce she had given up shopping expeditions, theatres and concerts and stayed at home. She spent almost no money on herself; she lived on as little as she had when studying for MBA. She took it too hard. She never got used to living alone. She felt isolation of the most desperate and soul-destroying kind, like being alone in a boat in the middle of an ocean and nothing to take you to safety. After a few months it seemed to her that in losing Mitchell she had been cut off from his life like a cataract, discarded and she began to feel that there was no future for her either. Silence was her only way of getting by, if she were silent long enough this moment of discomfort would pass by. However, this did not happen; now she felt sorry for her life which was passing so quickly and uninterestingly and kept thinking how good it would be if she were happy again.

Sometimes she felt she liked to live in this world; she wanted to go out and live a real life. "I fell in love I suffered; I fell out of love I suffered. Now the time has come when it is a mere memory, now I reason coolly and consider the whole thing absolutely trivial. But I am alive I want to live. I do not want to be depressed, I do not want to be anxious I want to be well, I want to be good, I simply want to live, to dream, to hope, not to miss anything. Life is short and one must spend it well." She had to find a way to live as other people do. Now besides a novel reading group, she also joined a cake baker/winemaker's club and an informal group where members entertained each other weekly over dinner parties that had a fixed cost.

She joined a musical club in the evening. There were not only music lovers but also a community of visionary artists and writers who orbited the place. Her first real acquaintance with Aamir came at the musical party where she sang Doris Day's "Que, Sera, Sera" and Cliff Richard's "Summer Holiday," with feeling which charmed all even Aamir. He fell in love with her at first sight and believed instantly in the integrity and uniqueness of her mind and soul. He saw that she was not content to be like other girls, she was special.

He sat down beside her and said in sweet voice, "It's soft and pleasing sonority is reminiscent of classical music." He listened and listened and suddenly a thought occurred to him that it would be nicer to get married. On the weekend his friend Aasim threw a party and invited him and Rhea. He told him everything about her. In amorous matters, especially in marriage an insinuation plays a major role. Everybody, his colleagues and friends from the club, started convincing him that he should marry her and that his age was also a consideration. Yes Rhea was interesting and good looking and above all, she was the first woman who treated him kindly and cordially And she was a stocky woman with a big deep alto and he had a sweet tenor and above all he had fallen in love There was nothing he could do about it and he decided he really did have to marry her.

In that mood, Amir wrote to his mother, "I find it somewhat sad and shameful to admit even to myself that my youth has been entirely without love and now in the real sense I am in love with Rhea for the first time at the age of thirty-two. Rhea is thin and her face is broad but with an expression of goodness when she smiles. Her voice sings and vibrates when she speaks. She is an exceptional being with a penetrating mind and high ambitions. She is Indian, very spiritual and that elevates her in my eyes. She has done her schooling in Kuwait, IIT from Delhi and MBA in Wharton." His mother was happy that he finally thought of settling down. Even then he did not propose at once; he was afraid Rhea might reject him and kept on postponing it to the great vexation of his friends. Finally, one day he picked up courage and invited Rhea for dinner to tell her how long he had been waiting for her.

They met at the restaurant of Westin Hotel and ordered, iced coke, mutton chops, mashed potatoes and apple pie. They went on eating in silence like strangers. Throughout the dinner he gazed at her in silent ecstasy, not knowing what to say. Then he pressed the napkin in his hand, and not recognizing his own voice he said, "There is no pure and joyous life without you. If you consent to be my wife I would give everything. There is no price I would not pay, no sacrifice I will not make!" This suddenness of proposal jolted Rhea. She stared at him in astonishment and dismay. Her mood underwent an immediate and radical change and in a petulant voice said, "What are you saying? What you are saying is inconceivable to me?" He said immediately, "It is not impossible I assure you. Take your time to decide I am in no hurry." But Rhea left the hotel in exasperation. She now regretted going with him because now something that had previously seemed simple had turned messy, difficult and complicated.

When Rhea didn't pick up his phone for a few days Aamir felt that it was all over, that he no longer had to spend the whole days in expectation, explaining himself, thinking only of one thing. He had to relinquish the prospect of personal happiness, live without desires, without hopes, never dreaming nor anticipating. Imperceptibly old age would overcome him and life draws to an end. His forehead felt taut, he felt a sensation of weakness in his whole body, and he lay down on bed but could not sleep.

After the initial shock of suddenness wore off Rhea realized that it was not that she had never thought of getting married. The possibility -- half a certainty -- had been in her thoughts. She had thought that it would happen, someday, but not exactly in this somehow queer way. "That's the crazy thing, wasn't it? We did not even really know each other," she thought.

Nevertheless, her anxiety increased with every hour of solitude because in the course of her life she had often met elderly unmarried women -- insignificant women who were bitterly and openly remorseful because once they rejected a suitor. Would the same thing happen to her? The other thought that rankled her was whether one should marry from passionate love or without it? In the scripture it is written wife must love her husband and in novels love is given vast importance. Since she did not love him, she asked herself if it was right to marry. Was there then no answer at all for a woman whose marriage had failed? She was already twenty-eight; at this age marriage was for companionship not for romance. Often she considered if she remained sunk in escapist tendencies/fantasies she would only harm herself. There comes a time when you have to let go of the past if you are going to keep moving, if you are to survive. She took a considered decision to move on in life and not to relinquish forever the dream of her having a place of her own, her notion of happiness and married life. Out of all the marriageable men she was acquainted with, Aamir, after all, had a university degree and spoke French. He was a healthy and vigorous man with black hair, an intelligent and pleasant face. He was considered handsome and had an air of a man already ready to oblige. A tall good looking person, sociable but serious the way as nobody is anymore. The placid nature of his demeanour suggested a genuine concern for others and a lack of selfish regard. In addition he also lived in Philadelphia where there are beautiful theatres, musical evenings, and superlative confectioners. Besides he was from Lebanon and had a rich ancestral home and loving parents in Beruit. Above all he was in love with her. If she married him he would love her more than she could imagine. That night, she said prayers, knelt down and with deep feeling said, "Oh Lord, grant me understanding and wisdom!"

Early in the morning when she was still wavering between yes and no there was a sharp ringing on her phone. She picked up the phone and was amazed to find Aamir on the line. When your attitude changes everything around you changes. She thought if now she accepted to choose him it would change her life. She agreed to meet him in the evening in the plaza. She dressed in her beautiful turquoise blue dress and met him that evening. From everything, her smile, her glances, even the way she held her head and shoulder when she walked beside him, he could see that something had changed and he was no longer a stranger to her. She had convinced herself that to refuse such a decent, good and loving man simply because she did not love him and especially when this marriage offered the possibility of changing her dismal, monotonous life when her youth was passing and future looked no brighter, would be madness, folly, caprice for which God might punish her. She said resolutely, "You know all this had happened somehow so suddenly I had to think. I was afraid. I thought for a long time; I accept your proposal." When she said yes, a wave of happiness came over Aamir. Now he had some hope for him, a belief in the goodness of things and in the capacity of people to turn around and change their mind He had read a sonnet True Love by Shakespeare where he writes that there are 'no impediments to the marriage of true minds' but he was astonished to see it happened in his life. Immediately he bent down and kissed her hands; awkwardly she kissed his head with her cold lips. Now he was at ease and spoke of her life after divorce, time of hardships, something hardly to be made up for by a whole lifetime of comfort, which he promised he would happily provide.

After she accepted his proposal, he finalized the details of their marriage. Instead of an elaborate wedding, dinner, music and dancing, he thought a quiet wedding might perhaps seem quite proper. As a man of principle, he took a trip to Lebanon, essentially, to make it known to his parents. His heart thronged with the foretaste of happiness; he laughed for joy, imagining how wonderful, poetic and consecrated life would be.

Both took the flight to Beirut where the wedding was organized by his parents. That wedding morning, she had been delighted that everything was turning out so well. Because everyone felt merry, she was filled with joy and somehow got convinced that she would be happy no matter what. "Oh, how happy I am," she thought. She recalled how delightful the wedding ceremony had been. The priests, the parents, relatives and the guests had been looking at her with curiosity. She had fallen in love with Mrs Imitaz, Aamir's mother otherwise it was not in her nature to be so worshipful. "When she put her arms around me, kissed me, spilling out unrecognized fragrance, showing none of her hurry or regret, none of her dissatisfaction with my appearance and nature, I felt she was not a stranger to me. I felt first amazed, then excited and hopeful," she told Aamir.

Mr and Mrs Imitaz were very social; they always partied on Sunday evenings. Mrs Imitaz was gentle, eager and witty and had been an engaging talker but her husband was quieter, slower and tolerant and their dinner conversations always seemed decent and novel. They told amusing stories in which the joke was on them. If the evening was cold they would light a fire and there was discussion of weather, the praise or apology for food. There were guests of varied backgrounds that Rhea even thought of teaching herself, Greek, French and Spanish.

Aamir, she had thought was a passionate man but his love was, much deeper, more pure and true and much more fulfilling. He dressed up and took her around the estate. He said, "How nice this place is! My grandfather built it and left us heredity, nobility this big estate and after his death father looked after it. I somehow had never had the time to stay much in the house. I rarely went upstairs to formal rooms which my father used only to receive the guests. Due to civil wars and its aftermath, I was sent to America for studies."

Instead of making her stay at home and talking to her mother as daughter-in-law usually did at such time, he took her around to be shown everything that was to see in Beirut. He said, Beirut stays very much the same, more or less the same banks and the same hardware and grocery stores and barbershops and the Town hall tower. Nevertheless, the places and things completely devastated by civil war did not escape his eyes.

The newly wed stayed with Aamir's parents in their house for two weeks and then returned to America. Now she shifted to his apartment, he went to work but for two weeks she did not go to work. Instead, she organized apartment, played violin and read the books and looked through the fashion magazines in the evenings. When he came back from the office he was as loving as before and he had carried take away with him on his way back from office. They ate a great deal of Chicken biryani and kababs and sundae as if it was a feast day. Occasionally Aamir took Rhea to the theatre and in the intermission he never allowed her to go a step away from him and walked holding her under his arm. When he greeted someone he introduced her as well. His speech was delicate and the gentle and dignified smile never left his face. After the buffet, she always wanted to eat something sweet; she loved chocolates and wild blueberry tarts.

As she joined her office they would go for a drive in the evening after office, stop for ice cream or hamburger. Aamir was not scrupulous about taking her to a bar. There was no fuss about doing the dishes and cleaning up the kitchen either. Aamir would hire a car; take her for a drive out to the countryside. There were outdoor grills, picnic tables where they sat having beer or lunch on warm winter days. She was glad to be beside him, driven by him, receiving this attention from him in front of the relatives and friends.

Her dream of her own house had never left her. Out of all the delights in Rhea's life none was more delightful than the idea of having a home. Out of all the desires if she wanted anything more dearly was her own home. The shine, the intentness of Rhea's eyes and the gaiety could not be imitated or inherited when she talked about it. She was saving out of his salary to buy her a house. She had been saving her salary. After a few months of marriage she said they would have a place of our own in New York. Not too close to our place of work and not too far. It would be a summer house, of course. Rest of the time they would live wherever his work would take them. That might be anywhere, Washington, New York, Seattle or Philadelphia. It was not the idea of such travels that delighted Rhea but more so she was delighted by the idea of their own home that he spoke with such severe pride. Secretly this was what she was pining for since her childhood because after the death of her mother the very house she had grown in had never seemed a real home. Women always have something, haven't they that keep them going? In Rhea's life it had always been the thought of her own home.

Now hers was a household just as peaceful and comfortable as she had imagined other households to be. His friends mostly said, "Theirs is a love story of how two people, joined together, became themselves. They cannot breathe right without each other."

During the Easter holidays Rhea saw a house of her dreams and wanted to buy it. This was a one storey house, the main roof continuing without break out over the veranda, on all sides. The house was surrounded by great hedges and sparkling poplar trees, screened windows, a lake in front, and a beautiful blue swimming pool. Perfect preservation and past intact and feeling of relief passed over her.

Of course, you can look for years and in the end you may not buy what you were dreaming of, at all. This was exactly what happened to Rhea; she had applied for a loan from the Bank of America and finalized the mortgage deals. On August 4, the series of devastating explosions destroyed most of Beirut's port, flattened surrounding neighbourhoods, damaged six hospitals and more than 20 health clinics, and destroyed 120 schools. The blast killed over 170 people, injured more than 6,000 and left thousands homeless. Explosion blew out windows for miles around and sent cascades of glass shards pouring into streets. It was a deadly blast caused by the detonation of nearly 3,000 tonnes of ammonium nitrate at Beirut's port that devastated the Lebanese capital and changed the city's life forever. There were foreigners among the blast, at least 150 people were permanently disabled as a result of the devastation. Most of the long-term disabilities were blindness or loss of limbs.

Aamir was badly devastated by this news. Lebanon had seen dark days, death and destruction during the civil wars days and now this explosion. He confronted the difficulty of knowing what he wanted. He was imbued with love for his country. He thought how great and beautiful his land was. UNO and humanitarian partners made flash appeals for blast victims. That night he wrote in his diary: Once we have seen, once we have known, we cannot easily unsee and unknow and so we cannot easily lose our sense of responsibility. Aamir wanted to make sense of his human life and values. Now he wanted to go back to Beirut, work for the victims of the blast. He talked to Rhea much more easily about this than before. He narrated to Rhea that once the Lebanese American poet, painter, and philosopher Etel Adnan was asked in a television interview who the most important person she ever met was, she answered without hesitation: "A mountain." He too loved Lebanon like Etel's mountain and longed to be there. He explained things much as if he was discovering them himself at the same time. Perhaps he was looking at the world from a different perspective/viewpoint. He said, "Rhea, life will end, let us leave something of sweetness and substance in the mouth of the world. I had to protect this precious and pleasant way of life in Lebanon from the ruin". Rhea replied, "Yes, touching people's lives in a positive way is as close as I can get to an idea of religion."

Aamir and Rhea applied for job on the internet. They were hired by the UNO humanitarian group for rehabilitation work of Syrian and Lebanon people. They packed their necessary articles and disposed of the others in a hurry and left for Beirut by night aircraft. Just a day after they reached Beirut from America they busied themselves to help Lebanese people in rebuilding their lives and recovering from the devastation with immediate humanitarian assistance and initial recovery efforts.

Rhea the UN humanitarian coordinator, sent appeals to national and international community for money to help people in need for food security, health, shelter and protection and the cost of prosthetic limbs and reconstructive eye surgeries, and Aamir immersed himself with other relief workers in immediate delivery of hot meals, food rations and grain supplies; provision of trauma kits and essential medicines, cash for shelter for families whose homes were damaged or destroyed and for repairs of common building areas and facilities affected by the blast and repair of schools and provision of educational supplies and psychological support for children.

All in a day's work he met the victims of blast like Nabha who said, "The moment I saw the smoke rise, I believed it was the end and I was dead... I couldn't feel my eye or my hands. My face was like dough, full of glass and drenched in blood." He recalled he saw bodies and dozens of injured people on the streets of Gemmayze, before he found an ambulance that took him to a hospital. He discovered Nabha lived to tell them his tale but there were others who were scarred for life and required extensive reconstructive surgery and many more suffer post-traumatic stress symptoms which would take much longer to overcome. Lebanon people found their homes shattered, their families killed, their hopes and their dreams killed as well, with no justice, in all impunity, they held a "corrupt government" and "neglect" responsible for what happened and they protested. Angry demonstrations accusing the country's political elite of exploiting state resources had already been raging for months. The outrage further flared following the devastating blast amid revelations that top Lebanese officials knew a dangerous amount of ammonium nitrate had been stored at the port in Beirut for years.

Three-year-old Alexandra Naggear, a rallying symbol in Lebanon against government corruption was one of the youngest victims of the tragedy, her death enraged, saddened, and galvanized Lebanon.

What kept Aamir motivated throughout was the entreating voice of his father, "As long as you are young, strong and energetic, don't weary of doing good. If there is meaning and purpose in life, then that meaning and purpose are not at all in our happiness but in doing good to others."

Besides this the relief work got further impetus when the relief workers heard victims: "I have a family that depends on me," said Da'douey. "I need to get up and provide for them." Likewise, Nabha said he had not given up on his dream of going to Canada but this time he wants to go with his fiancée Taj.

Despite their severe and life-altering wounds, the resilient men were adamant to recover and lead as much of a normal life as possible. Kindness eases change. Humblest tasks get beautified when loving hands do them writes Louisa Mary Alcott and time was also healing people who hoped Alexandra's memory could spark political change. Life was beginning to return to normal.

Aamir and Rhea had devoted all their time and energy in helping people. They were not at all thinking of making money as they could have made. They did not see life in those terms. Nor did they see it in terms of saving at least a part of their energy for good times, all this seemed unbecoming to them. As people returned to their routine life and Christmas was drawing near Aamir also thought of taking a brief break.

A long time before the Beirut explosion they were planning a trip to Tenerife in the Canary islands because his friends Mr Rahim and Mrs Nisa Abdulla who lived there had highly recommended this place. Now when he phoned they insisted they must stay with them. They booked their tickets and landed in Canary Island two days before Christmas.

Tenerife is a year-round favourite holiday spot for tourists from across the globe, but on weekends there was always a great deal of noise and activity. They enjoyed not only its beautiful scenery, extreme sun and ocean waves, great bars and restaurants, but also its secluded getaways and round-the-year spring weather. While visitors had come to swim and have drinks and to get a tan, Rhea relaxed on the gold sand beach after water rides in Siam Park and chilling on the mile long river. In the evening Aamir took her to The Malizia Show At Piramide de Arona. It was a great live performance that presented an incredible blend of traditional Hispanic cultures, and offered a mixture of flamenco opera and dance performance which was powerful and thought provoking.

The next morning they took a quick drive through the Teide National Park – a UNESCO World Heritage Site and took the cable car to the top and was delighted to have a heaven-like view of the Tenerife and surrounding islands. When they came back, Rhea said, "I always think it would be nice to live here around the year as these people do and discover the beauties and attractions of the island at leisure. It is really a wonderful thing living in a place to which you are not connected and it is possible to become a different version of you." The thought of life with Aamir, simple and easy, predicted on the notion/promise of his true love, seemed irresistible. Life would be wonderful and they could live in a beautiful house in Tenerife, with its garden, reading on sunny afternoons, the sharing of time, the sharing of responsibilities of anchoring themselves in the world.

On the Saturday of the new year eve they threw a Cocktail party in the hotel in Santa Cruz de Tenerife in honour of their friends Mr and Mrs Abdulla with whom they had been staying for a week. Rhea and Aamir got so fascinated by the place they decided that after a while they might move to this place. But this did not happen quickly as they had to finish their rehabilitation work in Beirut. In the meantime Rhea got pregnant and was blessed with a boy and that delayed their migration to Canary Islands.

Six months after the birth of the boy and accomplishing their remaining relief work they moved to Canary Islands and Aamir's parents joined them for the house warming party.

As they entered their new house that Aamir with the help of his friends had bought in Tenerife, Rhea laughed and gazed silently at the house for a moment, with tears in her eyes. She could not speak from all the excitement. It was the accomplishment of the long-held wish, a dream come true. She glanced at Aamir with a triumph of a child who has finally got his favourite toy. Aamir saw a happy woman whose cherished dream had so obviously come true, who had attained her goal in life, had for what she wanted, who was content with her fate and herself. He wanted her to be happy with her illusion as Pushkin has rightly said, "Dearer to us than a host of truths is an exalting illusion." As far as he was concerned there had always been something sad mixed with his thoughts about human happiness. But as long as the petty cares of life stir her not slightly, she is happy, everything is fine," he said to himself. Suddenly his father patted him on the shoulder he had come to tell him it was time for the guests to arrive. Aamir folded his father in a warm embrace and both moved to greet the guests, the music soft like the caress of wind through the trees was coming from the hall and Aamir knew soon the house would fill with guests in their beautiful dresses.

15

Ration Card

Varun was looking across the street which, usually quiet, was now on Diwali eve, full of life and movement. The eating places and sweet shops were busy and noisy. Varun looked at the men and young people and he suddenly felt a longing for the plain rough life among the crowd. He recalled vividly that he also used to be a part of this festive crowd when he was a little boy and used to go shopping with his mother and when tired would lie under the same quilt with his mother, while his grandmother who lived with them used to sleep in the next room and through the thin walls there came from the neighbouring flats the sounds of laughter, swearing, children crying, the accordion, and the whirl of sewing machines while his father was busy reading something. He longed to run to the park and school when he lived with his mother. How happy they were, those days! Never before had he seen his mother in such heavenly bliss as on the day when her dream of him (Varun) becoming an IAS officer came to fruition. And she was happier when he got married and after he was blessed with twin boys, her attention shifted from her son Varun to her grandchildren; now they were important he wasn't. There is a saying in northern India *mool se payara bayaz* (that interest is dearer than the capita). After the birth of his twins either his parents came to celebrate Diwali with them or called them to Shimla to be together on this day.

During those days how happy his boys used to be with the load of crackers, mounds of sweets and chocolates; the thought of those days for some reason touched him. Their excited voices, their attitude, their smile impressed Varun with their beauty and elegance. They would follow him to the living room where the gentry and eminent visitors were entertained, he could think nothing, he could only smile blissfully. Back then on this Diwali day and on other days as well, everyone was happy when the boys were in good spirits and played pranks and put on loud music. Besides, they could do as they liked without any fear of being sharply called to account for it. It so happens that when grandparents are around, parents don't scold their children and children know it. He remembered how cleverly and creditably they spoke at the dinner table and how he (Varun) spoke with eloquence and inspiration and always told them bedtime stories. His boys were carried away by his stories and thought that that every time they spent for such enjoyment was worth it and forgave him everything else. In those days Varun had a worry of nothing. His children went to the best school and he built a beautiful house that nestled among evergreens and oaks. He recalled what an immense surge of happiness had run through him when he first looked at his achievement: big house whose walls were hung with expensive paintings, drawings and water-colours, while the furnishings, the etageres, and the vitrines displayed a thousand knickknacks: large vases, statuettes, porcelain figures, ancient ivories and Venetian glassware.

His life was infinitely blissful and he anticipated that much affection and entertainment would be his forever, it would never end. Those days Diwali being a holiday he wanted to just relax at home, play/talk with his boys, but then the colleagues, his juniors officials, superintendents of Police, politicians, managers of some companies, officers of the secretariate doctors, civil councillor, barrister, CEOs of companies, eminent citizens, learned professors obliged for some reason or other would come to offer him their greetings, show their respect. Varun, a tall, good-natured, handsome, an honourable IAS officer, and a wonderful fair man with a slight sprinkling of grey on his temples, distinguished by his exceptionally elegant manners, would come with swaying steps from his study, bowed as it were reluctantly, and shrugged his shoulders as he talked and all this with an indolent grace. When he was passing through the headlong rush of sociality, at heart he wanted to escape from it all to celebrate Diwali with his family alone but the host of visitors would not leave him alone.

What an irony now he was alone on Diwali day. Suddenly the thought of children swoops down upon you like a locomotive, and bathes you in hot steam and deafens you with its whistle. Now he had to satisfy himself by looking at the walls of their bedroom where there were portraits of family members. Varun kept looking with amazement at his sons how they had grown up and how handsome they had become with their curly hair, their bold profile, their delicate ironical lips, and the tremendous strength in their shoulders, in their arms and chest and they were looking handsome, plump, healthy, young and fresh. With tenderness he looked at their photos on the wall that day. But the reality was his smooth-tongued and dignified sons had flown to America, those far off shores, so different in their nature and inhabitants. They did not care for his money, power, position, respectability and his big house. Now they had no time to listen how hard his life was and with what difficulties he had built this house and raised them, that he had been saving out of his salary for all these years for their education in India and abroad. Now they were strangers to him, busy in their world with no time to even wish his parents on this festival. Now they haven't had the slightest notion of gratitude and they never even pretended. Nothing fades faster than what you do for children. They take what you have to offer them and away they go. Now these souvenirs, bronzes, the albums and pictures on the walls representing a ship at sea, cows in meadows and views of the Kanchchanga, Himalayas seemed so absolutely stale that his eyes simply glided over them without observing them. Then all of sudden as always happened on all festivals and holidays, he began to be fretted by loneliness and the persistent thought that his life was primarily a celebration of what he had and what he was. He felt that his status, his wealth, his health was a mere cheat, since he was not wanted, was of no use to anyone, and nobody loved him. Wasn't it strange that despite everything he had a longing to run to overtake them, to embrace them, to forgive them? Still, he felt he would give all his life and all his fortune only to know that they were upstairs and were closer to him than anyone in the world, and that they loved him warmly and were missing him. The thought of such closeness, ecstatic and inexpressible in words, troubled his soul. In that big room Varun moaned and howled like the autumn wind in the chimney. "Ah unhappy wretch my life! It may be likened to a prison and there is no chance of escape for me." His world was so infinitely beautiful but it could be reduced to ruins so easily he could not have imagined in the wildest of his dreams.

He fell in silent conversation with himself: Varun, you are rich, you are free, you are your own master, you have a servant to look after you. One cooks for you, cleans the house, other does your laundry, dhobi irons your clothes, gardener keeps your garden full with fragrant flowers, still another comes to massage, to do your groceries and bring market stuff. You have so many people to look after you. Even during your visits to America, you were lonely when your children and their wives went to office, so it does not seem right for you to feel like an old lonely man in your own house surrounded by luxuries. Oh, you know how it is sometimes, when a man is dissatisfied and feels unhappy, how trivial seem to him the comforts of the house, the shapes of the trees, their shadows, the clouds, all the beauties of nature. When his wife, Apurva was alive the home held an abundance of comfort and inspiration all that a person needs to lead a life of joy. Earlier on after the children left, he had Apurva who offered liberating alternative from mutual desperation. She tried to fill the void created by them. She used to say love is a noble calling for the individual to ripen, to differentiate, to become a world in oneself in response to another. Nearly to the last, he and Apurva had swung off on their seasonal cycle of journey to Venice, Rome and America where their children lived. He reminisced: I adored Apurva my wife I loved her. We floated away together into the domain of the subtlest shades and there we blend into spectrum. One writer defines such relations better than anyone. He rummaged in one notebook and then another. (Not long before his notebooks were filled with extraordinary expressions which he had read in various authors now when he would search nervously, usually he failed to find them) not finding the right quotation to define their relationships, he sat down and started thinking. Never during their thirty-eight years of matrimony, had he and Apurva been separated for a night. After he lost her due to heart failure this place had become blank (empty); you lose your place in the world and your soul becomes disengaged and all the possibilities of happiness he had dreamed of then was lost to him forever.

Now everything in the room spoke of a loss, of an essence gone, of its soul and life departed. In all the rooms there were echoes of the past, of the flow of time, obliterating yet containing all that had gone before. All that he wanted to do at that time was to scream, "Come back." Since his wife died his children didn't worry about his being alone.

The more he thought of her, the gloomier he felt. This void was unbearable as he had never thought what existence would be without Apurva. She had become so thoroughly annealed into his life that she was like the air he breathed -- necessary but scarcely noticed. Now without warning, she was gone, vanished, as completely absent as if she had never existed. Isn't it the apt proverb that we never prize the music till the sweet-voiced bird has flown? Life seemed meaningless to him now. He prophesied to himself the foregone conclusions of the monotonous days ahead. Now there was only solitude, it was large and not easy to bear. To escape from loneliness, he longed for the company, that time has come when he would exchange it for any adult company that leads to conversation which he craved now to continuing life. Since his wife died his children didn't worry about his being alone. However, children are of that kind that you are likely to forget while they are present but remember distinctly after they are gone.

When his children had come on the death of their mother he talked about his loneliness. "If I could escape from all this, he said, imagining how the weight of the memories in this big mansion, would roll off his conscience, roll off his mind."

They told Varun, "You are comparatively young wealthy, independent, brilliant, bold and a clever man. You ought not to vegetate, my dear. You ought not to live like everyone else but to get the full savour of life and slight favour of depravity is the sauce of life. Revel among flowers of intoxicating fragrance in your garden, breathe the perfume of musk, best of all love life." All this conversation troubled Varun and he said, "For personally myself I cannot conceive of life without family; I am lonely, lonely as the moon in the sky and a waning moon. I feel this waning can be restored by your love and little attention. I want peace of soul, tranquillity. I want the very opposite of musk and spiritualism, in short, my children". They told him, "Why do not you get married? Well, you can do that. Do not deny yourself anything. But make haste and live, time is passing; it won't wait." The state of behaviour called "being reasonable" - that was all anyone asked him.

Inevitably, in recalling this, he was upset and uneasy. Varun thought, I cannot go on living like that or to marry someone at this age. I was married, for once and for all. It is too late for me to even think of this. Not a scrap! No frivolity, frivolity he said decisively.

"I am a fool, an idealist and to expect children to look after the old parents nowadays (even in India) is insanity, isn't it? How do they repay me for my honesty and sacrifices? Now that his children had become as remote, as strange and as distorted to him as some other country's colonial wars.

Whenever there was a moment free, he thought that his loneliness was quite natural because he had lost his wife; children never come to see him, he had no friends (few friends he had had left for summer vacation abroad), no family, no promising future but only money and the past, and its memories. People say with money, you can snap out of your grief, you can go wherever you like, you can travel, you can take your mind off your sorrows. All bullshit! What had money given him so far? What had power given me? In what way am I happier than anyone without it? Money didn't save one from emptiness. He was filled with the shame of a man humiliated, of a man who is disdained, who is not liked, who is distasteful, who is disgusting, who is shunned. But that was his fate. Fate had flung him out of the simple surroundings, in which he had felt so snug and at home with his wife and boys. Life gives those and then takes them away he thought but the great difficulty is to say "Yes" to life. "I am getting old. Ever since Apurva died, I've taken to constantly thinking of death. No sort of philosophy can reconcile me to death and I look on it as simply annihilation. I can never understand myself. I'm always in a gloomy mood or else indifferent. I never can adapt myself to life or become its master. Some people talk nonsense or cheat, and even so enjoy life, while I consciously do good and feel nothing but uneasiness or complete indifference. If you live in an atmosphere of emptiness, it is impossible for you to escape a deeper effect of it, loneliness will be yours whether you want it or not," he said to himself. He pacified himself with this thought, "No one knows what he has come into the world to do, what his acts correspond to, his sentiments, his ideas."

"Nothing is more unbearable, once one has it, than freedom," says James Baldwin. Somehow to bear this unbearable time, Varun clung to his choices, personal and social-habits, routines, the commitment of marriage and moralistic structures. He played an active and ardent role in awareness campaign, helped the cause of social justice by bridging the real and the ideal. After his retirement, he prioritized women's association working for women empowerment and non-profit cultural institution over glamorous commercial ones, critical praise and honours came cascading, trailed by invitations for lectures and acceptance speeches. When he did speak his words became almost a consecration; in his speeches he made them remember, the beauty and strangeness and wonder of the world that they can make them their own and also raised their social conscience by making them aware of what was happening in society.

Twin love of nature and love of literature had kept him busy till now. And, like many another wreck, he was throwing himself into the arms of literature. He was reading Aristotle and other western philosophers such as Marcus Aurelius, Michel De Montaigne, Friedrich Nietzsche and Simone de Beauvoir. Of course, Apurva and he used to go for long walks and spent time in the gym and meditation but after her demise he felt devastated and if his children had visited him often or had made long-distance calls even monthly or had corresponded with him to keep in touch, life could still be bearable for him. We must feel deeply before we can act rightly. Consequently, after Apurva's demise Varun had formed a little world of his own, and cared not to move beyond its precincts, there was hush in the house which is only known in station that stand solitary in the open country but his mind was like the forest where the wind howls and nothing else is heard and all-around emptiness and dreariness is felt. He didn't correspond with anyone, his telephone would rarely ring (there were no long -distance calls from his children either). He was glad his friends were away, for he was ashamed to be seen in this condition. He missed his children. When you miss someone but you can't even talk to them, the helplessness, the depressing mood and anger strangles your soul into sadness. The worst part is you can't even tell anyone. Instead, the voices of his children came to his ear in the midst of loneliness and caused his heart to bleed. What an irony of fate for a lonely old man nothing is of any kind of significance anymore. His life was without hope of personal happiness, without desires, without dreams, expectations and old age would come imperceptibly, and life would reach its end.

At that time the professor's words started echoing in his ears. Though, he regarded professor's words as nonsense, yet for some reason it had of late haunted his memory. He recalled that a long time back his professor had come to greet him on Diwali day. When he enquired about his family, with tearful eyes he showed his ration card, "The status of my family is posted here. We are three here and said sorrowfully my son has left me, now I and my wife are alone. If only I could explain things to you. Look at things I put up with, without complaint. Then he talked for the most part of his son's love, separation and frustrated hopes and held out his hands to him and said, "This ration card is the mirror that reflects the lives of the old parents in an empty nest whose children had flown for foreign shores. It is simply a reminder to face the inevitable facts of life in the right spirit. My son did not love me, though he never said so openly. Now I have grown calmer -- it doesn't weigh on my heart; but in the old days, when I was younger, it hurt me -- ach! how it hurt me. It is beyond all their (children's) conception.. They take no interest in our condition we suffer. Then the time comes when all this becomes a memory and you reason about it coldly and look upon it as utterly trivial. Do not expect too much and but only make the best of life as we do. Live for the minute, I would like to tell you. I think it will all come right of itself. Varun did not know yet that his children would also leave him or even that such a thing might ever happen to him as well. Therefore, he could not see anything in his words and the professor seemed to him most vexatious and stupid of all. But only now, for the first time in his life, he was sad and mortifying to acknowledge even to himself that all the professor had said and shown were not nonsense, folly and wilfulness. Professor was a learned, right, lofty and an honourable man. Varun felt shame at his previous thoughts and actions and that he had said something improper; he had disgust for his own lack of understanding and indifference. Now these words reminded him how uninteresting and absurd his own life was. How strange man is! He remains indifferent when others suffer calamity but when the same calamity afflicts him, he cries foul and howls.

Varun started reflecting deeply on the enormity and enigma called life. He started asking himself questions: What should be life's goal --happiness or contentment? Do I need others to feel fulfilled? Can people really change? How can I be the best version of myself? In his material-oriented living, he thought, he has perhaps forgotten to appreciate life. Blind to all -- caring experiences and its abundance, he has even become forgetful of the fact that he breathes and is alive. In the loss of his loved one he has let his capacity to love and laugh slip away. Instead of let him be driven by the love of life he has rather crippled himself by the fear of death and existential isolation. When pain is inherent in life, I need to manage my grief as elucidated by the "Two Arrows" parable of the Buddha that he discovered in the notebooks that his servant rummaged while doing spring cleaning before Diwali. The Buddha said that in any event of misfortune, two arrows fly our way, one is that of the event and the other of reaction to it. Being stuck by one is painful. Being stuck by the other is awful. One can't control the first arrow but the second one shot by you is more lethal. It made Varun look at worldly concerns in perspective.

He thought: We will all have to endure some misery in our lives but Nietzsche saw in this an opportunity, not a setback and did not let them destroy him. "What does not destroy me, makes me stronger." If your life is not exactly the way you want it to be by the time you are seventy, not much point in continuing, you might as well change it, he thought. It was clear to him now that he was himself dissatisfied with his life. He must think things over, reconsider and live in some other way otherwise, he would grow dull and old, die in the end, as the average man usually does die, in a decrepit, soured old age, making everyone about him miserable and depressed.

Finally, pulling himself together, Varun leaned with a passionate longing for a change in his life to come at once without delay.

Time and again he said to himself: For decades, I have thought of nothing but these boys in foreign lands but now I see I have wasted my time; I have let it slip by like a ninny! Ah I have been a fool, a fool!" As seventy or seventy-five strikes you feel your time is up and then you start thinking you still have bonus time to live.

I do not believe any longer that I can afford to say that it is entirely out of my hands. I made the world I am living in and I have to make it over, once again. Whatever ugly and unforeseen forces we might come across into this world, into the dispensation of chance contouring our lives, there is always the choice -- human freedoms -- to choose one's attitude in any given set of circumstances, to choose one's own way.

Perhaps the most vital things for me to realise, are the habitual ways in which I have imprisoned myself and have relinquished my freedom. I understand that I will no longer exist tomorrow. Today I am alive, I am feeling this moment, I can see my hand on the desk. I can feel the warmth of the sun. I can't afford to lose time as it waits for no one. If not used constructively, it passes you by."

Varun moved to the puja room where Apurva had a shrine for icons that came to her on her marriage; he recalled his mother's words: Life is short, my dear Varun, and one must make the most of everything. The art of living is nothing without the vast ongoing participation and collaboration of the real world, nothing without the thousand-fold harmonizing of things and beings.

Now Varun was steady, and devout as an old man, bowing down to the icons in his wife's puja room, she liked burning incense in his room. Then a relic of faraway childish feeling -- joy, that today was Diwali, suddenly stirred within him.

In this mood he called Ramdev, his housekeeper and said this year he would have a Diwali party for orphan children. Ramdev looked at him, blankly and in perplexity, evidently unable to understand. He did not believe what he was hearing as after the death of mistress of the house there was always darkness on this day of lights. He repeated after a couple of seconds, "A party, sir?" Then Ramdev drew near, "I will take care of everything, sir, I will send Raghu to bring sweets and other things he knows where to find them. Would there be crackers?" "Of course," said Varun. "We will have crackers also." Standing there, his face excited, he received the instructions from Varun then he left to frantically execute any and every order that was given by his officer. Varun handed him the money. The news of Diwali party spread like wildfire. An hour and half later, Raghu and a huge wagon, covered with a dome-shaped canopy and other materials arrived. All the servants gathered, their faces brightened, each man attending to his own duties. They began to work; decorated the house with lights and flowers, while the housekeeper had a lot of preparations to make for the party.

In the evening, when they all met again, they laughed upon seeing one another, well-scrubbed, well-groomed, very fresh in neat and new clothes as if on inspection and Raghu switched on the lights hidden in the trees and at the bottom of the dance floor. The throng of children surged/ trooped into the party area and the music exploded from the sound bar, assaulted the walls and shook the streets and interior of the house, awakening the irresistible yearning into the children to jump around and have fun. They jumped, pranced, shook, wiggling and flapping their arms like stumps of fatherless wings while others danced with earnest but clumsy effort and a comic furore. When Varun saw them enjoying themselves, something better than gems shone in his eyes, redder than rose in his cheeks and that danced like electricity anxious to be loosed from the tip of his tongue. At that moment his eyes filled with tears; it no longer mattered to him that they were ordinary urchins and he belonged to an IAS family. In a moment he realized that they were just the same -- they were orphans and so was he.

Outside his street, the city roared to him to come join in its dance. He might go forth unquestioned and strum the strings of jollity as free as any bachelor there he might carouse and wander until dawn if he liked. Varun realised that day how correct was Nietzsche when he did not look at happiness as life's goal but thought of it as a consequence of our actions. His actions must be making Apurva happy wherever she was, he thought.

16

Room with a View

September is a very pleasant month in Shimla like spring in Chandigarh especially in the morning when I draw the curtains and open the door. A gentle sun streams in touching everything in my room with a golden hue and suddenly the whole room is brightened up. It feels as if somebody bright and vibrant has entered it. The gentle touch of breeze moves the window chimes and my memories too. They also gain a voice. They start speaking to me in that silent sound that only I can hear. My room offers a view of Chail in the front, deodar and oaks on Jaakku hills, Dingu Mata shrine on left. The green valley down below, interspersed with two lines of meandering roads, but it is the numbers of concrete buildings in housing colony that completes the picture of this view.

Why do I call this room mine when I own the complete house? Is it because my husband has shifted to the adjoining room, which was my children's room, or am I facing the empty nest syndrome? I can't say. What if they have moved to greener pastures of New York and Sydney? Haven't my old octogenarian parents moved in to stay with me? Now their whimpers, their unexpressed needs, their feeble voices fill the void created by the loud music of my son. Why am I becoming so pensive? During those days of their childhood, they used to fight to take turns to sneak into my room and snuggle with me in the cozy bed in this sunny room. My son always had an excuse because he was afraid of sleeping alone in his room; he had to do his homework in my supervision. How he used to take complete hold of my study table, litter it with his notebooks and shout for his sisters to tell them all his regaling tales of his friends and what all they had done in school. I used to yearn to have this room all to myself but they all had decided to be with me. They all had their reasons to do so and being a mother, I could not openly tell them to give me my space to de-stress after the hectic routine of the college and juggling of multiple roles at home. Though it was called mama's room but only mama had no place to be there. I never got the time to prepare my notes. It is a common perception that a professor's job is very easy that they have to deliver lectures only but what hard work goes in preparation for the class lecture is nobody's guess. My children also believed in this popular myth. When they slept in their rooms, I used to snatch time not only to prepare my lecture but also to tidy up the room to call it my own. I remember teaching a story where both son and daughter go abroad to toil as hired labourer and housemaid in foreign land and mother bids a tearful farewell. The picture of a bewailing mother distraught with anguish still rankles my soul. I did not realize at that time that the pain of a mother is not country-specific, it cuts across the boundaries of time, space, rich, poor, educated, illiterate; it has universal appeal as well relevance. Is it not an irony of life that you are always shutting out something or the other -- sometimes it is children, sometimes their noises; you are never alone even if the room is literally yours now? My husband used to say, you will miss them, their messing up of the room, their sweet chattering. I never used to listen. I was busy disciplining them since the task of scolding and teaching them also had fallen in my share of responsibilities of raising children. How I would send them to play at odd times and allow them TV viewing so that I could complete the book I had started reading. Now they tell me how they used to befool me to take money when I was busy reading. Without listening to them I would say, "take it."

My room is empty, no one comes to it, no one speaks in it. It is silent, without the echo of a human voice, only the walls have something of the people who lived within, something of their look, their faces, their words. My room is empty otherwise but full of memories, like my life, and the thought of going back into that room all alone and sleeping in the bed and doing all duties of life terrifies me. When I stare at the watch and try not to think, I remember there was only one family photograph in a silver frame decorating my room, now on rows of bookracks; the mounted photos of children are sitting silently. Suddenly the computer substituted them. Now I have to surf them on photo websites. My room is empty, but I can see my children, nobody there but I can hear their voices. Are my nerves frayed or is it a trick of the mind? Oh no! I had left the Internet switched on when I went to give juice to my parents inside the room. They had really come for the voice chat. My son has sent the yahoo voice messenger and my husband installed it only last night. They must be wanting to check if it is functional.

Is it the room my friends used to come with platefuls of food to eat and relax or where I used to unwind talking with my sister late in the night or empty room with memories nestling in place of real ones or chat room with images appearing on my computer screen and I viewing them with a face sealed off, all emotions suddenly cropping up. Is it a real joy of having a separate room that I always dreamt of in my childhood or is it a picture of happiness which is it complete and frozen in time ? Virginia Woolf needed her room with a view to write her novels with psychological insights and an ordinary woman has her own reasons -- her own needs which keep on changing with the passage of time.

Do you know this, please introduce me to my room. I am an outsider viewing from my computer chair what their rooms look like. I want theirs to be full of what I am yearning for in these unspoken silences. I called my husband, my parents, and my helper Rajesh to come quickly to see them on screen. Once again the room is full of their sounds and my gaze is transfixed on them, my grandson is fidgeting with the web cam, his father is looking irritated. I want to tell them, don't deprive yourself of their joys of growing up; I felt a choking pressure around the heart. "No, no," said the inner voice. Let them learn from their experiences; wisdom comes from these experiences only. My eyes are involuntarily filled with tears that roll down my face. Then the room is full of continuous and incomprehensible sounds made up of different voices, near and far, vague and enormous, like my life but the thought of going and sleeping in that room all alone in my bed and doing all my duties of the day does not frighten me today. When you are young, you think everything is dispensable but memories are not. You don't know about the habit they have of coming back.

17

The Holy Land of Childhood

Almost all children look forward to their vacations because they can have fun at their *Nani's* house. My granddaughters Asmi, Aastha with their mother (my daughter) Neelam also came to visit me in Panchkula during their winter vacations. Aastha was an eight-year-old and yet did not leave her mother for a second. So they were obviously disposed to keep to themselves but Asmi was in the twelfth grade, of such an age that conversation was possible. Besides, she was very intelligent, soft spoken and spoke English fluently and with equal ease. After a long while I saw as she saw herself, as indeed she really was, as a dear little thing with a heart of gold.

When I came to know her I found her as simple as a child, touchingly grateful for any attention you paid her. She was a daughter any grandparent might have been proud of. She was five feet eight inches with a slim waist, dark black hair that waved slightly, brown eyes with long dark eyelashes. Her voice was deep, rich and full of colour; she spoke with her whole body, like a singer. She was not shy but there was a modesty in her demeanour. She was as honest, open and virtuous as she looked. I knew she liked to talk to me, but I lived a very quiet life and saw few people liked my company, my desk was my home and I was not bothered with the trivialities of social intercourse. I was plainly disinclined to strike up conversation with her but she was not.

Notwithstanding this she would hover around me but I never by so much as a glance gave an indication that I had seen her. I had guessed sometime before that she would not be able to resist making the first advance. Anyway, she grabbed the occasion of my golden jubilee to enter my study to wish me happy anniversary.

Till then I never thought that she looked up to me, respected me, thought the world of me, or took whatever I said as gospel truth; that she also loved me to distraction. I was surprised when she gave a handwritten card that read like this: *I could never find a Nani as modern, stylish, goal-oriented and so in accordance to my taste even if I looked for one. You are the best, Nani.* From that day onwards she was on perfectly friendly terms with me and I found her conversation very lively and there was heartiness of manner about her. In addition, she listened to my poems that brought us together.

One morning as I had just started writing the poem 'Dwarka' she walked into my study which was a large and comfortable room with a big desk, leather arm chairs and on the bookshelves were works of classic authors, fiction, nonfictions, stories of Hemmingway, Somerset Maugham, Anton Chekhov, Alice Munro, works of Susan Sontag, James Baldwin, Gabriel Garcia Marquez, Zadie Smith Eliot and other titans of literature -- classical novels of the nineteenth and twentieth century. Asmi was a trifle flushed with the excitement but seemed quite at ease when she started talking about libraries: They open up our lives and no one is alone who has a beloved book for company. You have a trusted companion in a book. Then she shoved her hand inside her baggy lowers and brought out a piece of paper from somewhere close to her waist, self-consciously unfolding the page on which she had scribbled a poem, she laid it on the table. Her poem was fresh and original and she had made little songs of her sorrows.

Asmi believed that poems connect people. I read her poem, and remarked, 'Yes, poetry is expressive and useful because it helps us to understand ourselves better. It also enables us to understand other people, especially people who are different than we are. The poet and reader share an intimacy that is irreplaceable. Sometimes you read a poem, you feel as if the poet is speaking directly to you. Poetry has verbal power to bring us together, care for each other, to recognize our sorrows and our sufferings, to heal our wounds and treasure our solitude. They are handles on the door of what we can know and what we can imagine. Each door leads to some new house and some new world that only that one handle can open." To encourage her I said, "Beside physical strength you have the divine spirit, a spark of the holy fire (creativity) which distinguishes you in the most striking way from others."

She was very communicative by nature and she started talking unasked about herself, about her school and her friends. She said, "I am a chatty girl and can't do without talking for a moment when I am not studying. Often my father chides me to keep quiet but I can never do. Can I talk to you, Nani?"

Without waiting for my opinion on it she embarked on another topic, she talked rather shyly, hesitatingly as though it was difficult for her to speak and yet she was forced on by some inner passion. I did not mind it because I like her vivacity and her talks. I love not only the beauty of her person, tall slim and straight, with the proud carriage of her head, but still more the beauty of her soul. With her truthfulness, her rigid sense of honour, her fearless outlook, she seemed to me to collect in herself all that was most admirable in this small-town girl.

In the evening again when I came back from walk, I saw Asmi rushing out of her room to greet me. "*Nani*, can I also join you in your evening walks?" Though we were happy to be together that conversation was unnecessary but it warmed my heart to observe her enthusiasm and I said, "Okay. Be ready by six pm tomorrow." Her face lit up at my words and her eyes flashed. She was excited. It was touching to see her delight. The next day I took her out for a walk. We conversed while walking in the winter setting sun. She found her greatest pleasure in nature. "How beautiful nature is! My God the scenery is awesome." Suddenly she drew my attention to the sky, "*Nani*, look across the evening sky, all the birds are leaving. How do they know it's time to go?" she continued because it seemed her only hope and because it was a relief to her to have someone with whom she could talk freely.

I found her talking without stopping on the way, she also said some very clever ones. Of course, she was witty, vivacious, philosophical and inventive. She had a point of view, original and sincere but the most striking thing about her was her eager, impetuous vitality and I listening to her with a grin and interjecting now and then in English to give my opinion. The good walk and Asmi's sprightly chatter combined to give these evenings a geniality I had never before seen in me.

The conversation that unfurled remained the most candid and revealing glimpse of Asmi's creative credo, a process which was at bottom her philosophy of life. Asmi's mind was richly stored and her conversation, however light was never flippant. "*Nani*, it feels good to talk to you," and she spoke now of her family in particular of her father.

"All members of the family have given up on advising me. You know my father. He worships himself and nothing is convincing to him but what he says. One evening I wore for my friend's birthday party the off-shoulder dress that you gave me last summer on my birthday. 'Immediately take it off,' he said. I knew perfectly well that the disdain for off-shoulder dress was founded not so much on his dislike of fashion but the fear that wearing these would set the whole town talking about me which was worse. He said, 'That, all your contemporaries are so simple and getting on well with their parents here you, my elder daughter is a rebel.' But I still sat on and how I longed to be understood. It is impossible, if you have sensitive nature, not to feel a certain melancholy, at the thought of all efforts/labour, the care and the pains, the thought, the trouble I have gone through to please him. In spite of everything I love my father and my sister and it has been my habit from childhood to consult them -- a habit so deeply rooted that I doubted whether I could ever have got rid of it, whether I were in the right or the wrong. I was in constant dread of wounding them. I keep myself aloof but aloofness is also offensive and my self-complacency is obnoxious to his vanity. I do not know how anyone can look at father without thoughts too deep for tears, after all he is the man who is supporting me since I have come into existence." She gave the impression of her self-assurance but wanted all the time to be assured by me.

I had heard a great deal of her parents during these previous three weeks but I have never understood how children presumably young can talk so articulately about their emotions these days. Now it was plain to me that people about them fail to notice that children are often lonely and afraid. They feel unprotected, manipulated by adults in ways they don't like or even understand. They try to address these feelings of isolations and loneliness in these outbursts. Her conversation seemed to have aroused in me a train of recollections, for I began to talk of my school days. I felt that I was once more in my childhood world of which I had so many charming as well unpleasant memories.

The holy land of childhood knows no boundaries or states outright. "The one flag we all share is the beautiful flag of childhood," says Naomi Shihab Nye. It is a colourful flag and waves over all our heads like a banner.

What an irony! Much about the childhood experience remains the same from 20th century to this moment. Before I could enlighten her on generation gap and differences of attitudes which I have also experienced, we had reached our house. At night certain voices, troubling and yet against my will refusing to still their clamour, were at last silent in the heart and I went off to sleep.

Soon after breakfast as I sat on the chair, I thought that this girl with her sack of worries on her head will show up in a minute and I won't be able to finish writing the end of my story, "Progress of Love". As she entered the room, I knew it so well that she was full of news and I could not supress the exclamation of delight. She also looked around with a smile. She sat down in the chair in front of me and looked at me with calm grave eyes. "Now what have you to say to me?" I asked. "I hardly know how to begin." And suddenly Asmi blurted out, "Do you know our class is divided in sections according to the merit of students?" "No," I said. There was a long silence before Asmi spoke again. It seemed it was a difficult story she had to tell; there were things that she could not bear to tell me and yet in justice to herself, she must tell the whole truth. She began like this: "I am in section A -- one of meritorious students and the other B is of mixed type, third C consists of sportspersons who excel in sports. You know our campus has two playgrounds respectively for primary graders and high schoolers." I said, "Yes I have done my summer job in your St Lukes School in 1965 as a substitute teacher for Rita Faria (who went to Bombay to see her ailing father) when I was graduating." "In that case you already know," Asmi said, "that there are two separate grounds for middle schoolers to eat lunch at. So, when it comes to break time the primary graders eat in their class, middle schoolers in two step grounds and high schoolers including me in our campus' base ground which can be seen as soon as one enters the premises. With four classes eating lunch at the same time in the same place, there's quite the drama to witness. There're people fighting, kids playing after finishing their lunches and also people hurrying their way around their never-ending saga of friend circles which of course includes me. There are for sure pranksters seeking their next prey. These are indeed the best 35 minutes of our daily school lives."

She had a flow of lively conversation which I knew nothing could discourage and went on narrating with amusement, "However, the students of one section consider it below them to mix with others but I have my own mind and few friends in each group and I try to mix with them, sit with them during school lunch break. I always hang out with my friends from C section even though I belong to section A myself and I did have some friends in A section too but my best friend belonged to sec C so I and her group were close friends too. Now this one girl Rita approached me, 'Asmi! Why are you standing with C section girls are you in A section or C section?' And I was like are you serious? Like c'mon is this some sort of an India-Pakistan feud or what? Nani, they do not approve of my moving freely from one group to others though I am the head girl of the school and captain of the basketball team (and I have my tiffin with juniors as well as with seniors.) To tell you the truth *Nani*, their small remarks/actions affect my whole life profoundly."

(The conversation meandered leaving me to marvel. The longer Asmi talked, the more I was filled with the conviction that life is a fascinating business and one's own experiences more fascinating than one had ever suspected it of being.)

I was still trying to understand the complexities and zest of life when Asmi interrupted, "Nani, how difficult it is to cope up with these pressures of peers and expectations of the juniors who look forward to talking to you. And sometimes even the fate of human beings is curious to consider. Whenever I try to tell at home that girls and teachers are indifferent and I cannot do what I want, to eat with whom I want or play whenever I want that I have undergone tremendous vicissitudes in my school, they are not at all significant to the elders in the family. If you talk about this stress, they ignore it as a silly thing. The story that began with the school is finished abruptly and it looks as though it meant nothing at all. It is a tale told by an idiot. Is not it odd that the event, of such an importance and so dramatic looks so trivial to my family? Do not you agree such incidents have consequences that are incalculable?"

I was just considering what to say to her last question when she moved to another topic in her bubbly manner. She said, "They say school life is really very fantastic and there are no cares and worries that mar this life. One has to have a peculiar sense of humour to see the fun of it. But *Nani,* is not childhood the time when you are in the midst of loneliness, in the midst of fear, in the middle of feeling misunderstood and rejected? Then suddenly forgetting about these problems and avoiding the complicated questions Asmi and me -- the chums of incompatible years would get engaged in familiar bantering and innocent laughter, and my heart would fill with delight.

After that day I was engaged in a rambling conversation with her on many topics. Some people have this this gift of infusing their own abundant energy into the listener and Asmi had it in plenty.

She had honed her love of life in childhood itself. She was not privileged but straight and not resigned to the era's conventional destiny for a girl. She often worked until the small hours and saved time and money and learned early in the world how to make her life full of sensorial enchantments. She loved listening to music. She had no formal knowledge of what she was singing and no theoretical rationale for why it was so soul-stirring. Her soul still had more understanding of classic music than aesthetic creatures. For her it was a matter of enjoyment through the five senses. She saw beauty all around her, everywhere and enjoyed it.

Walking with her for a few days I noticed that something troubled her. I knew every expression of her face and her denials now were useless against my keen instinct. Something told me that her harassed look had to do something with her family and I did not rest till I made her confess it. Asmi did not say anything for a while and when she spoke it was hesitatingly. "The fact is, *Nani*, my father tells me not to mix with boys, concentrate on studies. My mother is also of a very suspicious type. Whenever she hears about any scandal, she nags my father to keep a watch on me. Whenever I want to make light of suspicion, she asks me pointed questions: are not there instances of school romance in society? Did not Raghu's daughter elope with her class fellow? Is it altogether impossible for a boy to fall in love with a smart girl in co-educational school? I agree that those were not impossible but were improbable in my case but how to make her trust me. How to tell my father I am smart enough to avoid these romantic connections. To tell you frankly it was not that the fellow had not tried. I encountered one when he was boasting with his fellows, he was seized on a sudden with shyness and his conversation which had been fluent and ready, ran dry when I mocked him, I bantered him. The most devastating weapon is ridicule and his friends rocked with laughter. I did my best to show him his place and to put him to the shame and ridicule of his classmates and threatened him not to nurture such foolish ideas of falling in love anymore. It silenced not him alone, but many others as well received the signal that I am modern frank but not this type. Besides I have more freedom if I am on my own."

I was listening to her bold secrets quite attentively without commenting even slightly. She smilingly said, "Oh *Nani*, you are wonderful. I did not know there was anyone in the world like you. How can you be so good and kind? How can I ever thank you?" I responded normally, "I do not want your thanks. There's nothing in the world I want more than your happiness." Asmi felt very excited and said: "*Nani,* honestly speaking I think of nothing else but my studies, my grades, my aspirations. I dream of becoming a computer engineer at night, a scientist, a doctor or a writer. I reckon that it would be decided this year and I do not want to relax till then. My teachers say I work with more zeal as if I had been a painter or a sculptor creating a work of art. I think it was this eagerness that made my teachers like me. They tell me they like my zeal, they like my ingeniousness, they are so impressed by my passion for achievement that it makes me indifferent to the solitariness of my life, even to the thought of going home early in the evening but to play volleyball and basketball."

I asked her inquisitively, "Asmi, you have said that your teachers like you. You didn't tell me anything about them." Asmi said, "Oh! they are wonderful. All teachers teach fine actually but sometimes what they don't understand is that their teaching method may or may not suit a child. Most of them lack flexibility. It is important for them to know that each student is going to have his/her own approach to the syllabus and strategy of completing it. Transparency is required in the school's plan of marking the students so that a student can work out his way in planning for best grades. I tell you one big example is internals for boards. In class 12 specially in online school the teachers don't check the notebooks but just tell us to maintain it. Great. The problem is for students like me all of us are prioritizing our JEE or entrance exams and undergoing coaching while handling school so maintaining like 2-3 registers per subject for different institutions is very difficult even if we study 12-14 hours. And the difference in content to be written in school notebooks and coaching material is huge. Often teachers specifically even want the exact words they said in class to be noted down when in reality nobody actually listens. All of us are practically studying from our tuitions and coaches. School classes are attended so as not to mess up our attendance as it reflects on our report cards. What teachers need to understand is that even though we aren't directly writing down your words we are still at least studying and writing by ourselves. Majorly the teachers give homework as if theirs is the only subject we study.

However, Nani PT periods were always the best actually. Some days you would just play for fun. Sometimes for the sake of physical fitness, some days there were inter-class matches or inter-house tournaments. But playing against your enemies was always the best. I and my good friend had this arch enemy. Let's call her A. A was always the bossy kind but me and my friend weren't the ones who could be controlled. So, we were always the ones she hated the most. We would deliberately play against her team and go rough. Basketball is more fun when aggressive. We enjoyed those matches a lot." She told me all this with joyous glee and her eyes flashing.

When she blared out the stories of school, I fancied it all before my eyes. I could see Asmi striving hard to strike a delicate balance between her aspirations and her teachers' expectations. One morning I was sitting in my room and editing my story. It was the end of winter, for the last few days the temperature was freezing and almost unbearable. I was enjoying the warmth of a strip of morning sun that had alighted on my feet under the table. It was about 8:30 am and most of the early risers had finished their morning walk with their necks wrapped with scarfs and were returning home. Just then I heard some commotion in the other room. Putting together details from Asmi and Aastha I understood that they were having a row over the computer. I overheard Aastha, "Nani has given it to both of us. You being elder always bully me and do not let me do my project."

Asmi looked a little hurt by the statement and stood stupefied for a time, gazing at me with a fixed look. Then her face became purple in shame and she said coyly. "I try to practice kindness, but like most of us even I am not capable of perpetual kindness. I also transform into an ill-tempered girl with my loved ones, possibly we human beings are not wired for consistency of feelings, of conduct or self-hood," and then she left abruptly.

My eyes welled up with tears at the sight. This brought back memories of my childhood when I used to bully my younger sister Subha. In a moment I realized that we were both the same; Asmi is the bully and so was I. I said to Aastha who was standing close to me, "I will tell her to share with you. If she does not, I will give you a separate tablet."

At 4o'clock in the afternoon I would lean in my chair, put my feet on the desk and muse aloud, "I wonder what kind of new experience she would have today." That day Asmi narrated, "I hate this experience the most and regret the most for not speaking up. We were attending the intraschool Model United Nations Conference and of course we were to dress formally for that except for the school uniform. So, I wore this white knee length pencil skirt. I really loved my outfit and the others' too. Every boy and girl were looking so smart and intellectual. But then even before the conference could commence, a teacher called out all the girls wearing skirts. I was confused. We 10-15 girls went out to an empty classroom where the female teachers were.

This head teacher who summoned us told us to change our outfits or leave. Why? Because when one of our committee's skirted girl members was leaving from the washroom this teacher heard a couple of boys comment vulgarly on her short skirt. The thing is, those two boys were not even scolded rather not even approached but all the girls had to change their skirts. Disgusting. I remember I spoke up for myself; I refused to change my skirt and proceeded to the committee like that only. But my seniors and some juniors had to change. If only I was so confident as girl, then as I am now, I definitely would've searched for those two stupid chaps and given them a good piece of my mind. And also, to that teacher who saw the fault in our skirts but not those two."

Another routine exchange between us these days was: Do you have lots of friends? Are they good enough for you? But to keep quiet and not to respond to my questions was contrary to her nature, therefore, Asmi replied coolly:

There is a ton of social advantages and disadvantages that come with having friends. Having a lot of friends is a problem, having no friends at all is an even greater problem and having few friends makes you seem rude to your "non-friends" as if you are selective of your contacts out of ulterior motives. But if I have to choose, keeping close to everyone is important but only a few should be your real best-friends and priority. Maintaining a good relationship with juniors and seniors is necessary. Seniors help a lot in academics, hand me downs and tips for classes. Juniors make your school experience interesting and it's a reputation to hold up even when you're not any longer in the same school.

Sometimes your classmates start to dislike you for the fact that you are close to juniors/seniors and that they are not. It kind of reflects your "popularity" in school. How much people want to talk to you, be with you. So, popularity does matter in high school. It's like everybody treats the popular kids with more love and politeness just as their opposites -- the outcasts -- are ignored or disliked. Example – when there's a group project it becomes easier for popular kids to choose the best of teammates whereas less popular kids struggle. So, I am grateful that due to my naturally extroverted personality I was one of the popular kids and things were easy for me like not dealing with stage fright or social anxiety in the classroom activities."

Though it was quite clear that we belonged to different generations, but with me Asmi was franker than with anyone else. Even I had often sat entranced for hours while with the humour, which to me was her most astonishing characteristic, she regaled me with lurid tales of her friends. This was one subject in which her interest never failed. She pursued it with the same indefatigable energy as she pursued her studies. No obstacle prevented her from returning to it. All I did was to make suitable interjections at times. That evening over dinner that I always shared with the family that Asmi often ate heartily and thoroughly appreciating the food, I was surprised when she told me, "There are the elite girls that are the difficulty; they look at your clothes, in a glance take that arrogant air and freeze you with their indifference. I have friends in this group too I have known them so long their idiosyncrasies cease to trouble me. I accept them as you accept your own physical defects. Some girls are easy, cordial and natural they have interesting things to tell you. They are immensely kind. On the spur of moment, one gives them invitation and one is perfectly sincere about them but when one is taken at one's word, a slight dismay seizes one. Girls are so different at home from what they are at school. You are anxious when your turn comes to do something in return for the hospitality you have received. But it is not easy at my place. When they come everyone surrounds them though I have a room of my own. I introduce my friends to my family. I am afraid they would not amuse them very much because they are open, frank girls and find my family crashing bore and old fashioned. If my parents behaved like this, I could think of me having my tiffin by myself in the drab corner of the school alone in the playground and going back home with nobody walking beside me with whom I can enjoy chatting about school and no one to have my coke with during the interval."

The revelations thar Asmi had poured into my ears, sometimes only too willingly, sometimes with shame, with reservations, with anger, had longed ceased to surprise me. I knew by now that it was not for me to judge or to condemn. But day by day as these experiences were imparted to me, her face grew lighter. I felt that Asmi was at ease with me. The days passed in gaiety and fun; in picnics; I took them to the mall for shopping, gave them gifts for their birthdays, Christmas, Diwali. We laughed together and now and again they smiled when I read some stories to them.

On 20th of March, I received a phone call from Asmi's father that he was coming to take them home as Asmi's school classes would start from 25th March. I told Asmi, no matter how turbulent the times as long as children have dreams, there is a hope for the future. I read to her what the Chinese author Bin Xin wrote:

Children!

Within their small bodies

Resides a great spirit.

I urged her to stay brave, kind and considerate, and to thoroughly train her body and mind. Life is another name for struggle. While many challenges and hardships may await you on the road to your dreams, you should always strive bravely and strongly, and keep growing. Remember that obstacles and difficulties are great opportunities to become stronger and you would see your dreams come true.

While departing for Solan. They thanked me for taking good care of them. Asmi said, "You need a vacation, *Nani.* You haven't been away from the city in years. Please come to us for at least two weeks in summer." Her voice was exquisite, mellow, full of beautiful emotions that my heart melted within me. I had a most awkward lump in my throat when she finished and looking at her, I saw the tears were streaming down her face as well. When they left, I went to the terrace, the orange trees in full flower exhaled their heady perfume and there was a magnificent cedar in the garden and its dark branches were silhouetted against the evening sky. Asmi's words, "How beautiful nature is," wafted on the wind.

❑❑❑